The Burden of Evidence

By Buddy Howard

This is a work of fiction. Names, characters, businesses, places, events, and incidents are either the products of the author's imagination or used in a fictitious manner. Any resemblance to actual persons, living or dead, or actual events is purely coincidental.

Published by
Birch and Quill LLC
107 Windel Drive, Suite 211
Raleigh, NC. 27609

ISBN (Paperback): 979-8-9991881-0-6
ISBN (Hardcover): 979-8-9991881-1-3
ISBN (eBook): 979-8-9991881-2-0
ISBN (Audiobook): 979-8-9991881-3-7

Library of Congress Control Number: 2025913802

Cover art by Bojan Rekovic from PixelStudio

www.burdenofevidence.com
www.birchandquill.com
www.buddyhoward.com

Printed in the United States of America
First Edition

Dedication

For my wife Cathy and our two adult children, Tristan and Stephanie.

Acknowledgements

Writing a novel is never a solo journey. I owe thanks to many people who supported, challenged, and encouraged me throughout this process.

To my editors: your insights, patience, and skill were invaluable: Lisa Harris, Kerri Marikakis and Peggy Payne.

To those who offered guidance and encouragement throughout various parts of the writing process: Paula Munier, Irene Goodman, Michael Neff, Hannah Turner, Nora Gaskin, Alice Osborn, Lawrence Harte

To my early readers who helped shape the manuscript and offered thoughtful feedback: Paul Whit Howard, Mike Elledge, Marcus Jimison, Susan and John Cashwell, Michael Peeler, Debbie Laws, Scott David, Ellison and Karl Weist, Brooke and Gary Sweeting, Jeb Jeutter, and members of my immediate and extended family.

I'm honored to have had you with me on this path.

"No one in the world can change Truth. What we can do and should do is to seek truth and to serve it when we have found it. The real conflict is the inner conflict."

Maximilian Kolbe

Chapter 1

Before the trip to Grand Island, Paul had never heard his adult son Daniel scream. The trip had started innocuously enough: a six-hour car drive from their Detroit home to a ferry headed to Grand Island, a scenic isle in Michigan's Upper Peninsula with unspoiled beaches, soaring sandstone cliffs and a canopy of ancient hardwoods.

Paul and Daniel had boarded the ferry and now stood side by side, leaning against the railing as the boat cut through Lake Superior's crystal-clear waters. They surveyed the island in the distance—a green unspoiled wilderness surrounded by a deep blue expanse. Paul glanced at his son, who was busy snapping photos, and felt a pang of nostalgia.

Years had passed since they'd last been camping, and he hoped this trip would give him a chance to help Daniel think through some things: his longer-term plans, getting a place of his own and clarity regarding his career among them. More than that, there were other things to think through for himself, like how to patch things up with Katherine, his latest unfinished novel, his stalled career. Getting away was a good idea.

Disembarking at Williams Landing, Paul sucked in a deep breath of fresh pine-scented air. He'd chosen this island, which featured a twenty-one-mile hiking loop, for its rugged beauty, and had long been looking forward to seeing those towering cliffs up close. They'd planned this overnight hike for months, and now that they were here, they both felt the adrenaline rush of the pending adventure. They checked in with the welcome station, which was staffed by an affable park ranger, who confirmed their reservation.

"Ready to hit the trail?" Paul asked, pulling out some walking sticks.

"Absolutely!" Daniel exclaimed.

The first part of their walk took them west towards Juniper Flats, a camping area where they planned a short break. There was a nearby makeshift outhouse and a well water source close by as well, so when they arrived, they refilled their bottles and made a few adjustments to their packs. They resumed their walk, Daniel leading.

Their blatant lack of experience was comical. Seeing Daniel's overstuffed backpack wobbling back and forth with every step, Paul told him to hold up. "Let me cinch this down a little so it's more comfortable," he told his son, tightening the straps over Daniel's shoulders and under his arms. "Maybe also snug up that belt around your waist if you want," he added, which Daniel did.

"It's beautiful here," Daniel mused, taking in the surroundings with a thoughtful expression and appreciating the pause.

"That it is," Paul said, smiling. "I used to come here with your grandfather when I was a kid. It's nice to be back."

After Paul was satisfied with his backpack handiwork, they resumed walking—each lost in his thoughts against a backdrop of rustling leaves—and after a few miles came to a long, steep ascent leading to a bend ahead. As they ambled up the trail, breaks in the vegetation provided glimpses of the shoreline.

Daniel, in better shape than Paul, walked a little more quickly and arrived at the peak first. He walked to the edge to survey the scenery as his dad stopped to catch his breath. Paul laughed to himself. *I remember when Daniel was the straggler. Time eventually catches up.* He wiped the sweat from his forehead and took a deep breath.

After Paul had finally caught up, Daniel held out his phone and gestured toward some jagged rocks nearby. "Hey Dad, take my phone. I want a shot of me with those in the background."

Paul joined his son at the edge of the trail and saw the view was indeed spectacular. Looking downward over the island's steep sandstone cliffs that terminated about fifty feet below, he could hear the waves faintly lapping against their rocky edge.

"Wow. That's a big drop. Careful, Daniel."

"Here," Daniel said, handing him the phone before tentatively stepping backwards and inching into position. "Let me stoop down so that…"

And that was when the edge gave way.

Daniel dropped violently to the ground, desperately grasping for anything to arrest his fall. His right hand managed to grasp a two-inch-thick tree root protruding from the sandstone.

Paul dropped the phone and dove towards Daniel.

"Hang on!" he yelled. Frantically pulling at his son's arms, Paul realized he too was close to going over the edge and began looking for some way to anchor himself. When his right leg brushed against something solid—a small tree—he spread himself flat and threw his legs around it to lock his feet at the ankles. It was the best he could do.

"Dad… Dad…" Daniel managed between gasps. He was able to get both hands on the tree root, but it looked ready to break at any moment.

Paul grabbed him by the wrist and pulled with all his might. Making a guttural sound reflective of the effort, Daniel rose a few inches but kept slipping back whenever he tried to grab the root farther up. His lower torso was suspended in mid-air, his legs kicking frantically as he tried to get a foothold on anything solid.

"Can you pull yourself up?" Paul asked desperately.

Daniel didn't answer while struggling to maintain his grasp. Both were breathing heavily, their grips beginning to weaken.

Their eyes met.

"Dad, help!" Daniel pleaded.

Seeing the backpack still secured to his son's back and trying to conceal his own panic, Paul said, "I have an idea. If I can reach it, I'm going to try to run my rope through one of your backpack loops. Try not to slide out of your pack so it has a chance to hold you!"

In one swift motion, Paul removed the rope attached to his backpack, grabbed one end and—nearly toppling over himself— threaded the end through a sturdy loop at the top of Daniel's pack.

"Don't...let...go!!" Paul urged, pulling tight both ends of the rope looped through the backpack and frantically wrapping them a half-dozen times around the base of the small tree he'd used to anchor himself. He tightened a knot to secure it.

"Daniel!" Paul exclaimed, trying to catch his breath, "I think this will hold. When you're ready, slowly release your grip a little and start transferring your weight to the rope." He paused and added, "Daniel, this is important. If you can keep your arms locked in place down low, the chest straps will stay under your armpits so you won't slide out. Understand?"

Paul perceived a slight nod from his son between gasps for air.

Daniel began to loosen his grip, his body sliding down a few inches over the edge and the rope tightening.

"So far, so good," Paul said, trying to sound encouraging. "Let go a little more."

Daniel let loose of the root, and the backpack started to ride up his back. Instinctively, he jammed his elbows down and inwards all while dropping several more inches. He began swinging precariously in mid-air, suspended only by the backpack, and Paul wondered if the fabric would hold.

"Are you OK?" Paul yelled over the edge, seeing the top of Daniel's head but not much else.

"I…I don't know…" Daniel managed, the terror palpable in his voice.

"Lock your hands together in front of you so your arms can't come apart," Paul instructed him.

"OK, I'm doing that." Daniel responded.

"Can you stay like that for a minute?" Paul asked. "I mean, do you feel like it's going to hold you and keep you from sliding out?"

"I don't know…"

Paul inched closer to the edge and peered over the fifty-foot-high sandstone face that ended in the water. He had absolutely no idea if Daniel would bounce off the wall or just hit the water should he fall, or even if he could survive such a drop.

"Daniel, I'm not going to be able to pull you up. I can either leave you here and try to find someone to help, or I can try to lower you part of the way with the rope. I think the rope is maybe twenty feet long or so, not as long as we need but it's all we've got."

"I don't think I can stay like this for long. The shoulder straps are starting to dig into my arms."

Paul looked at the rope wrapped around the tree several times. By untying the knot and slowly trying to uncoil the rope, he figured there might still be enough resistance for him to lower Daniel part of the way. *Far from an ideal solution, but it'll shorten the fall at least.*

Paul peered over the edge once more, feelings of helplessness nearly overwhelming him. "Let me start trying to lower you," he said, trying to keep his composure.

Daniel looked down and back up at Paul, his lips moving without making a sound, mouthing silent words of desperation.

"Don't panic," Paul said. "Yes, that's a big drop, and you may graze the side of the cliff but you'll ultimately wind up in the water. Once you do, try to get out of the pack and keep your head above water. It will be cold, but you can do it. Okay?"

Daniel responded with a hesitant nod.

Nodding back, Paul backed up to the tree. He braced his feet against it a foot or so above the rope, wrapped the loose end of the rope around his wrist a few times and held it tight, slowly untying the knot. Much to his relief, the rope stayed put around the tree.

Paul glanced over toward the edge of the precipice. "Okay, Son, I'm going to start letting the rope out now."

"Okay."

Just as Paul began to uncoil the rope with both hands, the unthinkable happened: the rope suddenly began whipping around the base, ripping through Paul's hands.

Daniel screamed.

Tightening his grip, Paul winced at the searing pain from the friction as the rope tore through his hands. Then he heard it: a splash. He rushed over to the edge of the cliff and peered over, spotting ripples but no sight of Daniel. *Please God, no!* A moment later, Daniel's head popped out of the water. He looked dazed.

"Daniel! Are you okay?!" Paul yelled.

Daniel looked up, his backpack still on, and wiped his face.

"Um, I think so!" he yelled back while treading water. "I don't think I broke anything."

"Get out of the backpack and swim over to your right. There's a beach over there," Paul said.

Paul ran toward the beach. His hands felt on fire. He looked down and saw the skin intact—though beet red and badly chafed.

He found Daniel sitting on a rock, his backpack beside him. Paul rushed over and threw his arms around him.

"Son, are you okay!?"

Daniel stared at the ground. "I think so?" he responded, still looking dazed. "I seriously thought I was gonna die."

"Stand up and let me look you over for a second."

Daniel pushed himself up. "Ow! My shoulder is a little sore, but I don't think it's busted."

"Yeah, you're going to be sore for a while."

They both stood there for a moment, not speaking, but just staring at one another, processing what had just happened. Paul noticed his hands shaking, mainly from the trauma and the exertion. Daniel's body was beginning to shake as well, though his was also due to the cold-water exposure.

Paul said, "Let's get you out of those wet clothes. You can put on some of my stuff."

Paul grabbed Daniel's backpack and saw the back of it was ripped. "It looks like you hit the side of the sandstone. This thing saved you from getting really scraped up."

Daniel walked over and nodded. "Wow, you're right. Want me to carry it?"

"No, I got it," Paul said.

They walked back over to the trail and then made their way about thirty yards past to a less conspicuous area in case someone came ambling up the trail while Daniel was changing clothes.

Paul opened his backpack and pulled out a change of underwear, socks, pants and a pullover he had planned to sleep in. He handed them to Daniel, who had stripped. Paul noticed a purple abrasion on his shoulder.

"Hang on," he said, inspecting the area and touching it. "This hurt?"

"A little but not bad."

"Good. Here, put this stuff on."

Paul noted that the clothes fit Daniel pretty well. It was in that moment that the full gravity of the situation hit him. Overcome with emotion, he shook his head. "I thought I'd lost you." He hugged Daniel again and blinked back tears.

"Ready to head home?" he asked with a slight laugh.

To Paul's surprise, Daniel shook his head and said "No." He looked at Paul resolutely. "Look, I'm OK. Let's dry my stuff out and make a go of it. This can still be a great trip."

That moment was one that stayed with Paul for the rest of his life, and he often thought it was a defining moment, not only for Daniel in his own life but also in how he perceived his son. He was a good kid...no, a good *man*.

Paul smiled. "You sure?"

"Yeah. Are...are *you* okay with that?" Daniel asked.

Paul took a deep breath and exhaled slowly. "Yeah, I think so."

Daniel nodded toward the trail. "Let's try to make our way to the camp site."

They started walking and briefly stopped at the place where Daniel had fallen. Paul retrieved the rope, one side still coiled around the tree. Daniel noticed his dad handling it gingerly.

"Your hands okay?"

"Yeah, just some abrasions is all."

Pushing on, they hiked about four more miles and found the spot they'd reserved to make camp. They strung their sleeping hammocks—which Paul had mistakenly deemed more comfortable than a tent—across adjacent trees using the rope and adjusted the length so the hammocks hung a foot or so above ground.

Daniel emptied his soggy pack, dangling the items from tree limbs to dry, as Paul finished unpacking a few things of his own for the evening ahead. They gathered twigs to make a fire—desperate to remove the chill from the brisk October air—and pulled out a couple of packets of freeze-dried lasagna. Paul read the directions. *Just add water. Even I can't mess that up.*

He produced a small stove and filled a collapsible pot with water. Once it started boiling, he tore open the top of the package and stirred the water into the noodles. Steam wafted out, the cheesy, meaty aromas making Paul's stomach growl. "There's some water left for yours, Daniel," he said over his shoulder while looking for a place to sit.

Ah, he thought. *The hammock.*

Squatting down and holding the top of the lasagna pouch with one hand, he spread out the fabric with the other to make a comfy place to sit. The ropes strained but held firm in response to his weight, and he marveled at how secure the hammock felt under him.

"Here's hoping it's smooth sailing from this point on," he said to Daniel while pulling a spoon from his shirt pocket. Just as he was about to take his first bite, Paul made a novice mistake: he leaned *way* back. His feet suddenly went airborne, his head grazing the ground as he backflipped onto his chest with a *whoomph* that knocked the breath out of him. Daniel saw the acrobatics out of the corner of his eye and came running over, asking if Paul was OK.

"Yeah," Paul said after a few moments, rising to his knees and seeing the contents of the pouch now covering the front of his jacket. He cleaned up the best he could and shared Daniel's dinner that night.

After finishing supper, the pair found a couple of large stones to sit on and rolled them over by the fire. Staring into the flames, Daniel chuckled.

"What?" Paul asked.

Daniel shook his head and smiled. "You flipping out of your hammock."

Paul managed a modest smile and nodded in acknowledgement. He looked at his son. "We'll always remember this trip, you and I."

"Ah." Daniel said nodding, "That we will."

"How's the shoulder?" Paul asked.

"Alright," Daniel replied. After a brief pause, he asked a question that surprised Paul. "Dad, I don't want you to take this the wrong way or anything, but I've been wondering...Are you doing okay?"

Paul looked up from the fire, a puzzled expression on his face. "What do you mean?"

"I don't know…It's just that you've seemed a little distant lately, like something's been bothering you. Am I overstaying my welcome with you and Mom? I know you guys expected me to go to college and that I need to get my own place at some point. You know, I really appreciate you letting me stay there."

"It's not that. Well, actually, I *do* want to talk to you about your longer-term plans at some point…but that's not really what's most pressing on my mind."

Paul hesitated.

"I don't want to burden you with that, Son."

"Dad, I'm an adult. I'm *family*. You saved my life today…I think we can have a personal moment here."

"Saved your life? I've been telling myself I almost *killed* you."

"Dad, I was the one who stepped too close to the edge. You secured me so that when I did fall, it wasn't headfirst." He paused, then continued, "Before I got out of the water, I looked up where I hit. The backpack saved me, but had I been tumbling head over heels, I probably would have cracked my skull during that fall."

A chill ran up Paul's spine, both from the thought as well as the plummeting nighttime temperature. "Maybe so," he replied quietly.

Daniel waited for more of a response to his original question but there was silence.

Daniel finally said, "So what's going on?"

Paul looked into the darkened woods, as if they held a response.

"I don't know, Daniel. I just feel like I'm in a rut. My career is one example."

Daniel looked puzzled, "What's the problem with your career?"

"It's like I've hit a wall I can't break through," Paul began. "I've been writing novels for nearly thirty years, which felt right for a while, creating worlds and characters that resonated with readers. But it has started to feel stagnant lately, all fake and seemingly irrelevant. I mean, what difference do my novels even make anyway? The business is changing too, with more pressure for blockbusters and publishers that want fresh voices and new ideas from younger minds. I feel like I'm on the sidelines."

Daniel thought for moment. "What about trying something different, like screenwriting or podcasts?"

Paul shook his head. "That would essentially be starting over. I don't have the energy. I wish I felt like my words still mattered."

Daniel did his best to sound encouraging. "I guess it's tough when our identity is so tied to our work, but remember, you're more than your novels, Dad, and you have Mom and me."

Paul nodded silently. He thought about Daniel: twenty years old, having never attended college and still living at home as a movie theater employee with zero clue about his life plans. Then there was Katherine, his wife of roughly twenty-five years who'd seemed distant over the past several months. He worried they were drifting apart.

"I do have you two, but even with your mom, I feel like we're not connecting the way we used to." Paul looked up, surprised he'd said the words aloud to his son. "Sorry…I'm saying too much."

"No, Dad. I actually sensed that." Daniel chose his words carefully. "Do you think she feels the same? Maybe she's going through her own struggles."

"Maybe."

"What do you think about doing something out of the ordinary for her, something spontaneous like when you were younger, so she knows you still care?"

Paul frowned. "What do you mean? A gift or something?"

"More like an experience for the two of you," Daniel clarified. His eyebrows raised with the flicker of an idea. "Why don't you throw her a surprise party for her next birthday? Isn't she turning fifty this year? We could have a small shindig at the house."

Intrigued, Paul weighed the suggestion. "A surprise party.

That's actually not a bad idea. Her birthday isn't until May, so it would give me some time to plan."

Daniel grinned. "I could help you plan it."

Paul nodded, the idea growing in his mind. "Something to think about for sure. Thanks, Daniel."

They stared at the flames for several minutes.

"You sure you're okay?" Paul checked in again.

Daniel lifted his left arm and rotated it around above him. "Little sore but fine overall."

Paul shook his head. "I still can't get over that fall. I'll have nightmares about it for years."

Daniel nodded. "Trust me, I will too."

"And I'll never get your scream out of my head."

"I screamed?"

"Yes, you didn't realize that?"

"I guess not. It all happened so fast."

"Your mom will skin me alive if she finds out."

"Then let's make sure she doesn't."

Paul laughed, cherishing the moment with his son—both counselor and co-conspirator. *Yes, that kid'll turn out just fine.*

Daniel yawned and stood up. "I'm beat. Time to hit the hay, err, hammock."

"I'm turning in too," Paul said. Arriving at his hammock, he carefully lowered himself and shimmied into his sleeping bag.

As the hammock slowly rocked back and forth, Paul listened to the dwindling crackle of the fire. *There's something about being in the darkness of the woods with Daniel and being away from all the distractions that speaks to the importance of family.* The night air seemed to lighten, and hope, especially for a rekindled relationship with Katherine, began to calm his anxieties. He sensed an inflection point.

* * *

They spent two more nights on the trail and completed the

roughly twenty-one-mile trail loop in three and a half days of hiking. The return trip home to Detroit took about six hours—including an hour to fill up the car with gas and take a lunch break—and was filled with discussions about the fall, how it happened, how lucky they were it wasn't more serious and what they would do differently next time. Sprinkled in were lighter topics of conversation, parts of the trail they enjoyed most and brainstorming other things to do together.

Back at 350 Gordon Drive, Paul shouted, "We're home!"

Katherine looked out from the kitchen. "Oh, hi you two. Welcome home, how was the trip?" she asked.

"It was good. Nothing too exciting, we completed the loop just fine. Gorgeous area," Paul told her.

Daniel smiled, winked at his dad and gave his mom a hug. "I'm heading up for a shower."

After Katherine left an hour later to play tennis at the country club, Paul spent the afternoon unpacking and stashing away his camping gear.

In his home office later that evening, he found himself lost in thought—pacing the room and imagining how he'd execute the surprise party, wanting to put all the focus on Katherine and create a night she'd never forget. One filled with laughter and joy, elements that had seemingly faded from their lives. He would run several ideas by Daniel in the days to come.

Chapter 2

Paul woke to the faint melody of "Moonlight Sonata" wafting upwards from downstairs. He pictured Katherine's delicate fingers gracefully gliding over the keys with a self-taught skill that made the piano seem like an extension of her body. The notes plaintively rose and fell, and he marveled at her ability to render such emotion from strings under tension. Music often transported him, evoking memories and even shifting his mood. Even though she'd played that sonata hundreds of times, he never wearied of hearing it.

He thought about her surprise birthday party, scheduled for that Friday night. He'd taken painstaking care to make the arrangements over the past several months, and Daniel had advised him throughout the process. For the first time in several weeks, he felt well prepared for the event. Daniel and several neighbors had their instructions. All he had to do was get her out of the house. A lengthy dinner would do the trick.

After a few moments, he heard her moving about the kitchen. Clad in an old running shirt and a pair of yellow Patagonia shorts, he rose from the bed, his fifty-five-year-old knees making a cracking sound as he stood. He shuffled into the bathroom, washed his face, and walked downstairs to the first floor of the sprawling colonial home: a product of Detroit's exploding growth in the 1920s when it bustled from the twin economic engines of easy money and optimism. He entered the kitchen where Katherine was already eating breakfast, her face shielded behind the morning paper. He glanced out the rear bay window, yawned, and stretched.

"Good morning."

She lowered the paper and acknowledged him with a restrained smile. "Good morning. I left you some toast," she said before returning to the article in front of her. Paul glanced at the headline on the front page of *The Detroit News*—"Recent Violence Linked to Gang Activity"—and sat down at the breakfast table with black coffee and toast.

From behind the paper, Katherine said, "Remind me where your book signing is today?"

"McIntyre's."

"Sounds nice."

"The owner told me they expect a hundred or so, so it won't be a big crowd like last week, but I enjoy these smaller venues. Much more intimate. What kind of day do you have?"

"Not too busy. Frank has some briefs that need to be filed, and Tony has a deposition he wants me to help him prepare for. I may be a little late tonight since I want to stop at the art supply store to pick up some new brushes."

"Okay, I'll pick up some takeout for us. Chinese sound okay?"

"Sure."

"Hey, I was thinking…How about if I take you shopping after dinner to get you something for your birthday? Maybe we can go to The Black Dress or Neiman Marcus or some other nice dress place? I have something for you, but it isn't quite enough, and I thought maybe you could pick something out."

"That's sweet, but you don't have to do that."

"I want to. Let's do it, okay?"

Katherine laughed softly under her breath while carrying her plate to the sink. "Okay. Thank you, Paul."

"Daniel up yet?" Paul asked.

"No. He doesn't have to go into work until five o'clock today."

"Did you ever think he'd still be living with us at this age?"

Katherine smiled. "No, but I also never figured I'd enjoy having him in the house at this age."

* * *

That evening after dinner, Paul and Katherine finished cleaning up and opted to go to Neiman Marcus, given its larger selection. Katherine tried on several dresses, and with each one, she asked Paul what he thought. For the first three—each conservative outfits Katherine could easily wear to McGee and Crampton, the law firm where she worked —Paul offered muted responses.

"Looks nice," he said, his enthusiasm lacking.

There was a fourth dress, a cherry red, Italian ruffled number with a surplice neckline that showcased her neck and shoulders. It didn't look like anything she would typically wear, and Paul loved it even more for that reason. Katherine balked at trying it on but acquiesced to his prodding.

When she walked out of the dressing room, Paul's eyes spoke before his lips. "Oh…Katherine," he managed to utter, his mouth agape.

Katherine laughed. "It's not me."

Paul's eyes admired, almost hungrily, her figure: the product of an active lifestyle that included swimming and Zumba classes.

"Oh, but it is. You don't know it, but it's you in spades."

"It's expensive. It's a Chiara Boni."

Paul laughed. "I don't care." He forced his eyes away from

her body to look into her eyes and said, "We're buying it."

Driving home, Paul said, "Let's have a nice dinner Friday night to celebrate your birthday. Maybe you can wear that dress for me." He shook his head. "Katherine, you look gorgeous in it."

"That sounds nice."

* * *

That Friday night, Paul and Katherine dined at their country club just as Paul had arranged. She'd resisted wearing the dress at first, saying she felt silly wearing it for just the two of them, but he laughed and said, "Honey, look. Let's act like we are going somewhere special. I'll dust off my tuxedo."

"You are one-hundred percent crazy, but okay."

To Katherine's relief, it was a quiet night at the club, and they saw none of their friends at dinner before leaving around eight o'clock to return home.

Once in the driveway, Paul held the car door for Katherine. She got out, frowned, and said, "That's odd…I thought I left the lights on. Maybe Daniel flipped them off when he left to hang out with his friends."

Paul acknowledged her statement with a neutral "Hmmm" and walked into the house ahead of her. As they turned a corner to enter the main part of the darkened place, he flipped on the lights. Suddenly, friends from years past and present jumped out from behind curtains and furniture. "Surprise!"

Katherine, mouth open, stared for a few seconds as if her brain had not caught up to her eyes. She slowly turned to look at Paul, who laughed with delight.

"Oh, Paul!" She leaned in and hugged him before a swarm of people converged on her.

"Katherine, you look absolutely stunning," Paul overheard one of her girlfriends say, stepping back from her embrace to fully eye the red dress. She added, "When Paul sent out the invitations several weeks ago and said no one would be allowed into the house unless they were wearing black or white and *only* black or white, I could not for the life of me understand why!" She looked around the room and added, "Well, one thing's for sure: All eyes are on *you* tonight!"

A band situated in the corner of their expansive, marble-floored parlor began to play KC and the Sunshine Band's "Get Down Tonight," the furniture having been removed to make room for dancing. As the evening wore on, champagne and cocktails flowed liberally. Katherine danced much of the evening. She even danced three songs with Tony Leone, one of the senior partners at her law firm who had briefly trained, in dance no less, at Julliard.

In fact, Tony moved with such command and grace that Paul was reminded of old movie scenes with Astaire and Rogers. At one point, Tony looked over at Paul, smiled and winked, and said, "Hey ol' man, want to give it a try?" Paul shook his head and managed to say, "No, you look like you've got it under control." He was relieved that he wouldn't have to follow Tony's dance moves. It was an enchanted evening, even for Paul.

The next morning, they slept until nine—quite late for them both—and Katherine stirred Paul upon waking. He looked at the clock and groggily managed, "Wow. Nine o'clock." Paul thought about their relationship and how he'd hoped the party might give a boost to their intimacy. He rolled over, saw Katherine gazing dreamily at the ceiling, and said, "I love you." She responded by laying her head on his chest. He put his arm around her and shut his eyes, oblivious to almost everything in the room except the feel of her body next to his and the warm, rhythmic pattern of her breath against his skin.

Chapter 3

June 2018

The day had gone much like any other, with Paul grinding out a few pages and Katherine assisting with legal documents, culminating with the two of them retiring to the den for dinner and to watch the news. "Want me to pour you another glass of wine?" Paul asked, rising from his chair.

"Thanks, but I better not. I need to head to the grocery store to pick up a couple of things for when the Cashwells come over this weekend."

She grabbed a list stuck to the refrigerator door and walked to the back door. "I'm heading out...shouldn't be long."

"Okay," Paul responded, changing the channel to a nightly business report that started at eight o'clock.

At about nine-fifteen, he glanced at this watch, thinking she must have had more things to pick up than she'd originally anticipated. She was still not home thirty minutes later. With only a mild sense of concern, he dialed her phone. After six or seven rings, it went to voicemail. Odder still. She would normally pick up or otherwise send the call straight to voicemail if on the phone. He tried her again at ten o'clock and once more at ten-fifteen, each time with more anxiety when he got her voicemail.

By ten-thirty, he was frantic and called Daniel to see if he'd heard from his mom. Daniel said no, and when he asked if something was wrong, Paul acted as if he wasn't worried. "She must have just gotten tied up."

"Okay, Dad. By the way, I might be out a little late tonight."

"Sure."

Paul hung up and decided to go try to find her. The store was only ten minutes away, and he knew her usual route. He had just turned off the TV and grabbed his empty wine glass when he heard the back door open.

"That you? I was worried!" he yelled toward the rear of the house.

Silence.

He walked from the den to the kitchen and dropped the glass in his hand. Katherine stood in front of him—blouse ripped open, bra askew, skirt twisted. Mascara stained her face.

"I was assaulted. I was…raped."

"Katherine!" Paul went to throw his arms around her, but she collapsed to the floor and erupted into uncontrollable sobs.

At first, he thought she'd fainted and he'd tried to catch her, but she landed like a ragdoll with no strength in her legs. She wrapped her arms around herself and balled up into a fetal position. Paul tried to control his shock, gently pulling her close to him and whispering, "I have you… You're safe… It's okay now…I have you…" He looked down at her blouse and saw her left breast exposed. Feeling his eyes on her, she quickly pulled her blouse tightly around her before hugging her arms against her chest once again.

They sat without speaking for several minutes, Paul rocking her gently back and forth and reassuring her that she was home and nothing more could happen to her. Her crying began to subside, and Paul noticed her eyes were closed. Her face did not look bruised.

"Honey," he said, "Talk to me. What happened?"

She didn't respond, and he waited a moment.

"Should we go to the hospital?"

She shook her head no.

"It may be a good idea to get checked out. Maybe we should call the police."

She shook her head no slowly and resolutely.

Paul's voice became firmer. "Who did this to you?"

Katherine rolled to her knees and shakily stood up, Paul helping her.

"I just want to sit for a minute and not talk, okay?"

She walked through the kitchen, carefully navigating the shards of glass and straightening her clothing, and entered the den. Paul followed closely behind and sat beside her on the couch.

He asked once more, "Honey...what happened?"

She began crying again. "I can't talk about this now."

Her eyes suddenly shifted toward the ceiling. "Oh no. Is Daniel here? I don't want him to know about this."

"No. He's out, remember?"

"Oh. That's right." Katherine sat in silence for a few minutes before asking, "Would you fix me a glass of wine?"

"Of course," Paul said, standing and heading for the kitchen.

She stood. "I'll be right back. I'm going to the bathroom."

Paul stopped and turned. Hesitating, he said softly, "I don't mean to be...insensitive...by asking this, but should we go to the police first?"

Katherine glared at him, her words tinged with resentment, "Paul, I *need* to go to the bathroom. Besides, I'm not sure I want to go to the police anyway."

Paul nodded, "Okay, sorry. I was just asking the question."

"Make it a generous pour."

Paul did as he was asked and then waited on the couch for several minutes before walking to the bathroom door and asking, "Are you okay in there?"

"I'll be out in a minute," she said curtly.

"Okay."

She returned in another minute, taking the glass of wine with trembling fingers and consecutive swigs before draining its contents completely.

Paul looked pleadingly into her eyes. "Katherine, look, I know this is incredibly difficult, but there may be details you can recall now and not later." He reached out and touched her arm. "What can you tell me?"

Katherine sighed heavily. "He was white with short hair, almost a buzz cut. Maybe forty years old. Southern accent, and he had a couple of tattoos: a tiger on his left bicep and two teardrops on his right eye."

"Had you ever seen him before?

"No."

"What did he do to you?"

Katherine shook her head. "Paul, I just don't know that I can talk about this right now."

"Okay." He waited a moment. "Honey, we *need* to report this."

She looked at him and then looked away.

He pulled out his cell phone. "I'll call the police, and you can tell me what to say."

Her eyes filled with tears of anger. "Paul, do you have any idea what's involved in reporting something like this? I don't think you do. I've read depositions of women who were attacked and had to testify. The only way *anything* is going to happen to the attacker is if he is brought to trial." She waited a moment and then added with emphasis, "And that doesn't even consider the embarrassment and humiliation of people talking about it behind your back. I'm not going to relive this in the courtroom nor have friends in the supermarket whispering, 'She was attacked, you know, a guy got into her car and made her drive...'" Her voice trailed off, and she started crying again.

Paul beheld her with eyes concealing his fury. Who was this man? Could he find him? What would he do if he *did* find him? Would Katherine relent and let the police investigate? One thing was clear: Katherine was not going to report anything that night.

"Would you like me to draw you a warm bath? Maybe with some bath salts, and I could put on some soft music while you soak?"

Katherine said nothing and simply nodded yes.

Paul asked as they headed to bed a few hours later, "Honey, don't you think your doctor should at least check you out?"

"I was thinking I might do that. I wanted to ask him about..." her voice trailed off, leaving Paul to wonder if "sexually transmitted diseases" had gotten caught in her throat. "I'll just call him in the morning," she rushed to finish.

Paul tossed listlessly in bed that night, listening to Katherine's rising and falling breath and trying to calm the adrenaline-fueled rage pulsing through his body. Every time he closed his eyes, he saw the man with the tear-drop tattoos and imagined his hands on his wife and her struggling. At twelve-thirty, he heard a noise downstairs and jerked upright in bed—initially fearing a burglar or even Katherine's rapist who might have followed her home. He quickly realized it was Daniel returning from his evening out, but his unease lingered. He finally got out of bed at two o'clock, went into the study, and turned on the television. The adrenaline slowly dissolved. By four o'clock, he was asleep.

Chapter 4

When Paul awoke a little after nine that morning, Katherine had already left for work. On top of the coffee maker, she'd left a note, "Hope you eventually got to sleep. Went on in to work," and signed it with a "K." He poured his cup of coffee and opened his laptop.

He googled "sexual assaults" and began reading about long-term psychological impacts on victims, the fact that as many as eighty percent of such assaults went unreported, and the toll they took on marriages—intimacy in particular. He also googled teardrop tattoos, learning they were a common gang symbol signifying the person had killed someone. Typing the words "tiger tattoo meaning," he found definitions suggesting power, fighting, and resilience.

Daniel walked into the kitchen.

"Morning. Are you working today?" Paul asked, looking up from his laptop.

"Yeah, leaving in a minute," Daniel said groggily as he retrieved a muffin from a box on the counter before abruptly walking out.

Paul pulled out his phone, typed, "You OK?" and hit send.

Moments later, a text arrived saying, "Yes. Trying to get some work done. Not easy. Thank you." A curt message and yet, Paul wondered: *What did I expect? I'll try to get more details tonight.*

Paul ate breakfast and showered, then got into his car and drove to the grocery store. On the way, questions peppered his mind: *Had she seen the car the attacker might have been driving? What was he wearing? How tall was he? Where had they driven?* And of course, the thing he most wanted to ask but least wanted to hear the answer to: *What did he do?*

He found himself peering into drivers' windows as he drove down the boulevard, looking for a man about forty years old with short, cropped hair and sporting a dark mark on his eye that would indicate a tattoo. The absurdity of finding him made him shake his head. "Needle in a haystack," he muttered. And yet, he continued to squint to spy the man behind each window he passed, wondering, *Is this him?*

Paul arrived at the grocery store and sat in the parking lot for thirty minutes. He watched as women with groceries walked out nonchalantly, totally oblivious to the fact that an abduction had occurred the very night before. His mind imagined Katherine in the car with the man, and he felt his jaw muscles tighten as questions plagued him. *Who was he? Would he ever be caught?* Paul was clueless about the answers, but he did know one thing: the man would never be caught if the crime was never reported.

He wondered: *What would I do if I saw him?* For several minutes, he got totally lost in his imagination, confronting this man and envisioning the physical struggle that might ensue. Paul—with his five-foot, ten-inch, one-hundred-seventy-five-pound frame and sagging mid-section—was not physically imposing, much less skillful in a fight, and hadn't been in an altercation since he was a young boy.

He didn't *think* he would confront him physically; but what if it couldn't be avoided? He was not a violent man by nature. He had friends who loved to watch Friday night fights, buddies who loved to go hunting—even Daniel—and yet Paul had no interest in doing those things.

This was different, though. His protective nature had been reinforced in his own upbringing by a loving but military-hardened father, now dead twenty years. Paul drove back home and spent the rest of the day trying unsuccessfully to add a thousand words to his manuscript. Nearly every sentence he wrote had an edge to it.

Katherine came home about six o'clock. She walked into the house as if nothing had happened the night before, simply saying "Hey" to signal her arrival when the back door closed. Paul was seated in a recliner in the den, watching the beginning of the news. She walked in and sat on the couch.

"How…are you?" he asked.

"I'm okay," she responded. "Bit tired."

"Were you actually able to work?"

"Yeah….um, Tony had some briefs that needed to be filed. It was the mindless sort of stuff I needed." She seemed eager to change the subject and added, "Any ideas for dinner?"

Paul looked at her, unsure how to proceed.

"Katherine, we need to talk about this."

She looked at him, a bit coldly. "Why?" It was less a question than a statement.

"That man is still out there. He could do the same thing again."

"So, in the interest of protecting everyone, you think I should go to the police and report it, to essentially relive last night to them, with all the probing and…" she thought for a moment, then added, "…humiliating detail. I won't let that be who I am Paul, the woman who got raped at the SuperMart. I won't be remembered that way."

Paul watched her to see if she would go on, trying to imagine what she meant by "humiliating." If only she would talk.

He nodded.

Neither spoke for a moment. She started for the kitchen.

"Wine?" she asked.

"No, thanks."

He heard the clink of a glass against the quartz countertop, the refrigerator door open, the pop of a cork, and the glub-glub-glub of an extended pour. Katherine returned with an overfilled goblet of Chardonnay in one hand and a box of Wheat Thins in the other.

The news announcer was talking about the weather.

"Katherine, even if we don't report it, I'm your husband. I *have* to know some answers."

She didn't respond. Taking a big gulp of wine, she looked down at the box and retrieved several crackers.

"Katherine."

She stopped chewing and looked at him.

"Yes."

"What happened?"

She nodded slightly with what seemed like resignation that Paul wouldn't accept no for an answer.

"Okay." She put her glass down. "What do you want to know?"

Paul rose from the recliner and sat beside her. "Can we start with what happened?"

She looked down at the floor, as if trying to focus, before proceeding.

"I got there...to the SuperMart...and the parking lot wasn't too crowded. I got out of the car and noticed a man sitting in a black pickup truck parked a couple spaces away. At first, I just figured he was waiting for someone. I walked in front of his truck toward the entrance and could feel his eyes staring at me. You know that feeling? I just kept walking."

Paul nodded.

"So, I go in, do my shopping, and notice the truck's still there when I leave the store. Seemed a little strange he'd still be there."

She took a sip of wine.

"Anyway, I felt like he was sort of creepy, so I walked behind his truck on the way to my car and glanced at it out of the corner of my eye when I walked past. There was a Confederate flag decal on the rear window. Not big but clearly visible…driver's side."

Paul processed this new information. At least it was a start.

"I go to my car and open the front passenger-side door to put the groceries in the front seat."

She hesitated and took a deep breath before continuing.

"All of the sudden, I feel myself getting shoved forward and land on the center console. The guy said 'Don't scream' and pushed me again, getting in behind me."

Paul realized he was clenching his fists.

"He closes the door, and I say, 'What do you want? Get out! I'll give you my money, just let me go,' and he looks around to see if anyone is near and yells, 'Drive!'"

"I start pressing my horn…I hold it down, and he knocks my hand away, and I notice he has a knife in it. He punches me in my side, and it knocks the breath out of me, and I start…" Tears begin filling her eyes, her voice trembling. She struggled to continue. "…gasping for air…I couldn't breathe …"

Paul put his hand on her shoulder. "Stop for a minute, Katherine. Take your time."

Nodding, she got up and retrieved a box of Kleenex from the bathroom before returning to her seat next to Paul. Taking a deep breath, she continued.

"So, he grabs me by the hair and…holds a knife to my throat. I'm guessing it was the blunt side because I could feel the metal, but it didn't cut me. I can still hear his voice," she said, shuddering. "'I'll slice that pretty little throat of yours if you try that again. You won't get hurt if you do what I tell you to do. *Drive*.'"

Paul tried to appear calm despite his racing heart and rapid breathing.

"So, I drove."

She stopped and looked at Paul, almost as if that were the end of the account.

He sensed her reluctance to proceed and asked in a reassuring voice, "Where did he make you drive?"

"To a dirt road a couple of miles away." She didn't elaborate.

"And that's where it happened?"

She nodded yes, putting her hand to her throat and beginning to cry again but more softly this time.

"Honey, is there any chance at all you can vocalize what exactly he did?"

She bit her lower lip, her face contorting, and shook her head no.

Paul nodded slowly.

"How can we not report this?"

Katherine's countenance immediately shifted from one of vulnerability to desperation and even anger. She said in a raised voice that echoed throughout the house, "No! I...said...no!"

She began crying inconsolably, loudly.

Daniel, who was now at the top of the stairs, yelled, "Mom?! What's going on? Are you okay?"

Katherine was too wracked with sobs to respond. Hearing their son bound down the stairs, Paul glanced at his wife. She shook her head back and forth with a look that said, "Don't you *dare* tell him."

Daniel stopped at the doorway and stared at them.

"It's okay, Daniel," Paul said. "I've got it."

Daniel stayed silent, eyes shifting hesitantly from one parent to the other.

"Um...alright," he said indecisively, his eyes lingering on his mother as he turned to head back to his room.

Katherine's face was buried in her hands. Paul gently pulled them away.

He whispered, "Look at me."

She slowly lifted her eyes to his. He cradled her face in his hands and kissed her cheeks, wet with tears. He whispered softly, his eyes filled too, and said, "We won't tell anyone. I promise."

Paul wrapped his arms around Katherine, and she returned his embrace. "I know this is hard for you too," she whispered.

They silently remained that way for several minutes, Paul stunned by how two lives could be thrown into such turmoil so quickly.

He eventually stood up and said, "Let me go check on Daniel. I'll tell him it's work-related."

* * *

Several times over the next few weeks, Paul drove to the SuperMart and parked, hoping to get a glimpse of a black pickup truck with a Confederate emblem on the back. He tried to imagine what he'd do if he saw the man. The fact was he didn't know, and each time he played out a scenario, it changed from the one before. In one unlikely situation, he might confront the man, maybe even attack the guy, without saying anything—throwing himself at him with fists and knees until the rapist was rendered helpless on the ground. That scenario, Paul realized, was a bit unlikely. This was a younger man, likely a much tougher guy. Paul was more likely to be on the losing end of any violent exchange; he could be killed. Other scenarios were sometimes less violent, but they all involved some level of interaction, of justice, and that brought at least a measure of, ironically, "peace" to his mind.

He wondered how Katherine would react to his efforts to find the man. There was an easy solution: he simply wouldn't tell her. Paul would sometimes say he was running out for an errand, or heading to the pharmacy, sometimes truthfully saying he was "running to the grocery store." He would often arrive back an hour and a half later. Katherine never seemed to wonder about his evening jaunts, except for one evening when she said, without expression, "You're sure going out a lot. What, are you seeing somebody?"

Paul had playfully said, "Honey, come on," and dismissed her question. She remained expressionless and didn't say anything in response. After thinking about the exchange, it dawned on Paul how much her demeanor had changed over the past few years. Five years ago, she had an engaging, playful demeanor, and now in its place was either apathy or a hair trigger temper that could be set off by the most innocent of comments.

Katherine had stopped eating breakfast, and her face began to take on a drawn look despite extra time spent in front of the mirror every morning—extra makeup used to cover eyes swollen from weeping or lack of sleep.

One evening, Paul came up behind her and kissed her neck as he'd done many times in the past. But this time, she recoiled, jerking away in fear and shrieking, "Paul, don't you *ever* do that to me!" Paul felt like a violator himself, and he wondered if they would ever experience intimacy in the same way as before.

"Darling, I'm so sorry. I'm so sorry! Please forgive me..." he implored, but the damage was done. She stormed out of the kitchen with Paul left to wonder if the rapist had been behind her in some similar way. It stirred up his rage at the man anew.

She began sleeping more, often taking a sedative at bedtime, and seldom ventured out of the house. Paul would suggest, "Honey, why don't we go grab dinner after work tonight and maybe take in a movie?" hoping to alleviate her despondent demeanor. She invariably refused.

She also refused him in bed. One Friday night, Paul placed his hand on her arm, saying, "Honey, you know, it's been a long time. I miss...being intimate with you."

Katherine looked at him and said, "I know, I'm sorry," before turning over and going to sleep.

The only thing she seemed more engaged in, as it turned out, was work. Paul had heard of people doing that—throwing themselves into their jobs—after enduring personal tragedies, and he figured maybe that wasn't all bad. Their relationship, though, silently suffered. What little hope he had summoned within himself after her surprise party, and the brief thawing from what had become a somewhat cool and distant demeanor, quickly vanished.

Daniel, for his part, still had no idea about the assault. He'd sometimes ask, "Mom, are you okay? You don't look like you're feeling well."

Her response was always some version of the same: "I'm fine."

One night, Daniel asked if she was going to the grocery store soon and mentioned a couple of items he needed. She asked him to put it on "the list." But it was Paul who always went to the store, and he never complained, as it was an excuse for him to linger in the parking lot and to keep watch for the black pickup truck.

Early one evening, when Paul was on his way home about a mile from the grocery store, he picked up the phone to ask Katherine if she needed anything. He pulled out his phone and hit the speed dial as he was approaching a stop light. As he looked up, he realized the car in front of him had stopped suddenly, and he had to slam on brakes to avoid rear-ending it. The phone call went to her voicemail, and he hung up. "Whew," he muttered under his breath. He looked around casually.

And then he saw it: a black pickup truck—a Ford F-150— one car ahead of him in the next lane over…with a Confederate flag on the back windshield. His heart began racing, the adrenaline kicking in with such alacrity that he felt as if his entire body were buzzing with an electrical current.

He stared, unblinking. His eyes shifted from the truck to the light, which finally changed to green. Where was the truck heading? Paul panicked. *What the hell do I do now?* He looked in the back seat, eyeing an old baseball bat of Daniel's he'd stashed under some papers when he first started trying to find the man—figuring he'd need to rely on more than his fists should a fight ever break out.

Paul squinted, trying to make out the driver. His lane began to inch forward, his car now five feet behind the pickup in the adjacent lane. Paul could see a man's hand holding a phone. He was either dialing or texting but put it down as the cars in front of him started to move.

Paul put on his blinker and looked back to see if he could pull in behind the pickup truck. The car behind him flashed its lights and Paul pulled in behind the black truck as the line of cars accelerated through the intersection. *The tag...get the tag.* Paul reached into his console and managed to find a pen and scrap of paper.

He furiously scribbled "KCS 2899 Michigan" while attempting to steer with his knees, glancing up between letters to avoid a collision. He reread it to confirm just as traffic picked up speed and the space between cars grew. The Ford pulled into the left lane to pass a slower car, and moments later returned to the right lane. Paul followed, staying back a bit to avoid notice. The truck slowed and turned right onto a residential street.

Paul slowed down to add a little more distance. As he proceeded down the dimly lit street, he noticed boarded-up homes and graffiti painted on dumpsters, signs, and buildings. The truck made a left and a quick right onto Pineview Street before pulling into a driveway.

Paul stopped short, pulled over against the curb, and turned off his automatic headlights while leaving the engine running. From about three houses away, Paul watched as the man got out of the truck illuminated by a nearby streetlight. He relaxed his clinched grip on the steering wheel, wiped the perspiration from his hands, and tried to slow his breathing. He had no idea what to do.

It's actually him... the man who assaulted Katherine. He reached back and positioned the baseball bat on the floorboard with the handle pointing towards him in case he needed to grab it quickly.

The man walked to his mailbox. Paul assessed the man's

physique, which looked to be about Paul's height but a bit stockier. He opened the mailbox, appeared to glance at the letters under the dim light, then ambled back toward the house. *If I wait much longer, it'll be too late to confront him in his yard. What would I even say? Should I say anything? Should I just rush in wielding the bat, which is what I feel like doing?*

The man walked onto the dark front porch of a modest light-colored clapboard house and paused at the door, presumably to unlock it. He walked inside. Paul took his foot off the brake and inched his car forward so that he was angled to see inside the house. A light in what must have been the living room came on. Paul saw the man walk past the window, then back. A car turned down Pineview and began approaching, the headlights briefly illuminating the interior of Paul's car. Paul turned off the engine and took his foot off the brake, not wanting to draw any attention. The car passed and continued down the street.

For several minutes, Paul sat motionless, just watching the lights from the television flicker against the side wall of the man's living room. The darkness had prevented Paul from ever really getting a good look at his face, and he wondered: *What does this guy look like?*

He quietly opened his car door and, as an afterthought, grabbed the baseball bat from the floor behind him. He eased out of the car and gently pushed the door shut. He stared for a moment at the open view into the house and looked around. No one was in sight, the stillness of the evening broken only by the distant bark of a dog.

Paul took several hesitating steps towards the house, stubbing his toe on a brick that was lying in the yard. He swore under his breath and gingerly moved forward. He paused when he got to the truck, walking to the driver's side and peering in. He couldn't see anything. He reached for the door handle to see if it was unlocked, but he quickly lost his nerve, fearing it might have an alarm. Its polished exterior beamed under the streetlight; it looked new.

He carefully made his way to the darkened front porch, eyeing the number "231" beside the closed front door. Inching closer to the window, he hugged the front of the house to remain out of sight and angled his head out from the wall to peer into the room: spotting a Confederate flag on the wall and a small bookcase. He could hear the television. Moving closer, he had a partial view of the man's head mere feet away. If he turned around, he'd most assuredly see Paul.

Paul's adrenaline-fueled heart pounded, his breathing rapid and shallow. With his right hand tightly clenched around the handle of the bat, he felt the anger rising within him and yet—at the same time—was afraid of this man. The combination of rage and fear anchored him motionless for a full minute as he struggled with the incompatible objectives of revenge and safety.

The man reached up to scratch the left side of his neck and tilted his head slightly to the right, turning slightly toward Paul who could now see the two black marks high on his right cheek near the corner of his eye. *The teardrop tattoos.*

Paul looked at the rest of the room. On the other wall was a poster of a football team with the Detroit Lions emblem on it, and in the far corner, an old-timey rifle that looked of Civil War vintage along with a few kettlebells and a lava lamp on top of the bookcase. A floor lamp stood in the corner. The man shifted on the couch and turned his head as if preparing to look outside. Paul jerked back away from view…waiting…listening.

What the hell do I do now? he asked himself and weighed his options: ring the doorbell, wait for the guy to open the door and attack him (probably a terrible choice since the guy probably had a gun somewhere and would likely wrestle the bat away from Paul anyway), or ring the doorbell and threaten to kill him if he ever got near Katherine again—probably a bad option as well. Then there was the third option: wait for another opportunity to avenge Katherine's attack. That seemed like the most prudent one.

With his eyes fixed on the back of the man's head, he silently and warily inched backwards, retracing his steps, and then stepped off the porch and into the front yard. He quickened his pace, watching where he was stepping, and noticed the brick he'd kicked earlier. He paused, looked back at the truck and then at his own car twenty feet away.

Paul pictured the man waxing his big, black Ford F-150, probably his most prized possession probably. He shifted the bat to his left hand, picked up the brick, and walked over to the front of the pickup. Rearing back and with all his might, he hurled the heavy crimson block directly into the front windshield right in front of the driver's seat. A thunderous crash ensued, and the window shattered—spider-web fissures covering the entire plate of glass. He looked at the house and saw the man peer out the window and rush for his front door.

Paul sprinted to his car and pushed the "Engine Start" button as quickly as he could. Nothing happened. He jabbed at it wildly, looking up at the front door as the man bolted out of his house and straight toward Paul's car. Paul quickly locked his doors, still desperately pushing the button, and his arm grazed the console gear shift that was apparently not in the right position. He looked down frantically and saw he'd left it in "Drive." Ramming it into "Park," he put his foot on the brake and pushed the start button again. Success. He floored the accelerator right as the man reached the car.

Paul's tires screeched as he peeled away, and he saw the man rushing toward the F-150 in the rear-view mirror. Paul was a block away and preparing to make a left turn onto a street he hoped would lead to a main road when he saw headlights bounce as the truck bounded over a curb in pursuit. Paul timed his high-speed turn well, his tires emitting a high-pitched "eeeerk" as he struggled to keep them in contact with the pavement.

He narrowly missed a car parked on the right side of the street and once again gunned the engine, looking back and seeing the truck make the same turn. It was gaining on him. Paul looked at his speedometer—a little over sixty and climbing on a narrow residential road—and with increasing dread realized there was a good chance the altercation he'd dreaded was becoming much more likely. He made another quick left, as did the Ford, which was now only about thirty to forty feet behind him.

Paul searched for another street to turn onto and, to his relief, saw one just ahead. He slowed as he approached it, the truck only feet behind his car. Paul looked again in the mirror. The gaping hole on the driver's side was the only way the man could see—the windshield completely shattered otherwise—and the two cars barreled under a streetlight. Paul got a momentary glance of the man's illuminated and enraged face, inches away from the opening as he struggled to see.

Paul could see an intersection ahead with a red light and feared a collision if he rushed through it, still going at least sixty. Stopping was a poor alternative. With another side street ahead on the right and in a momentary flash of perception, it occurred to Paul that the man's view would be obscured by any quick *right* turn, no gaping hole to see through on that side amidst all the cracks. He sped up, as if preparing to bolt through the upcoming intersection, and the truck did as well. Paul turned sharply at the last minute, his tires screaming while barely gripping the pavement, as both cars pushed the limits of physics—friction pitted against centrifugal force. In Paul's case, friction won. In the case of the Ford F-150, centrifugal force.

Paul watched in his rear-view mirror as the pickup truck fishtailed and slammed into the curb, no doubt wrecking the axle and its wheels. Paul was amazed it hadn't flipped and saw it had stopped in a perpendicular position to the street, its lights still on.

He wondered if the truck was drivable but wasn't going to wait around to find out. He made the first left and then approached the main road and made a right. He stared and drove, unblinking and trying not to draw any attention to himself. He wiped his forehead with the back of his hand, drying it on his shirt, and took a deep breath.

After Paul's breathing had finally begun to moderate, he made a left at the next intersection to drive back home. He pulled into his driveway fifteen minutes later and shut off his car, sitting there for another moment before exiting and hearing the *click* of an overheated engine cooling down. He walked into the house.

Katherine was in the kitchen and stared at him as soon as she saw him. "Good heavens, you're as white as a sheet," she said, her face showing concern. "Are you okay?"

Paul, looking down, shook his head no and struggled to find the words. He wanted to tell her.

"Paul…What happened?"

Paul looked from the floor to her. "I nearly had a wreck."

"Where?"

He went on to recount an imaginary near-head-on collision with a "likely" drunk driver, the details of his account convincing. Katherine, for the first time in a long time, seemed genuinely concerned about him.

She shook her head. "Well, I'm so glad you're okay. Why don't you go sit down? The news is coming on…How about I get you something to drink, or eat?"

The rest of the evening was uneventful. After Katherine went to bed, Paul powered up his laptop and googled phrases like, "Ways to trace people through license tag information." He also went to the Wayne County property tax site and typed in the man's address, finding a name. Digging deeper, he googled him and found a LinkedIn profile for a real estate investor. When he studied the photo, though, it was a completely different person than the man who had attacked Katherine.

Chapter 5

Over the next week, Paul didn't return to the man's house, though it was never far from his mind. He spent a few more hours trying to research the tag, all to no avail, and began thinking about alternative ways to find out more about the man. It dawned on him that perhaps the easiest way was to simply ask one of the attorneys Katherine worked with…if he could do it without arousing suspicion, that is.

Which attorney should he call? He wasn't sure he wanted Katherine to know about this, so maybe he'd tell the lawyer he was just trying to identify a suspicious vehicle in the neighborhood and didn't want to unnecessarily alarm Katherine. He thought about Tony. "I bet he'd do it," Paul whispered to himself. He looked up the number for the firm and called it before he had a chance to think it through any further.

A receptionist picked up.

"Hi, is Tony Leone in, please?"

Seconds later, Tony was on the line. "Paul, how good to hear from you. I was just telling Katherine the other day what a wonderful party you threw for her. The band was terrific."

"Thanks, Tony. It was a fun party to plan. I appreciated you joining us." Paul paused. "Umm, Tony, I have a question and thought maybe you have the answer being in criminal litigation and all. Is there any way you can trace a vehicle tag number to see who the owner is?"

"The firm doesn't, but I have people who can help. What exactly are you trying to find out?"

Paul hesitated while his mind crafted a response.

"Well, it's probably nothing, but we've had a string of break-ins in the neighborhood over the past few months, and one of my buddies said he saw a suspicious car driving down the street and wrote the tag down."

"Why don't you just give that information to the police?"

"I could, but I sort of doubt they ever really pursue things like that."

"Totally get it, but Paul, what would you even do with that information? I mean, let's say I get you the name and information about the person. What good does that do? It's not like you can do your own investigation."

"I know, but let's say I have enough information to at least run a background check and find the guy has a long rap sheet. It may make the police take the tip a little more seriously."

Tony laughed. "Paul, I don't know."

"Well, look Tony, don't worry about it if it's a hassle. I might be able to find some sort of online source I can use instead."

"No, it's not that much effort, but I wouldn't want you to do anything if it led to trouble. I mean, candidly, I could get in trouble if something bad resulted from my getting you this information. If I am able to turn something up, let's just keep it between us, okay?"

"Listen, Tony. I understand and wouldn't tell anyone. In fact, I was going to ask you not even mention this to Katherine. I don't want to upset her or make her worry about this sort of thing any more than she already does."

"Sure, understand. What's the tag?"

Paul read the number, and Tony repeated it back. "Give me a

couple days to look into it, and I'll get back to you. I won't mention it to Katherine."

"Thanks, Tony. You've meant a lot of Katherine over the years. She really thinks a lot of you, and I count you as a friend as well."

"Well...Paul...of course. Happy to help."

* * *

Tony called Paul two days later. "I have some information for you on the matter we discussed the other day."

Paul, in the middle of writing in his study, grabbed a notebook and pen.

"It's a Ford F-150 pickup truck, year 2017, does that sound about right?"

"Yes."

"Okay. The tag belongs to a man named Marcus Roberts. Lives at 231 Pineview Street. He has an extensive criminal background. Larceny, attempted murder, and multiple assault charges and convictions. Did time in a Georgia correctional facility for six years in fact. Paul, this is a tough character you're not going to want to mess with; but if you're trying to strengthen your case to go to the police, the information can't hurt."

Paul scribbled notes as he listened.

"That's helpful, Tony. Anything you can email me?"

"I'd rather not, Paul. As I said, it's a little unconventional for me to even give you this in the first place. Sorry."

"No worries, Tony. Thanks a million for your help. If I do turn this over to the police, I won't mention how I got the information."

"Thanks. Glad to help. And Paul, don't approach this guy, okay?"

"Got it. Thanks, Tony."

Paul hung up and considered going to Katherine with the

information. Would it help convince her to go to the police? Now that a few weeks had passed, would anything even happen though? There was no evidence and no known witnesses, so it would likely be her word against his. Why would he even want to put her through the process if a conviction was impossible? Moreover, as she wanted to "just move on," would introducing his name hinder her ability to recover from this? She already seemed so distant. Paul worried that bringing up the name would set her even further back.

Turning his attention to his computer, Paul typed "Marcus Roberts" and "Detroit, Michigan" into the search box. A number of links popped up, none seemingly relevant until Paul saw one titled "Mugshots." His eyes traveled down a corresponding page full of names and stopped on the man himself. *Marcus Roberts. Arrested for aggravated assault.* He clicked on the site, and the face of the man Paul instantly recognized as Katherine's attacker appeared on his screen. It felt like a gut punch.

The first thing Paul noticed were the teardrop tattoos. Behind those eyes, Roberts had a defiant look that seemed to challenge whoever was on the other end of the camera. His face was swollen and bruised under his left eye—something Paul figured had happened during the arrest—and unshaven with what looked like a good two- or three-days' worth of dark stubble. His t-shirt was filthy, and Paul could only imagine the stench of this man whose defiant expression sat atop a muscular neck—the vein running up one side reminiscent of weightlifters.

It was a good thing Roberts hadn't caught up with Paul that night, who likely would've been killed notwithstanding the baseball bat. Tony was right. Roberts was one person Paul shouldn't ever confront.

He wondered what to do with the information, something that weighed on his mind most of the day and past the dinner hour during which he watched TV with Katherine and Daniel over lasagna he'd picked up from their favorite Italian restaurant.

After dinner, Daniel excused himself and went upstairs. Paul glanced at Katherine, who seemed lost in *Entertainment Tonight* and the latest Hollywood couple escapades.

"Can I get you a glass of wine?" Paul asked, standing and walking toward the kitchen.

"Actually, that might be nice."

Paul glanced upstairs and, seeing Daniel's door closed, figured he must be talking to friends or listening to music. He returned a moment later with chardonnay for Katherine and pinot noir for himself. She took the glass without meeting his eyes and murmured a quiet "Thanks" while staying glued to the TV.

He studied her for a moment. Her color was paler than normal, her cheeks less full. He'd noticed her on several occasions excusing herself from the room and going upstairs for fifteen minutes or so, coming back down with red, swollen eyes. Whenever he asked if she was alright, she'd simply say, "Yes, I'm fine." She also refrained from discussing her workday like she used to, only occasionally filling Paul in on various cases here and there.

When the segment wrapped up, Katherine glanced at her watch and Paul picked up the remote. Turning down the volume, he said, "Hey, I want to talk to you about something."

Katherine looked at him without speaking, and it seemed to Paul she sensed the general topic that was coming.

"I know who did it."

She turned from the television and looked directly at him. "What do you mean?"

"I know who did it. I know who the attacker is."

Katherine blinked, her face unchanging, waiting. It was unnerving to Paul, as he'd expected a more emotional response and didn't know how to read her expression.

The seconds of silence that elapsed as Katherine processed felt like minutes to him. She eventually opened her mouth and said, "How did you find out? Who did you *tell?*"

Paul quickly processed the questions and realized she assumed he'd gone to the police or a private investigator or something along those lines. He wasn't sure exactly how to respond either. After all, the only thing he'd asked Tony to do was to look up a license plate number. Katherine's real secret was still intact.

"I didn't go to anybody. I saw his truck, the one with the Confederate emblem on the back, and followed him. I know where he lives."

Katherine closed her eyes and shook her head from side to side, as if trying to fling Paul's words from her mind. When she opened them, they were filled with tears.

"Katherine," Paul said softly, "how can we not go to the police?" In an angry, hushed voice, she said, "When...when... will you give this up?"

Her face contorted as tears began to flow more freely.

"A trial, Paul. Is *that* what you wish for me, for me to get on a witness stand? And with *what* evidence?"

"He has a long record and will do it again! If we don't report him, who will?"

Katherine stood, unable to listen to any more discussion, and said in a raised voice, "Paul, you weren't the one who was raped. Do you have any idea what it's like to try to put something like this behind you? Do you? Do you know what it's like to wonder if you're about to be killed or if you'll ever get to see your home and family again..." She pointed to her neck, and in a shrill voice, exclaimed, "or if...if...your throat's about to be sliced open?"

She started out of the room but stopped at the doorway suddenly, raising her hand to her mouth and whispering, "Daniel!"

Paul walked over and saw his son standing just around the corner of the doorway. Based on his expression, he'd surely just overheard most of his mother's words. His eyes were fixed on hers, and he said softly, "Mom...when?"

"Oh, Daniel, I didn't mean for you to know. I'm okay, I really am. It happened, and it's over. There's nothing any of us can do about it now. I just need to..." She walked over and hugged him, and they stood motionless in each other's arms. Daniel looked up, and his gaze met Paul's. He was wondering what was going through his son's mind.

Katherine broke the embrace and put a hand to Daniel's cheek. "Really, I'm okay. There's nothing more to talk about," she said before walking to the counter to refresh her glass of wine. Daniel and Paul stared at each other for a moment, neither knowing the right words to say.

After Katherine had left for work the next morning and Paul was getting ready to head downstairs, he heard Daniel yell, "Dad, are you free?"

Paul walked down the hallway and stuck his head in his bedroom door.

"What happened, Dad?"

Paul recounted the limited details he knew.

"She won't tell you any more than that?"

Paul shook his head no.

"And she won't go to the police?"

"Trust me, I've tried."

Daniel looked around the room as his mind processed what he'd just heard. "And who is he, exactly?"

"Marcus Roberts. He lives at 231 Pineview Street and has a rap sheet. In fact, you can find him online thanks to the mugshot they took after an arrest. Very recognizable, with two teardrops on his face."

"Means he's killed people, Dad. It's a gang symbol."

"I know."

"Should *we* do something about it?" Daniel asked.

Paul had no intention of mentioning the incident with the brick. "No. There's nothing to do. It's just one of those things in life, like your mom said, that we all just have to move on from."

Daniel agreed in an unconvincing tone, and Paul wondered if he shouldn't have disclosed Roberts' identity.

"Daniel, please keep the information I shared private. Your

mom is hell-bent on making sure no one finds out."

"I hear you," Daniel said and looked from Paul to his cell phone, which he'd started typing into.

Paul walked downstairs.

Over the next several weeks, Katherine began working longer hours. Paul figured it was her way of distracting herself but was also a bit surprised since she seemed so listless at home. She'd long since abandoned their long, leisurely walks at Belle Isle—an island park in the middle of the Detroit River—and seldom conversed over breakfast. Nothing elicited laughter from her anymore, something Paul could often summon from a witty remark, and of course there was the lack of intimacy. They hadn't made love for several months.

One evening after dinner, he sat down beside her on the couch and put a hand on her knee. "Honey, how long do you think it'll be until you're ready to…" but his voice trailed off when her gaze averted from his. He nodded softly in acknowledgement and decided to try a different approach.

"Katherine, I'm wondering if we should see a marriage counselor."

"I don't know," she said, looking down at the floor. "Maybe you're right Paul, but I think I might need to see someone on my own first," she suggested amid tears.

And so she began visiting a therapist, a woman her primary care physician had recommended. Paul was relieved, her depressed demeanor a concern to both himself and Daniel. Running errands with his dad one evening, Daniel asked, "Do you think Mom is going to get better?"

"I don't know, Daniel."

"Do you ever think…" Daniel hesitated, and Paul sensed the subject, "…about this Roberts?"

"I do," Paul responded. "It feels very unresolved."

That night as Paul prepared for bed, he noticed two prescriptions on Katherine's bathroom vanity: one for Xanax and one for

Zoloft, which Paul knew treated anxiety and depression, respectively. Katherine hadn't mentioned either, a stark reminder of the diminished communication between them.

Paul walked into the bedroom and found Katherine sitting on a chair, staring at a blank wall.

"Honey, are you okay?" he asked.

She gave him a vacant look and avoided the question. "I might go watch TV downstairs for a while. I don't feel like going to bed."

Paul himself slept badly that night, waking with a start from a nightmare where Roberts was chasing him in the truck again and unable to shake the image of the man's face glaring through the windshield. He got out of bed, walked down to the den, and found Katherine asleep on the couch before returning to bed himself.

Chapter 6

Tuesday, August 14, 2018

It was a typical Tuesday evening when Paul and Daniel decided to head to a sporting goods store around eight o'clock and spend a little over an hour there before returning home. When Paul yelled to greet Katherine upon entering the back door, he heard nothing in return and so headed upstairs.

He found her asleep, a good bit earlier than normal given her typical routine of watching the ten o'clock news with him in bed and perhaps reading for a few minutes. Paul went to kiss her forehead as he watched her breathing but feared waking her. She looked so peaceful, lying on her back with her left arm draped across her stomach and the other bent slightly at the elbow but raised over her head as if she was asking a question.

He eased into bed an hour later and did his best not to disturb her.

When Paul awoke about six o'clock the next morning, he stared at the ceiling for a few minutes while thinking through the day ahead. He was giving a talk to a writing group in a few weeks and needed to begin preparing his remarks, plus he wanted to get some exercise…perhaps a walk. He stretched and looked over at

Katherine.

When he initially saw her in the exact same position as the night before, he thought, *Wow, she slept soundly.* Looking closer, though, with mounting alarm he realized something was wrong. Her torso, after rising and falling rhythmically mere hours ago, was barely moving, her color pallid.

He shook her gently. "Katherine…Katherine…" No response. Paul jerked upright and turned on the bedside lamp, the room still dim in the early morning light, and saw two open pill bottles on her bedside table.

"Oh God, no…" Paul gasped. He rose to his knees on the bed beside her, his hand frantically moving to her wrist in the hopes of finding a pulse. It was barely perceptible.

"Daniel!" he screamed. "Daniel, get in here, quick! Daniel! Daniel!"

"Call 9-1-1!" Paul ordered once Daniel appeared. "I think your mom might've overdosed!"

Paul jumped up and ran around to Katherine's side of the bed, lifting each bottle and finding both empty. He sat back down and caressed her cheek, whispering, "Hang on honey, please, just hang on."

By now the 9-1-1 dispatcher was on the line, asking questions and directing Paul through the speakerphone. "Do you know how many pills she took? What kind of medicine is it? Can you see if anything is lodged in her throat? What is her pulse count? Any movement whatsoever?"

Paul did his best to answer the laundry list of questions.

In minutes, an ambulance siren wailed outside. Daniel directed the medics upstairs, and they lifted Katherine onto a stretcher and into the rig. Paul and Daniel followed it to the hospital.

They spent the next two hours in the emergency department waiting room, doctors occasionally coming by to say they were still working on her and that her condition was critical.

"Can we see her?" Paul asked.

"Not yet," they'd respond.

Another two hours passed before they saw a doctor again. Seeing the man's grave expression as he walked up to them, Paul's heart sank.

"Mr. Nelms, Daniel, follow me into my office for a minute, will you?" he directed them.

Once they were seated, the doctor looked back and forth at each of them and shook his head slowly. "There's no easy way to say this. It isn't good."

"What?" Paul said incredulously, "What do you mean?"

"Mr. Nelms, the EEG is showing minimal brain activity. We can keep her alive, but honestly, the team doesn't see any way that she will come out of this. If you want to wait for several days, even weeks and keep things just as they are to see if there is any improvement, we can do that. But again, the brain activity is...not even registering."

Paul's voice cracked. "Doctor, this can't be happening..."

The physician brought a box of tissues over to Daniel and Paul and said, "I'm very sorry." He added, "Feel free to stay in here as long as you'd like. I have rounds, but if you need me, please tell one of the nurses. This way you can give things some thought before we touch base in a little while. I'll be here another few hours."

"Thanks. Can we see her first?" Paul asked.

"Yes," the doctor responded before walking over and speaking to a nurse who escorted Paul and Daniel back to a curtained partition where Katherine lay attached to multiple tubes.

Sobs followed, and the two men embraced.

Chapter 7

Sudoku stilled Paul's mind as something painless to focus on. He paused and looked up, spying the multitude of books filling his library, and rose from his chair. Walking over to one of the shelves, he lightly rubbed his fingers over the spines and pulled out a hardback edition of *The Catcher in the Rye:* riffling through several pages and fondly recalling Holden Caulfield's cynical and jaded perspective on life. He knew the feeling.

He took a step back and perused the titles. Singly, they were stories of triumph and tragedy, humor and sorrow, hope and desolation. Together, though, they emitted a comforting chorus of voices he knew would never leave him totally alone; it was for that reason he loved them—not so much for what they were but rather what they represented: a remedy for isolation.

He returned to his puzzle, the grinding engine of a diesel truck outside diverting his attention a few minutes later. He rose and peered through the window. Three men exited the cab and rang his doorbell, and Paul opened the door.

"Hi. I'm Sam from Wright's Piano. Are you Mr. Nelms?"

"Yes. Come in."

Paul turned and led the men into an adjoining room anchored by a large black Steinway & Sons baby grand piano. He motioned toward it. "This one goes out, and the player piano comes in."

The men looked confused.

"We're picking one up?" one of them asked.

Paul answered, "Yeah, this is a trade-in, a piano I bought from you all several years ago. You're supposed to pick it up and take it back to the store. I assumed they would have explained that."

"Oh…okay," Sam said. "We can handle that."

The piano swap-out took about thirty minutes, the new one looking identical to the old one save for a few wires snaking along the floor.

Sam handed Paul a sheet of paper. "Okay, Mr. Nelms, I think everything is set. If you'll just sign here saying it was delivered, please."

"Sure. Before you go, let me make sure I remember how to work it."

He walked over to the piano and turned it on. Fiddling with the buttons, he cycled through the beginnings of a dozen songs, frustration evident on his face. "It's not on here. The one song I specifically said must be on here—it's not."

"What's the song?"

"Moonlight Sonata."

Sam walked over. "Let me look." After a minute, the Sonata's opening notes filled the room.

"That's it," Paul whispered. "Yes. Cut it off now, please."

Sound gave way to stillness. Paul smiled apologetically. "I'm sorry for getting a bit agitated. Things have been a little tough lately; I've gotten about four hours of sleep the last couple of nights."

"No worries," Sam said, smiling, "Glad it was on there after all."

"Thanks, fellas," Paul said, fishing a twenty-dollar bill from his wallet and handing it to Sam. "I really appreciate it."

Sam pocketed the twenty and headed for the truck to find his two cohorts awaiting him.

In the fading afternoon light, Paul stood at the door and watched them leave before ascending the stairs to his bedroom. Moments later, he descended carrying the pink terrycloth bathrobe Katherine used to wear that had hung on the back of their bathroom door for the past five months. He had fought the urge to take it down, or wash it, or put it away. The belt dangled at his feet as he sat down and pushed a few illuminated buttons on the piano.

"Moonlight Sonata" graced the air once again, and he closed his eyes—rubbing the end of the belt against his face to catch the lingering fragrance of perfume he'd given Katherine on her last birthday. As he inhaled the faint but unmistakable aroma and heard the notes she'd loved so much, it felt as if she were in the room with him. "I miss you," he whispered. The terrycloth absorbed his tears.

Paul, fully immersed in the moment, failed to notice the front door opening or the hand reaching in to turn on the light. The sound of "Dad?" instantly jarred him to attention, and with evident embarrassment, he stammered, "Daniel! Don't sneak up on me like that, please!"

Daniel hesitated and said, "I…uh…sorry, Dad. I didn't mean to startle you or anything. The lights were off."

Paul leaned back in his chair and sighed as "Moonlight Sonata" played on.

Daniel looked at the piano. "To be honest, hearing that song playing sort of creeped me out when I walked in the door." He paused. "It felt like Mom was here for a second."

Paul nodded softly. "I know."

Daniel's attention returned to the piano. "So, this is some kind of self-playing piano I guess?"

"They delivered it while you were at work." Paul shook his head. "I'm having a tough time adjusting to this. I don't know what my life is supposed to look like now."

"Have you thought about seeing somebody?"

"I'm not ready for that yet. People say give it a year."

"I don't mean a woman. I mean a *therapist*."

"Oh. Actually, I have. I made an appointment with a grief counselor and go in a few weeks."

Daniel nodded. "Sounds like a good idea."

"I thought you had a date tonight."

"I do. Darla. I'm going to pick her up in ten minutes, so I better go. Sorry about…interrupting you." Daniel started to close the door but hesitated. "You want the light on or off?"

"On."

Paul stood up, turned off the piano, and gently placed the robe atop its smooth black surface.

Chapter 8

Thursday, January 17, 2019

P aul dreaded his first appointment with Dr. Harris. It reminded him of routine physicals where doctors poked and probed, all in the interest of uncovering some lurking threat only they could ascertain. He walked up to the door and read the black lettering displaying the name, "Dr. Thomas G. Harris, MD – Psychiatry."

"Hi, you must be Paul Nelms?" a woman in the reception area greeted him.

"Yes."

She nodded and tapped lightly on a closed door behind her, opened it a few inches, and announced, "Your ten o'clock is here."

"Thanks, Margie," a voice replied.

Moments later, a lean, gray-bearded man entered the waiting area.

"Mr. Nelms? Come on in."

"Yes, hi, Dr. Harris. Thanks for seeing me."

The doctor shut the door and sat in a chair opposite a couch meant for patients. He gestured for Paul to sit.

"Is it Paul? Call me Tom, by the way."

Tom's baldness made him look older that Paul, though he figured he was about the same age—fifty-five, give or take. He looked sporty yet casual, with a tan sport coat, no tie, and dark-framed glasses.

"Yes, Paul is fine."

"Good. So…Paul…What brings you to me today?"

"Well, as I mentioned to your assistant over the phone, my wife died last year. I'm having a hard time dealing with some things. For one, I'm not sleeping well and often wake up in the middle of the night and can't get back to sleep. I'm not motivated to work or really do much at all, in fact. I'm just…" He paused as if searching for the right words before ultimately settling for "…not myself."

Paul continued. "Sometimes when I wake up, I try to read or watch TV, but I'm always exhausted the next day. I'll doze off at two in the afternoon or after dinner, and that makes the nighttime routine even worse. I need to talk to someone, but I was also thinking maybe I need to get a prescription of some kind for my nerves and a sleep aid."

"There are some good ones out there; I can probably help you with that. How did your wife die?"

Paul hesitated, saying it out loud still difficult. "Suicide. August 15, 2018." He took a deep breath. "She'd been struggling with depression."

"How long had you been married?"

"Twenty-eight years."

"That's a pretty long time, particularly these days. I'm sorry to hear about your loss. Was there anything that prompted her depresssion?"

Paul hesitatingly asked, "This is all strictly confidential, right? I mean, if I tell you something, it goes no further?"

"Absolutely."

"I promised her I would never tell anyone about this. Other than her own therapist, my son, me and now you, no one knows this."

Tom nodded with a nonchalance that reassured Paul.

"She'd been dealing with a very traumatic event after being sexually assaulted last June. It was never reported to the police since she said she couldn't stand the humiliation of all the neighbors and her friends knowing if it went to a trial. The prospect of having to testify, the news…She was very outgoing and yet also very private."

"I understand," said Tom. "Those types of feelings are not uncommon. Do you know who did it?"

Paul looked away to a wall filled with books, his jaw muscles pulsing as he fought to hold his temper in check.

"You don't have to answer if you don't want to," Tom assured him. Paul remained silent, and when Tom noticed his eyes fixed on the books, he asked, "Do you like to read?"

"I do. To both of your questions."

Both were quiet for several seconds.

"Have you ever confronted him?"

Paul thought about the brick through the window, the chase, the wreck. He didn't want to disclose any of it. So, he lied.

"Not directly."

"What does 'not directly' mean?"

"Well, I mean no. She didn't want me to and made me swear not to, saying she wanted to forget it happened and just move on."

"Are you able to discuss what happened?"

"She'd gone out later than normal one night to pick up a few things from the store for friends coming over the next evening. When she got back in her car with the groceries, he forced his way in behind her and ordered her to drive. They drove about a mile away, and that's where it happened. She was never able to give me every detail, but she did finally tell me he forced her to…" Paul stopped speaking, clearly having difficulty with the next part.

"Did she come right home and tell you?" Dr. Harris asked as a reprieve.

"Yes."

"And you never told the authorities about it?"

"No. We argued about it, but every time I insisted, she became so upset that we didn't."

"How did you figure out who he was?"

"I saw his truck. Katherine described it, and it had a Confederate flag decal on the back. You must admit there aren't many of those in Detroit."

Tom nodded slowly, intently.

"Anyway, I was close enough to see his profile and saw the distinguishing tattoos on his face she had mentioned. That's when I knew it was him."

Paul paused and then said, "Katherine never had time to recover. She was seeing a therapist, and like I said, she told her about it. That was the exception to her keeping it all a secret. A therapist doesn't count, she'd said, because they're sworn to confidentiality."

He sighed. "In the end, it didn't help…or at least there wasn't enough time for it to help."

His forehead was damp with perspiration. "Can I have some water?" he asked.

Tom said, "Of course" and left the room before returning with a cold bottle of water. "You've been through a lot, and I know it's been very difficult."

Paul looked at him. "I guess it probably needs to get out. I've been keeping this a secret for a while now, trying to explain to friends why she'd had such a sudden change in personality. She was happy once."

"So, you have other family then; you mentioned a son a minute ago?" Tom asked.

"Yes, Daniel, who's twenty-two and lives at home. He hasn't figured out what he wants to do in life yet. He's a good kid but not the most responsible, and he likes having a good time. He's really the only family I have left."

Tom offered an understanding nod and then asked, "The suicide...Who found her?"

"I did, in the morning after waking up. She'd overdosed on pills her doctor had prescribed. We called 9-1-1, but it was unfortunately too late."

Paul recalled Katherine stretched out on the bed the night before and felt tears forming in his eyes. "She looked so...peaceful...as if she was sleeping. I'd seen her so many times looking just like that, maybe on a Sunday afternoon when we were taking it easy in the late afternoon, me in my recliner and her napping on the couch."

He wiped his eyes. "The hardest part is that I keep thinking she's coming back. I'll be in the study and hear my son come home and for a moment think, 'Oh, that must be Katherine.' Then suddenly I realize she's *never* coming back."

Tom said, "That's not uncommon."

"I hear that." Paul paused and then added, "Her death is the worst thing that's ever happened to me."

"A friend of mine once told me that the worst things in life are never the final things in life."

"And what would he say to Katherine? The worst thing was her taking her own life...That seems pretty final."

"I guess that depends a little on whether you think anything happens to people after they die." Tom removed his glasses and pinched his nose where they'd just rested.

"Yeah. Sometimes it feels like I can sense her presence. The other day I was thinking about her on my back porch, and a butterfly landed on the edge of the railing about a foot away from me. It just sat there, opening and closing its wings before flying off. It was beautiful and reminded me of one of her favorite paintings that had several butterflies in it. Sometimes I like to think that was her in some way, or maybe her sending me some kind of message."

"It could have been...You never know. I agree with you, by

the way. I don't think things end when we die."

The two men were silent for a moment.

Tom asked, "What do you do for a living?"

"I write. I've published three novels, one of which did very well. Between that and an inheritance from my parents, I'm financially secure and don't have to work."

Tom started to say something, hesitated, then went ahead and said, "You know, I've always wanted to write something. Fiction, I mean. I started an outline once but never got to writing it."

"If you want my advice, skip the outline—at least until you're several drafts in. I find my best stories emerge as they're written."

Tom rubbed his beard and laughed. "I'll keep that in mind. So, what's a typical day for you these days?"

"I wake up about six and spend the first hour or so taking a shower and having something to eat while reading the paper. Usually from about eight until eleven, I write. Sometimes I exercise before or after lunch, and I usually spend the afternoon running errands or thinking through any writing assignments I want to take because I still take on some small freelance jobs. Daniel's usually home at night, so we'll watch a ball game and have a pizza or something else like that. Takeout, usually."

Paul glanced at his watch. The hour was almost over.

"Do you feel depressed?" Tom asked.

Paul responded with thinly veiled sarcasm, "What do you think? My wife is dead."

"Well, let me ask you this: Do you ever think of harming yourself?" Tom clarified.

"Who doesn't?"

"Most people."

Paul noticed Tom make a note in his notebook. *Suicidal*, he assumed.

Paul said, "Maybe they don't, or maybe they do and just don't admit to it. I guess I don't think about it seriously. Besides, I tend to deliberate things. The people who kill themselves always seem impulsive. Katherine was like that. She was very decisive and would act on things right away. It served her quite well professionally. Not so much when she became suicidal."

He paused before continuing. "But to answer what you're getting at, Tom, no, I'm not planning to kill myself. I worry sometimes I might slip into that state of mind, but for now, no."

Tom nodded, and Paul wondered how routine a conversation this was for a psychiatrist.

"So do you think you can help me?"

"Tell me what you need help with the most."

"Sleeping, probably. I need something just to get me through the nights. Beyond that, I want to be able to write again. I can't maintain a continuous thought for more than a few moments these days, and it feels impossible to open my mind to a creative process that allows a plot to emerge. I work on jigsaw puzzles sometimes or Sudoku, but doing something that takes much more focus is very difficult. I just feel like I'm going through meaning-less motions."

Tom nodded. "I do think coming to see me on a regular basis would help." Reaching for his prescription pad, he added, "And I can prescribe a sleep aid. Actually, I'd like to start you on an antidepressant as well, particularly given that what I'm prescribing for sleep can sometimes cause depression."

"When would you like me to come back?"

"How about Thursday three weeks from now? Give some time for the new meds to kick in a bit?"

"That's fine," Paul said, standing and taking the script from Tom.

"Thank you for seeing me."

They shook hands. On his way out, Paul walked over to a huge antique chest with numerous drawers and Chinese writings on the front of each.

"Interesting piece," he commented, walking up to inspect it more closely.

"Ah," Tom said, "my Chinese apothecary cabinet." He placed a hand on one of its six-foot-high sides. "I fell in love with it the day I saw it; it spoke to me."

"So many drawers...How many?"

"Seventy-five, to be exact: three large ones on the bottom plus seventy-two above, each of those with three sections," Tom said, pulling out one of the empty drawers. "More than two hundred compartments. The Chinese doctors would use these to store their medicines."

Tom removed a drawer and handed it to Paul, saying, "Here, smell it."

Paul inhaled the fragrant remnants of a mix of herbs now infused in the wood.

Tom reinserted the drawer, saying, "When I first saw it, I knew what it was and started to think about all the people who'd looked to it for answers, for cures, for hope. I began imagining the stories this piece could tell if it was able to speak." He smiled, saying hesitatingly, "You're going to think I'm crazy at this point, but as soon as I had that thought, a voice popped into my head that said something like, *I can speak; the question is whether or not you can hear.*

"Sometimes I'll be working on something," Tom said, nodding toward his desk on the other side of the room, "and get a whiff of what you just smelled...It sort of comes out of the blue. Granted, it probably has something to do with the humidity or temperature in the room, but on my more open-minded days, I like to think it's trying to get my attention—as if it's trying to tell me one of those stories."

Paul smiled. "What you just told me has the makings of a good book." He took a step back to better assess the piece. "I will say this...It's *stunning.*"

"Thanks, Paul," Tom said, seeing him to the door.

Paul left the office and drove to a drug store about a mile from his house, taking the prescription to the pharmacist who said,

"That should be about fifteen minutes. We'll page you when it's ready."

Paul ambled over to the magazine section. He perused the covers, picking up a *Sports Illustrated* with a photo of Andy Reid, the football coach for the Kansas City Chiefs. He thumbed through to an article about Reid, then put it down, and glanced through two or three other magazines. One was about cruises, and he wondered if he and Daniel should take a trip.

The book section nearby caught his eye, one title in particular: *Surviving Loss*. He picked it up, opened to the table of contents and let his eyes scroll down. "You're in Shock: What to do First," "Self-Care, Your Next Investment," and "Creating New Beginnings" ranked among the topics.

He heard his name paged over the store's intercom. He tucked the cruise magazine and book under his arm and proceeded to the counter.

A few minutes later, Paul walked out of the drug store with a small bag containing a bottle of the sleep aid Ambien, and one with the antidepressant Effexor, as well as the magazine and book. He smiled and held the door for a young woman entering the store, responding "You're welcome" when she thanked him with a smile that Paul almost interpreted as flirtatious. He surprised himself by whistling a tune on his way back to the car. A good night's sleep would be a welcome change.

Preparing for bed later that night in his bathroom, Paul thought about the woman. *Was* she flirting with him? He wondered how long it would take to become interested in women again and whether a woman would even find him appealing. He inspected his balding head—its gray wisps tinged with a few surviving darker strands—sitting atop bloodshot brown eyes flanked by crow's feet. His wrinkles had deepened in the past year. He also scrutinized his neck, beginning to sag, and glanced down at a stomach now blocking the view of his toes. *I need to start exercising,* he thought, the face in the mirror nodding slowly as if to forge a contract.

He went to bed at eleven o'clock that night after watching the local news, popping his new medications before opening the book he'd purchased earlier and reading a few pages. Within about twenty minutes, he began to feel groggy and turned off the light.

Paul slept deeply. He awoke to the alarm at eight o'clock, which was a full hour later than he could remember having awakened in several months. He sat up on the side of his bed and rubbed his eyes. Other than feeling a bit sluggish, he felt surprisingly good.

Chapter 9

For the next two weeks, Paul followed the same nightly routine and was anxious to tell Tom about his progress, particularly in terms of sleep.

"So, how are you sleeping?" he asked as if right on cue when Paul entered the office.

"Better, thanks. I've only woken up in the middle of the night a few times. One interesting thing, though, is that I've begun to have vivid dreams. They aren't bad...In fact, some of them are quite pleasant and fodder for a story I'm tempted to write. I still feel a bit down from time to time, especially with all the Valentine's Day decorations and candy in stores. But I did write a few pages for a project I'm working on."

"That's good. The dreams you mention aren't uncommon and show your mind is in a deeper state of sleep. As you know, the grieving won't be a short-term process, and it's important to go through."

"If I could skip that part, I would."

"I have a story that'll make you think otherwise. When I went on a mission trip several years ago to Uganda, I met a woman whose daughter had just been assaulted and killed by some guerillas who were terrorizing the villagers. Her husband had tried to save her, but he was bludgeoned and left paralyzed. She had two other younger children at home and was desperately trying to survive amidst incredibly impoverished conditions, not knowing where her family's next meal would come from or how she would pay for medicines her husband desperately needed. Left to fend for her ten-year old daughter—who she feared would be victimized in the same way as her sister—and her five-year-old little boy, she washed clothes for pennies a day."

"That's terrible."

"It is, but do you know what she told me? She called grief a privilege. A *privilege*, Paul. She said she was too busy trying to keep the rest of her family alive to stop and grieve for her daughter. She wished she could and knew she'd struggle for many more years simply because she couldn't experience what so many others do: 'The healing power of grief.' And she was right. Her recovery will probably be much slower than yours, and while it might not feel like it right now—and I'm not saying your grief is pleasant—you must give your grief its voice. It has to come out somehow, otherwise you can never move on."

Paul focused intently. "How does one do that, exactly? Give grief its voice?"

"I can't answer that for you. It's different for every person and something only you can decide."

"Maybe I could write about it. Not like the book I'm reading now, my 'how to cope' book, but something more subtle, weaving it into a story."

"Yes, I suppose you could. Paul, do you and Daniel talk much about Katherine? About her...death?"

Paul looked away as if peering at a distant object, "No, not really." He shrugged. "I mean, she will come up of course. 'Your mom used to do this, your mom and I went there one time,' things like that, but nothing much otherwise."

"Do you think he needs to talk about it?"

"I don't know. It's the sort of thing Katherine would have figured out. It's complicated."

"Just know that I'm in touch with some good therapists who work with young adults. I could refer him to them if he wants to talk."

"I'll keep that in mind."

"Paul, what do you do in your spare time? Do you have any hobbies like golf or any physical activities?"

"Never liked golf, but yeah, I enjoy hiking or just taking walks."

"In the neighborhood?"

"Or area trails. Daniel and I camped at Grand Island on Lake Superior a couple years ago. These days, I usually walk the Iron Belle Trail. Do you know it?"

"I know Belle Isle, is that what you mean?"

"No, the Iron Belle Trail. It connects Belle Isle State Park to Ironwood in the Upper Peninsula. There are actually two trails that each run a couple thousand miles, one for bikes and the other for hikers."

"Ah."

Paul glanced at the foliage outside Tom's window and said, "I like the unpaved, wooded sections and to stop and listen to the breeze blowing the tops of the trees. It's calming, one of the few places where I can forget about things."

"Mmm."

Paul and Tom talked for another twenty minutes, mainly about Paul's work and establishing a routine. When it came time to leave, Paul stood up and said, "I want to thank you for working with me. I think this is helping."

"You're welcome, Paul. I will see you again in a couple of weeks."

As Paul left Tom's office, his mind returned to the Ugandan woman. He wondered if she was hungry, if the husband was still alive, and (with greater perspective) felt a kinship with this total stranger. He could envision a novel built around her character, maybe about her search to find an outlet for grief. Then again, perhaps it'd be about someone else—or maybe even him.

Chapter 10

About a week and a half after his visit to Tom, an odd thing happened when Paul went to bed: he entered a hybrid state between sleep and consciousness, beginning to dream and yet conscious of doing so.

He's in the front hallway of Marcus Roberts' house and hears the television blaring as the light from the screen flickers against the adjacent white wall. He feels trapped, fearing that if he opens the front door to escape, the noise will alert Roberts. He freezes. When the voice of an announcer introduces two opponents in a televised fight, the crowd erupts loudly and gives him a chance to creep toward the rear of the house in the hopes of slipping through the back door.

"I've got you now," whispers Marcus Roberts, suddenly at the doorway blocking his exit. "I'm gonna kill you!" he says in a sinister voice and then lunges at Paul. Paul screams, but it's not his scream, it's Daniel's from when he fell at Grand Island. Paul throws Roberts aside, runs into the living room and looks for something to defend himself with. Seeing a baseball bat, he picks it up and flings it at Roberts who jumps aside as it crashes through the front living room window. Paul looks for another weapon, glancing past the bookshelf and the Confederate flag on the wall before spotting a rifle in the corner of the room. He rushes for it at the same time as Roberts, each struggling to wrench it from the other's hands. Paul cocks the hammer and attempts to point the muzzle at Roberts, but the man pulls the rifle away from him.

Paul dashes into the front yard and looks back and sees Roberts, not chasing him but standing at the front door. He realizes in the dream he can stop running, no longer being chased, and looks back toward the street. He sees Katherine parked along the curb with the driver-side door open. She's trying to get out, but a red dress—the one she wore for her surprise party—is snagged on something below the seat. She's trying to work it loose, though apparently afraid of tearing it, and eventually gives up trying to free the dress. She slowly closes the door and begins easing down the street.

Paul, realizing he's still dreaming, imagines himself calling out to her and yells "Wait!" in the dream. To his amazement, she stops and turns her head to look at him, gesturing for him to come to her. He imagines himself opening her door, and back in the dream, he does: unhooking her dress from the place below the seat where it was snagged. She smiles.

She gets out, and they hold each other. He kisses her and looks into her eyes, beginning to fill with tears and then suddenly becoming swollen as if she'd been crying for an extended period of time. An emotional wave sweeps over him, and he feels himself on the verge of tears while saying to her, "I am so sorry, Katherine; I didn't realize you were so sick."

She breaks their embrace, takes a deep breath, and whispers, "I have to leave you now."

Paul suddenly awoke clutching his pillow, his chest heaving with sobs. "Oh, Katherine…oh, Katherine…oh, Katherine…"

He sat up in bed and, feeling the moisture on his pillow, recalled the morning after Katherine's fiftieth birthday when he'd laid his head on that very pillow—her head resting on his bare chest. It had reminded him of their early days of marriage when they'd lie on the couch to watch a movie, and she'd doze off in that same position.

He wiped his eyes, walked into the bathroom, and splashed cold water on his face. He blew his nose before climbing back into bed and flipping on the television. Numbly flipping through paid programming selections, he eventually became drowsy and drifted off.

The dream still lingered in his mind when he awoke the next morning, especially the memory of Katherine and seeing her face. The red dress specifically created a feeling of despondency and loss unmatched from the past several weeks, a reminder of one of their last happy days together.

He walked downstairs and outside to grab the newspaper before heading into the kitchen, finding Daniel already there eating cereal. "Morning, Dad."

"Morning, Son."

Paul poured a cup of coffee and sat down at the table, opening up the newspaper. Within five minutes, he was through glancing at the headlines and laid it on the table. "Real Estate" was across the heading of the section on top.

Unsure how Daniel would take it, Paul said, "This house is too big."

"What do you mean?"

"It's just you and me here in this huge 6,000-square foot home. It's more than we need, and at some point, you'll probably want to have your own place."

"Yeah, I've been thinking about that…I mean about getting my own place. Dad, I do appreciate you…you and Mom…letting me stay here the past couple of years. To be honest, it's helped to be under the same roof as you over the past several months. I think we've needed each other."

"I do, too."

Daniel asked, "So, you want to sell the house?"

"I'm wondering about it."

"Well, at some point, it probably makes sense. It's a lot to keep up with."

Paul got up with his half-empty coffee cup and walked into the living room. Reminders of Katherine were everywhere, the house well-appointed from a lifetime of accumulating things she'd loved. There were numerous paintings, many from highly re-garded artists, commingled with a few of her own pieces including a family portrait of the three of them and a painting of a wildflower-strewn field with butterflies. It wasn't her best work, but she had liked it. That alone had been sufficient to display it prominently on the wall.

He'd once loved being surrounded by her paintings, now constant reminders of her absence. More to the point, it felt as if they were keeping him rooted to a life he wanted to move beyond. He felt a sudden urge to sell everything he owned, not just the house but everything in it.

He headed to his computer. Pulling up a realtor site, he typed in his zip code and properties for sale began to populate the screen. He looked at condos in the downtown area with balconies overlooking the city, so airy and full of glass and light. The absence of a yard and other responsibilities of owning a large house appealed to him. Gazing at one image of a balcony, he imagined himself working on a novel and hesitating as he surveyed the city—searching his mind for just the right word and then returning to the laptop to finish the sentence.

Daniel got up from the table and yelled "I'm gonna shower!" Paul went to Google and typed in "real estate agents." He wrote down four names.

Chapter 11

Friday, February 22, 2019

Paul had a quick check-in appointment scheduled with Tom and several things he wanted to discuss. He'd only had a few other vivid dreams, none allowing him to affect the outcome, and planned on mentioning them to Tom as well as the idea of selling the house.

As soon as Paul sat down in his office, he began telling him about the dream involving Katherine. "It felt so real. When I woke up, it took me several moments to realize it wasn't. I wasn't sure what 'reality' was."

"Tell me what happened in the dream."

Paul recounted the dream to him as well as the surprise party for Katherine and significance of the red dress.

"Those types of realistic dreams are often called lucid dreams. They're not uncommon. Have you noticed any other sleep irregularities?"

"No. As I said, I've slept pretty well…a little groggy in the morning when I wake up, but overall, much more rested."

"Good. It sounds like the combination of meds is working pretty well."

Paul nodded.

"How are you otherwise?"

"Pretty well. I've been thinking about selling the house, maybe moving into something smaller. What do you think about that?"

"Big step. How does Daniel feel about it?"

"He doesn't really care, or so he says."

"If you downsized, what would you do with all your things?"

"Storage maybe or sell some of the stuff."

"It's probably something you should think about. Not the best time for a quick decision."

Paul nodded.

Tom shifted in his chair. "I wanted to ask you something...What do you think should happen to the man who assaulted your wife, this...Marcus Roberts? Now that Katherine is gone, do you ever wonder if you should go to the police?"

Paul thought for a minute before speaking. "What purpose would it serve? She's no longer alive to testify, so there'd never be a conviction. Besides, she was so opposed to going to the police when she was alive anyway."

Tom nodded. "I understand. I just wanted to hear your thoughts."

"Candidly, it bothers me to even think about it; it feels very unresolvable."

They spoke another few minutes before their session was up.

Tom rose and said, "In the meantime, let's keep you on the Effexor and Ambien. When I see you back in two weeks, I want to hear about at least one step you're taking to do something you look forward to doing."

The following day, Saturday, Paul got more writing done than he had in several months. He celebrated by going to the grocery store and picking up a steak to grill out that night, as well as one of his favorite bottles of wine. When he returned home, he pulled into the driveway and got out of the car. Looking down and seeing that he had stopped on top of a hose he had left in the driveway, he got back in the car and pulled forward a few feet until clearing it, then parked and walked into the house.

Daniel was taking Darla, his new girlfriend, to a Red Wings game. It was only about five o'clock, but Paul was hungry so he started the grill and opened the wine. He'd finished his meal and was on to his third glass by six-thirty, and by eight was unusually drowsy so decided to turn in early. He was in bed an hour later.

"Quite the partier, going to bed at nine on a Saturday night," he mumbled to himself as he slipped under the sheets. He reached over to his bedside table, took his nightly medicine, and flipped open a travel magazine. The description of a cruise "Treasures of the Greek Isles" sounded inviting:

Discover the magic and mythology of the Greek Isles, one of the most storied regions of the world. Sail across the azure waters of the Aegean Sea and visit the hidden ports of Nafplio, Monemvasia, and Patmos and the legendary islands of Santorini and Mykonos. Windstar brings you close to unique island cultures, ancient treasures, and the breathtaking beaches of Greece.

By nine-fifteen, he was asleep.

Around two-thirty that morning, Daniel awoke to the sound of his father making choking sounds—as if something was caught in his throat—and rose from his bed to check on him. The bathroom door was ajar, and he saw Paul standing over the toilet.

"Dad?" he said, slowly opening the door. "Are you okay?"

Paul made another hacking sound as if clearing phlegm and said, "I have a musket ball caught in my throat." He hacked again.

Daniel said, "What? Dad, what are you talking about? A musket ball...What do you mean?"

Paul repeated, "I have a musket ball in my throat. I'm just trying to get it out."

Daniel stared at him. Then, casually, Paul walked past his son and back into his bedroom. Daniel followed and heard the rustling of sheets as his dad got back into bed. Hearing his deep breathing, Daniel stood there for a couple of minutes, listening, and went back to his room when his dad began to snore.

Sunday morning, Daniel was already at the breakfast table when Paul came down the steps about seven-thirty. "Morning, Son," he said.

Daniel looked up from his cereal and said, "Dad, what in the world were you doing last night with that musket ball business?"

Paul frowned. "Huh? I have no idea what you're talking about."

"You told me last night...at about two-thirty in the morning... that you had a musket ball caught in your throat. You were in the bathroom hacking."

"You're pulling my leg."

"Dad, I swear. I'm not kidding."

"What did I look like? I mean... Did I look like I was sleepwalking or something?"

"You seemed normal and looked straight at me when you answered. Had it not been a nonsensical response, I wouldn't have thought twice about it. You don't remember anything about it?"

Paul thought for a moment. "That's so strange. Standing at the toilet I can vaguely remember, but I don't recall anything like talking to you and certainly not saying I had a musket ball in my throat." He focused, searching his brain for any recollection. "No, I don't remember anything else, but I can picture myself looking down at the toilet...that's all." He thought another moment. "I guess I was sleepwalking. It must be the medication I'm on. I'll talk to Tom about it."

Paul added, "I'm getting the paper," and walked towards the front door. Once outside, he looked at his car and noticed one of the tires adjacent to the hose. *That's strange. I thought I pulled up farther than that.* He came back into the kitchen.

"Hey, Daniel, did you move my car last night when you came in?" Paul asked.

"No, why?"

"I could have sworn it's in a new place. I must be mistaken.

Never mind."

As he sat down to his cereal and coffee, his mind was already crafting additional details to weave into the story he'd nursed along the previous day. It brought him the same satisfaction he felt when snapping the right piece of a jigsaw puzzle into place.

Opening the paper, he saw an editorial about the growing presence of gangs in the Detroit area, some of which had been aggravated by the city's ongoing economic malaise. The column mentioned the city's historic filing for bankruptcy in 2013, achieving the dubious distinction of being the largest municipality in the U.S. to do so. It had exited bankruptcy in 2014, but since then, the city's rebound had been hit or miss. Indeed, it was a city in search of renewal. Paul knew the feeling.

Paul had also heard about gangs pushing into suburbs and communities west of the city. He looked up at Daniel eating a piece of toast behind the Sports section. "Do any of your friends ever run into gang members?" he asked him.

"No. Why?"

"I'm just reading an article about the growing gang problem and how they're increasingly expanding into the suburbs."

"Hmmm."

A few more pages in, Paul saw a headline stating "Drive-by Shooting in Chavis Heights," only two or three miles from where they lived:

Police say three alleged gang members are in custody following a drive-by shooting and subsequent chase that began in Chavis Heights and ended with a crash near North Hills. Officers cruising the Chavis Heights area, the site of several gang activities, apparently witnessed the drive-by shooting and pursued the alleged perpetrators until their vehicle collided with another car in North Hills, injuring several.

Two people were shot and killed in what police believe was a gang-retaliation shooting that targeted members of a rival gang.

According to police spokesperson First Deputy Superintendent Michael Byrd, "Our officers were at the right place at the right time, and along with backup, they did a great job apprehending a very violent group."

Deputy Byrd indicated the men were also believed to have conducted an assassination-style murder of another individual several blocks away from where the drive-by shooting occurred.

Police confiscated handguns and a shotgun from the suspects' wrecked car.

Killed in the drive-by shooting were Mateo Pasquez and Jose Garcia, both purportedly members of Detroit's Latin Kings. The other fatality, which occurred on Pineview Street in Chavis Heights, was Marcus Roberts.

Paul read the line twice, as if he couldn't believe it, and felt a shudder run through his body.

Questions raced through his mind: *Could there be more than one Marcus Roberts? Is this THE Marcus Roberts?*

He stared at the name for several minutes. *Maybe there is justice after all,* he thought and spent the rest of the morning combing through online news reports about the story.

He picked up the phone the next morning to call Tom's office. While he was not scheduled to go in for another week and a half, he figured perhaps he could at least speak to him for a few minutes. After several rings, Margie picked up. "Dr. Harris's office. May I help you?"

"Hi, Margie. It's Paul Nelms. Is Tom in?"

"Sure, hang on."

A few seconds later, Tom came on the line. "Hi, Paul. What's up?"

"Marcus Roberts has been killed. There was a news story about it in the paper this weekend."

"Good heavens. How are you? Do you need to come in today? We could try to shift some things around if so.

"No. I just wanted to tell someone, and you're the only one I could."

"Of course. I'm sure this creates some difficult emotions. Tell you what...I can squeeze you in for fifteen minutes this Wednesday the twenty-seventh at three o'clock. Why don't you come in then?

"That sounds good. Thanks, Tom."

That night, Paul decided to take a break from his Ambien. It wasn't so much that he had a strong aversion to taking it but more a lingering worry about becoming too dependent on it. Internet accounts of people who'd become addicted to painkillers and other medications only added to his misgivings about its long-term use.

Sleep didn't come that night. He felt very drowsy and yet still couldn't sleep at two a.m., as if his body craved it yet his brain wouldn't allow it. He tried watching TV to no avail and then reading, which didn't help. Every time he put the book down to shut his eyes, he only found himself more frustrated that he couldn't drift off. At four a.m., he finally relented and took his Ambien and slept until ten o'clock that morning, barely remembering Daniel sticking his head into his bedroom before leaving the house.

He felt drained but had a strong urge to drive by Marcus Roberts' home despite his weariness, though not sure why he felt so compelled to go. Perhaps it was his desire to confirm it was the same man or maybe an attempt at some level of closure or even just morbid curiosity. In any event, after about an hour of trying to convince himself against it, he started driving in that direction.

Paul turned on Pineview Street and passed the spot where he'd parked his car on the night of the chase. He saw a police car parked in the dirt driveway of the home, apparently now a crime scene replete with the infamous yellow tape, as he continued down the street and tried not to look conspicuous. He made two right turns and headed back home via a long street parallel to Pineview. It was clearly the same Marcus Roberts.

Back in his own driveway, he turned off the engine and stared straight ahead. Any satisfaction in knowing Roberts was dead was simply not there, and for several minutes, he sat motionless in stunned silence.

Chapter 12

Paul walked into Tom's office, who looked up from what he was reading and said, "Hi, Paul. How are you doing?"

"Well, the news about Roberts' murder was a shock. I've been reading a good bit about it."

Tom took a deep breath, as if pondering the appropriate response. "Well, I suppose in some ways this might bring closure for you."

"I doubt it. I don't feel any satisfaction in knowing he's gone. I just miss Katherine."

"I'm sure you do, Paul, having been only…what…only five or six months?"

"Roughly, yes."

"How was Marcus Roberts killed?"

"He was shot."

"Do they know who killed him?"

"Yes, a gang. There's apparently been a big increase in gang activity in that area and speculation that some of the people killed were in a rival gang. I don't really know. The paper didn't say a lot."

Both men paused, neither speaking for a few moments. Paul hated the awkward silences therapists always seemed so comfortable with.

"So anyway…" Paul offered, breaking the silence.

"How are you doing otherwise?" Tom asked. "How are you sleeping?"

Paul explained the situation with the musket ball and his assumption that he'd been sleepwalking.

"Interesting. Was it just the one time?" Tom asked.

"Yes. At least, I think so. I had no recollection of the exchange I had with Daniel in the bathroom."

"Hmmm. I do know sleepwalking has been reported among patients taking this combination of Effexor and Ambien, but it's quite rare. If you want me to try something else, we can do that. It's up to you."

"I tried not taking anything last night, and it was a disaster. I hardly slept at all and ended up taking the Ambien about four o'clock in the morning."

"Yeah, don't skip your meds unless you speak to me first."

"Okay. What do you recommend?"

"We can cut back or even eliminate the Ambien, but it needs to be gradual," Tom said, grabbing his prescription pad. "Let's try gradually scaling back the dosage and then dropping it altogether. If you need something to get you over the hump, go with an over-the-counter antihistamine like Benadryl and let me know if you have any withdrawals—which sometimes do happen."

Tom handed him the prescription, adding, "Call me if there are any more problems with it. I also think it's important to try to add as many normal things back into your life as you can in terms of your routine, getting back to writing, exercising, and just a structured schedule overall. Maybe even take that cruise we'd talked about. Where was it again? Greece?"

"Yes. The Greek Isles."

"Yes, that's right. I remember now. Why don't you think

about that, Paul? It would be good for you to get away."

"You're probably right. I should also try cleaning out the house. Everywhere I look, I see Katherine and need to get rid of a lot of things if I'm serious about selling."

* * *

Returning home later that day, Paul called the local art gallery where he'd purchased some of his artwork in the hopes that an auctioneer could arrange for a private sale. He spoke to the owner and was pleased to hear he could host the event in one of the back sections of the gallery and would contact qualified bidders in advance. The fifteen percent commission seemed a small concession for someone to handle all the details.

The auctioneer stopped by the next evening for them to select the pieces and arrived at about seven o'clock. Entering the house, he looked up admiringly at the elaborate two-story entrance and then into the adjoining great room housing many pieces of sculpture and art. "My, what a lovely home!" he exclaimed.

"Thank you. Please, come in," Paul replied. He ushered him throughout the house, pointing out several paintings he intended to sell.

After studying them, the auctioneer said, "You have some very nice pieces here. A lot of these are emerging artists, and so I'm not sure if they'll receive top dollar, but I think you're conceivably looking a total value of around eighty to ninety thousand here."

"That's fine," Paul said. "To be honest, I'm almost more concerned about making sure they wind up in the right hands."

"What do you mean?" the auctioneer inquired.

"Just that I care about them. Sentimental value is involved, and I just hope they'll go to people who will love them like my late wife did."

"Oh. They will, they will," assured the auctioneer.

Paul walked up to a painting of a basket of fruit. "This is one of my wife's pieces. I'd like to sell it as well."

The auctioneer looked at the canvas and studied it for a moment.

"Hmm. Please don't take offense to this, Mr. Nelms, but she's pretty much an unknown in the art community. I won't be selling her work."

Paul responded in a slightly irritated tone, "Actually, you *will*...at least if you want to sell any of the others, anyway. Katherine's piece will in fact be the *first* one you sell."

The auctioneer shook his head with unconcealed exasperation, saying, "Well, whatever. You'll see that it won't." He removed a piece of yellow tape from the roll he was holding and placed it on the edge of her painting along with all the other pieces to be sold.

He then said, "Why don't we shoot for a week from Saturday, meaning March ninth? It's a small sale, but I'm sure I can pull together a good number of collectors."

"Is that enough time?" Paul asked.

"Mr. Nelms, didn't I just say I could? I have elite clientele, a select group of buyers who are well off, and hardly think you need to worry about it."

They wrapped up the conversation as Paul walked the man to the door and said goodbye.

* * *

When the day of the sale arrived, about twenty people were milling about the art gallery examining the selected pieces of art carefully displayed throughout the rooms. Brief descriptions of the artists, including several recognizable names, accompanied them. Most of the collectors spent several minutes assessing the noted artists' works, jotting down notes and checking their phones for information about the artist. Only a few paused at Katherine's painting, glancing at her piece before sauntering to the next one.

It was hard for Paul not to take it personally. Katherine would have been heartbroken to see something she'd painstakingly labored over so summarily dismissed. He walked over and stood by it, the sole piece of his wife's art portfolio for sale, and his mind flashed back to when she'd worked on it—the outlines emerging as she blended the colors and textures, creating shadows and dimensions with such realism that it made the fruit in the bowl look photographed rather than painted.

The auctioneer walked up to Paul. "We'll start the auction in about ten minutes."

"Okay."

"Let's begin with your wife's piece and then move to the others, the last being the most valuable one. The LeRoy Neiman."

"That's fine."

One of the bidders, a woman Paul guessed was in her forties, walked over and introduced herself. "Hi! I'm Ginger Hammond. I own a gallery in Ann Arbor. Why are you selling these?" she asked.

"My late wife was really the collector. I'm probably going to sell my home soon and am trying to let go of some of the more valuable pieces since I won't have room for them in my new place." Paul pointed toward Katherine's artwork. "She loved to paint and always wanted to sell one of her own pieces, believing it would sort of validate her as an artist."

"I see," Ginger responded, smiling. "Well, I look forward to the bidding. Nice to meet you."

By ten o'clock, everyone had taken a seat. There were twenty-one bidders, each with a numbered paddle in hand. The auctioneer walked to the front of the room.

"Ladies and gentlemen, thank you for joining us. Most of you have had the opportunity to review the pieces up for auction today. We'll start with a piece painted by the owner's late wife before proceeding to the others, as noted in the program."

He turned to Paul. "Mr. Nelms, would you mind bringing up the first piece?"

Paul positioned his wife's painting on a central table with a large stand. The auctioneer began, "Ladies and gentlemen, our first piece—a still life painting by the late Katherine Nelms—shows a wicker basket perched on the edge of a table with fruit. You will notice the realism and high level of detail in the piece, such as the bruise on the pear in the foreground. Who will give me five thousand...anybody at five thousand...will ya bid five thousand...who'll bid five thousand...?"

The bidders remained motionless, paddles still.

The auctioneer, barely suppressing a smirk, glanced at Paul before returning his attention to the crowd. "Can I have forty-five hundred...can I have forty-five hundred for this piece... Mrs. Nelms painted this herself...who'll bid forty-five hundred...."

The lack of a bid was agonizing for Paul to watch, and it seemed that the more the auctioneer argued for someone to make a bid, the more resistant they were to do so. The price had dropped to a thousand after a few minutes passed, still with no bidder, and Paul was tempted to call the whole auction off. The auctioneer, seemingly satisfied with his successful prediction, looked over at Paul and said, "Mr. Nelms, I tried to tell you. Would you like to table the sale of this painting?"

Paul stood and addressed the crowd. "My wife loved to paint but never felt validated as a painter. She was good, albeit with an unknown name. If you only knew how much of her is in this, though, and the type of woman she was, you would buy this piece."

Paul glanced at the group of bidders, and his eyes met Ginger's. She was expressionless. He resignedly walked over to the table to remove Katherine's piece but then heard the auctioneer's voice cut the silence in the room.

"We have a bid of one thousand...anyone at eleven hundred, will ya bid eleven hundred?" Looking up with this heart quickening, Paul saw that Ginger had placed the bid.

Another paddle went up. "We have eleven hundred…will ya go twelve hundred?"

The auctioneer's gavel came down after the price reached two thousand. "Sold! To bidder number twelve." The painting would go home with Ginger.

Relief and then raw emotion washed over Paul as he imagined Katherine somehow bearing witness to what had just taken place. He looked over at Ginger, who smiled and mouthed "I love it" with a reassuring wink. Not only had the painting sold, but it went for a good price that—at least in Paul's mind—would have given Katherine what she'd always desired. He was more than appreciative.

Paul walked over to the auctioneer. "I told you it would sell."

The man chuckled and said under his breath, "Sure it did…You begged."

Paul, who typically contained impulses of anger, had heard enough. "The auction is over," he said.

"What do you mean?" the auctioneer asked, confused.

Paul continued in a volume loud enough to be heard by everyone in the room, "I've decided not to sell the other pieces and instead donate them to my wife's favorite charity, St. Jude's Children's Hospital. That is, all except the LeRoy Neiman piece. That one will go to the successful bidder of my wife's painting."

Stunned silence followed.

"What?!" the auctioneer exclaimed in a hushed yet incredulous tone. "You can't do this! I have important collectors who traveled all the way here to bid on one of these pieces."

The bidders, even more furious than the auctioneer, mouthed their own versions of "What the hell?" around the room. Paul turned to Ginger, who'd just made a profit of at least ten-thousand dollars from a two-thousand-dollar investment. She was shocked.

The auctioneer, meanwhile, was livid. "This is unbelievable. You can't do this," he said again, "and are contractually obligated to pay me fifteen percent of the total sale's proceeds."

Paul opened his wallet, pulled out three one hundred-dollar bills, and handed them to the auctioneer. "Fifteen percent of two thousand is three hundred. We're all square."

He looked at Ginger, still stunned and speaking to a woman beside her as if trying to confirm what had just happened. Others began filing out, most with piercing stares at Paul or snide remarks about him. The auctioneer was pleading with them to not hold what had just happened against him.

Ginger walked up to Paul and said, "Mr. Nelms, thank you. I really don't know if I can take the Neiman though."

"Why?"

"Why do you think? It's worth at least ten thousand."

"Look, Ms. Hammond. I am financially comfortable. I wish I were as comfortable on the personal side of things. I know you didn't make that bid because you wanted the piece. I could see that in your eyes when you held your paddle up."

"But still, it isn't necessary."

"I know. By the way, do you have a business card?"

Ginger fulfilled his request with a card containing her Hammond Galleria information and then left the gallery after Paul thanked her once again.

Back at home, he fetched the mail from the mailbox and began sorting through it in his study. One piece had a return address of the Superior Court of Michigan that said, "Official Jury Summons Enclosed." He opened the envelope, the contents of which had boldly emblazoned across the top: "By order of the Superior Court of Wayne County, you are hereby instructed to appear at eight forty-five a.m. on the date above for jury duty." Paul looked at the date, July 15, 2019, and noted the number 704 beside "Pool Number" and 122 beside "Juror Number."

Daniel stuck his head in the room, "Hey, Dad! Whatcha doing?"

"Oh nothing…looks like I just got selected for jury duty."

"Interesting. When?"

"July fifteenth."

"You going?"

"I have to…or at least I think I do. Who knows, maybe it will be interesting."

The next few months passed quickly. Paul continued to see Tom every few weeks and felt as if he was making progress. He was feeling less depressed, getting back to writing and enjoying a decent night's sleep without any more sleepwalking—having weaned himself off Ambien. He was also feeling more stable emotionally from the Effexor and happy for Daniel, who was still seeing Darla and inviting her over to join them for dinner on some nights. The house still felt too big to Paul, but he knew he needed to start working on eliminating the clutter, the boxed-up memories and excess personal items before getting serious about selling it.

Chapter 13

At eight-thirty in the morning, Paul, summons in hand, parked and walked into the Criminal Justice Center building in downtown Detroit. After going through security, he was instructed to head to the jury assembly room on the second floor where he was given a pencil and a personal history questionnaire and asked to watch a video about the task ahead of him. Looking around the room, he saw about two hundred other prospective jurors talking loudly on phones, slurping coffee, and munching on bagels that had been laid out on tables flanking the walls.

He whipped out his legal pad and began scribbling notes, noting their features and creating stories about some of them. It was a game he and Katherine sometimes played for fun while out to dinner, saying things like, "They're not talking...probably married awhile" or "Check out that May/December thing going on over in the corner. Must be his third wife." Paul would occasionally strike up a conversation with some of these people and learn his and Katherine's version of someone's story was usually off the mark. They'd chuckle about it afterwards.

Observation was the essence of writing, Paul always said. Writers, he once told Katherine, are excellent observers. Just like artists, authors—at least the decent ones—wrote what they saw akin to how painters used brushes to express their observations.

Most of the people in the room were now transfixed by The *Price is Right*, and Paul walked over to grab a cup of coffee and a bagel.

"Have you done this before?" he asked an attractive woman in line ahead of him.

She smiled. "No, what about you?"

"Nope," Paul said. "I don't know exactly what to expect."

"Neither do I. If I get selected, I just hope it's an open-and-shut case. I don't like the idea of deciding what constitutes reasonable doubt."

Paul chuckled and said, "I know what you mean."

He watched the woman as she turned and walked away, his gaze lingering as he wondered who she'd reminded him of. Then it hit him: Jennifer O'Neill from *Summer of '42*, plus about 15 years. "Wow," he murmured under his breath.

He was asked to report to Courtroom 7A, where a judge was already seated and attorneys were in discussions at their respective tables. He shuffled in with a large number of other potential jurors, all instructed to take a seat in the spectator bench behind the railing at the back of the courtroom—the *Summer of '42* woman among them.

Judge George Mayer introduced himself and Mike Edwards, heading up the district attorney's team, followed by Liam Olsen, the court-appointed attorney representing the defendant. Then he looked at the potential jurors and said, "Ladies and gentlemen, thank you for appearing this morning as potential jury members. The case we are preparing to hear today involves a capital offense of first-degree murder."

If I get picked, this could take a while, Paul thought.

His suspicion was confirmed when the judge estimated a two-week trial. "As a first step," the judge went on, "we'll tell you a little about the case and then ask you some questions to better determine if we believe you can serve independently without bias or prejudicial perspectives, knowledge, or relationships. The victim in this case was a man named Marcus Roberts who lived at 231 Pineview Street in Detroit."

Paul's heart raced, his blood pressure suddenly off the charts, as his breathing became quick and shallow. His mind threw questions at him: Would he disclose that this man had assaulted his wife? What about his promise to Katherine? More to the point, what about the brick through the window and the chase? Could he simply say he knew the man without saying how he knew him? What if they pressed him on that question? *"How do you know him, Juror 122?" What if the court demands that I respond to this question?*

On the other hand, what if he kept quiet and actually served? Could he render an unbiased verdict? He began to rationalize. *Would the fact that I hate him even matter in terms of my ability to assess the evidence presented and determine innocence or guilt? Can I handle this emotionally? What would Katherine want?*

Had Marcus Roberts himself been on trial, sure…He could see how his knowledge would compromise his judgment. *Less so,* he thought, *with a man who might have killed him.* If Paul kept his and Katherine's history with Roberts a secret, as Katherine would have wanted, how would anyone find out anyway? Tom Harris was the only person other than Daniel and himself who knew. *Can Tom be pulled in and potentially brought in for questioning?* The answer was a quick "No" in Paul's mind. *Besides, Tom said everything I tell him is strictly confidential.*

Paul was still so stunned and wrapped up in his own internal questionings that he barely heard the judge say, "I will ask the question one more time: Does anyone here feel they can't serve as a juror in this case?"

Paul started to raise his hand, but Judge Mayer had apparently decided to confirm the results based on the silence that immediately followed the question asked a moment ago. He then casually added, "Very well then. Would the following people make their way to the seats in front of the jury box? Julia Taylor, Wilson Smith, Nathan Cashwell…" The judge ran through the list and called Paul's name about midway through.

As soon as Paul's name was called, he stood and walked to the appointed area where he took a seat. After the final name was called, the judge said, "Ladies and gentlemen, you all will constitute the group from which we select the jurors and alternate jurors. We will be asking you a few questions about your background and anything that could disqualify you from serving. Both sides, in other words, the prosecution and the defense, are allowed to strike a certain number of potential jurors from selection if they choose."

After all the potential jurors were seated, Judge Mayer looked down at his paperwork and said, "Juror 089, Mrs. Harper. Where are you?"

"Here I am, Your Honor" a large middle-aged woman responded, raising her hand.

"Fine," the judge replied, "Mr. Edwards, Mr. Olsen, you may proceed."

Mr. Edwards began, "Mrs. Harper, it says here you've served as a security guard in a juvenile detention center. Is that correct?"

"Yes, sir."

Edwards proceeded to ask about her job responsibilities, her experience dealing with subjects who'd committed violent crimes and whether that in any way compromised her ability to render a fair verdict. She assured him she'd have no problem doing so. He said, "I also assume you'd have no problem sentencing a person to life in prison?" as what seemed like a parenthetical comment as Michigan had no death penalty. She responded, "Oh, yes, I mean, that's correct. I would—uh, excuse me—*could* give him life in prison." Both attorneys took notes.

Both Edwards and Olsen spent the next thirty minutes asking

various people about their backgrounds, moving through most of them quickly. Paul knew his turn was approaching and was still unsure about how to respond.

After what seemed like hours, Judge Mayer said, "Number 122, Mr. Paul Nelms. Are you present?"

Paul raised his hand and said, "Yes, sir."

Edwards began, "It looks like you are a writer. Is that correct?"

"Yes, that's correct," Paul responded.

"Do you have a regular job where you have to report to work, or do you work on your own schedule?"

"My own schedule."

"Okay. What do you write about?"

"I write novels. Most of my writing is historical fiction."

"Have you been published, and what period of history, exactly?"

"A few of my novels have been published, most of them taking place in the 1800s in New England." He debated whether to elaborate or not, but Edwards' dismissive nod seemed to imply he'd said enough.

Then finally, the question: "Do you have any reason to believe you can't be an impartial juror in this case?"

Paul glanced at the judge, who was staring intently at him, and his heart pounded. For reasons he would question for years to come, he simply said, "No." He questioned the decision as soon as the word left his mouth, and with a mounting sense of gravity, realized there was no backing out now.

His breathing slowly returned to normal. *What did I just do?* Saying "No" had almost happened automatically, and he knew it had the potential for huge implications. Still, maybe he'd be stricken from the pool for other reasons.

Liam Olsen had no questions for Paul. Ten minutes later, he was not among several jurors dismissed and instead asked to remain in the courtroom. The judge announced they'd take a brief recess before beginning the trial.

Paul thought to himself, *I'll tell Tom about this. Therapists are sworn to confidentiality, and he can help me think through it when I see him Thursday.* He quickly realized something else, though: *I can't see Tom on Thursday due to the trial.* Paul took a deep breath, hoping it would allay the growing fear that he'd just made a colossal mistake.

Chapter 14

While a few jurors excused themselves for the break, Paul remained sitting. He shifted in his chair, wondering if jurors' seats were intentionally uncomfortable to discourage anyone from nodding off. The sound of a door opening drew his attention. In walked Mike Edwards accompanied by an associate with whom he was engaging in muted conversation. They looked self-assured, Edwards chuckling as if his partner had uttered an amusing quip.

Liam Olsen walked in moments later. He was in his late thirties, Paul guessed, with blue eyes and fair hair that gave him a youthful Scandinavian look. Olsen walked past the prosecution team to the table on the far side of the courtroom, offering a glance of acknowledgement to the jury members he'd just screened earlier. He dropped his satchel on a table as two other suit-clad men entered through the same door followed by a sheriff's deputy.

The deputy, standing inside the doorway, watched with trained eyes as one of the men calmly made his way to the table and took the middle chair. Paul stared at the man. Levi Johnson was of medium build, clean shaven and with light brown skin. *Probably about five foot nine,* Paul assumed. He was sporting a gray suit with cornrows neatly pulled back on his head.

Levi tugged at his collar and then turned to the rear of the courtroom, flashing a subdued smile to someone in the back. Paul followed his gaze and saw a young woman standing and holding the hand of a little boy who looked about four or five years old. The little boy waved, and Levi waved back before returning his attention to the front of the courtroom.

For several moments, Levi sat stoically, staring straight ahead. Then, as if it had suddenly occurred to him to assess the twelve people holding his fate in their hands, he shifted his gaze to the jury. Paul and Levi's eyes met and remained fixed on each other's until Paul suddenly felt uneasy. For inexplicable reasons, he nodded slightly—as if in some sort of acknowledgment—and Levi nodded back, almost imperceptibly. Paul would later recall that moment and wonder if there'd been any hint of recognition in Levi's gaze.

The judge entered the courtroom, and the bailiff loudly announced, "All rise! The Court of the Third Judicial Circuit of Michigan, Criminal Division, is now in session, the Honorable Judge George Mayer presiding." The judge sat.

Paul scanned the other thirteen jurors, which included two alternates, and wondered, "Is it too late to get out of this?"

His stomach tightened. Memories of that night were never far away: The mental image of Katherine rushing into the house crying hysterically, choking out the words that she'd been assaulted, her refusal to let Paul call the police, and his reluctant consent to her demand. He thought of the many times he'd second-guessed that decision along with the brick and the ensuing chase. Disclosing such facts wouldn't only violate his promise to Katherine but could in fact even make *him* a suspect. He knew he shouldn't serve, but…if only he could talk to Katherine. If only she were still alive.

Questions peppered Paul's mind: *If the court somehow discovers I perjured myself when I said nothing would compromise my objectivity during the pretrial proceedings, will I face prosecution? Was Levi Johnson, in fact, the killer? Can I even be objective since Roberts ultimately got what he deserved?*

The stern-looking Judge Mayer, with his sagging jowls and bushy gray eyebrows, asked both sets of attorneys if they were ready to begin the morning's proceedings before glancing at the jury as if to confirm the same.

If there's any time for me to back out, it's now, Paul thought. He started to raise his hand to signal the judge's attention, lifting it a few inches, but Judge Mayer's attention suddenly shifted to two men in the rear of the courtroom whose discourse had become increasingly disruptive.

Paul watched with mounting trepidation as the judge glared at the men and slammed down his gavel, shouting, "Order in the court!" He lowered his trembling hand.

The judge took a deep breath, looked down from his towering bench to the district attorney and asked, "Mr. Edwards, you ready?"

"Yes, Your Honor."

Judge Mayer then eyed the defendant and his team of lawyers. "Mr. Olsen?"

"Yes, Your Honor, the defense is ready."

Judge Mayer then turned to the jury and told them he had some introductory remarks. "This trial is likely to take a couple of weeks. You'll hear witnesses for the prosecution as well as the defense and be shown evidence from the scene of the crime, some difficult to see. However, it's important you not form any conclusions about guilt or innocence prior to the conclusion of the presentation of the evidence. You may take notes, but you're not to discuss the case with anyone. That includes your fellow jurors when you're not deliberating."

Removing his glasses, the judge continued, "The Court has already called this morning the case of the State of Michigan versus Levi Johnson, Case Number 08 CF 137. In a few moments,

I will give you some opening instructions in this case, but before that, the clerk will swear you in. At this time, I ask that you all please rise."

After the jury was sworn in, Judge Mayer continued, "Members of the jury, before the trial begins, there are some things you must understand about your role as a juror and your responsibilities. Your duty is to decide this case solely based on the evidence presented and the law given to you by the Court. If you come into contact with any of the parties, lawyers, or witnesses, do not interact with them; they will do the same. The jury will not be sequestered during this trial."

Paul hadn't even considered the notion of staying in a hotel during the trial.

"Nevertheless, you're forbidden from listening to, watching, or reading any news accounts of the case during the trial or even discussing it with anyone including members of your family or other jurors."

Paul watched the judge speak and immediately thought of Tom, knowing he'd likely be unable to follow the judge's instruction on that point.

The judge continued. "It's critical that you do not browse the web or read or listen to any news reports about this trial, nor are you to join any conversations about the case. To ensure this lack of exposure, the Court is ordering that—for the duration of the trial—you not watch or listen to local news or consume local print or online media unless you task someone else with previewing the content first. Should you be exposed to any reports or communications from any source concerning the case during the trial, you should report that information to the bailiff. Also refrain from investigating the case on your own or visiting the scene."

Already violated that, Paul thought.

"You'll notice there are fourteen of you, with twelve of you reaching a verdict. Two alternate jurors will hear all evidence but remain absent from your deliberations unless someone becomes incapacitated or is excused for any reason."

Paul played out how an alternate could figure into his situation, not hard to imagine as he guessed the Court would immediately disqualify him if it became privy to his connections to Roberts.

Judge Mayer continued on for another ten minutes, instructing them they were only to consider what was presented in the courtroom and could take notes at any time except during opening arguments and closing statements. Said notes would be taken from them each day but returned the next morning and then destroyed after the trial was over. They were not to consider *any* evidence successfully objected to, were the sole judges of the weight of the evidence, and were to assess the credibility of witnesses. With each word the judge uttered, the seriousness of Paul's failure to disclose his history became more worrisome. *What would Tom tell me to do right now?* he asked himself.

After the judge dismissed the court for a brief recess, all the jurors filed back down to the assembly room. Paul had a chance to speak to some of them, most of the conversation focused on where people grew up and other "safe" topics not in violation of Judge Mayer's orders. Paul walked up to the *Summer of '42* woman. He introduced himself and learned her name was Rebecca.

"They could use some better Danishes," he said, picking one up and taking a small bite. "Less stale."

She laughed. "Yes, but at least they have coffee. I think I need an extra dose this morning."

A few minutes later, the bailiff summoned the jury back into the courtroom. The jurors filed in and Judge Mayer began, "Members of the jury, to help you in evaluating the evidence, I am going to read portions of specific jury instructions for the offenses with which the defendant is charged. At the conclusion of the presentation of evidence, I will read them in their entirety."

He continued, "There is a single count against the defendant that charges Levi Johnson, who is seated in this courtroom, with the first-degree intentional homicide of Marcus Roberts. Section 750:316 of the Criminal Code of Michigan provides that first-degree intentional homicide is committed by one who causes the death of another person with intent to kill that person. Before you may find the defendant guilty of first-degree intentional homicide, the State must prove, beyond a reasonable doubt, that the following two elements were present: first, that Levi Johnson caused the death of Marcus Roberts or aided and abetted another in causing the death of Marcus Roberts. Second, that Levi Johnson acted with the intent to kill Marcus Roberts, irrespective of whether he did so directly or aided and abetted another in doing so."

Paul listened carefully, trying to reassure himself he could render an unbiased verdict.

The judge added, "When it says, 'intent to kill,' that means the defendant had the mental purpose to take the life of another human being or was aware that his conduct was practically certain to cause the death of another human being. *Intent* to kill, if found at all, can only be determined from the defendant's acts, words, and other facts and circumstances. Intent is not the same thing as motive, which refers to a person's reason for doing something. Proof of intent is necessary for a conviction; proof of motive is not. While motive may be shown as a circumstance to aid in establishing the guilt of the defendant, the State is not required to prove motive on the part of a defendant in order to convict. Evidence of motive does not, by itself, establish guilt. You should give it the weight you believe it deserves, given all the circumstances."

Judge Mayer paused to look up at the jurors, seeing all were paying close attention and thus continued. He explained the concept of reasonable doubt, how the law presumed everyone innocent, and that the burden of proof lies solely with the State.

"If, after all evidence has been presented, you can reconcile that evidence with any reasonable explanation consistent with the defendant's innocence, you should do so and return a verdict of not guilty."

Finally, he concluded with, "In just a few moments, the lawyers will make opening statements. The purpose of an opening statement is to give them an opportunity to tell you what they expect the evidence will show so that you will better understand it as it's introduced during the trial. Keep in mind, however, that these opening statements themselves are not evidence."

The judge looked at Mike Edwards, who rose from his seat to set up an easel before proceeding with the prosecution's opening statements. "Ladies and gentlemen of the jury, you have a difficult task in front of you, which is to decide whether Levi Johnson is guilty beyond a reasonable doubt of the charges the judge just read to you. It's obviously a very serious matter because a man's life is at stake, but it's also a very serious matter from the other point of view as an innocent man was murdered in his home. It's important not only to make sure you don't convict a defendant if you have reasonable doubt but also to make sure justice is done."

Paul took careful note of his delivery, which was polished. He could imagine Edwards as one of the characters in his books.

Edwards made a few more introductory comments and then strolled in front of the jury while looking accusingly at Levi Johnson. He stated, "The defendant is charged with the offense of first-degree intentional homicide of one Marcus A. Roberts. The evidence will show that on the evening of February 23, 2019, Levi Johnson, along with two other men, Joseph Adams and James Turner, all members of the Bloods Street Gang, were driving on Pineview Street, and that Mr. Johnson—upon arriving at the decedent's address—exited the vehicle, rang Mr. Roberts' doorbell, and when Mr. Roberts opened the door, shot him in the chest with a 12-gauge shotgun, killing him instantly."

He then provided details of the police report, beginning with a neighbor calling in to report what sounded like a gunshot on Pineview Street, with a nearby police unit responding and how, while in route, this police unit saw shots fired from a car occupied by Levi Johnson, Joseph Adams and James Turner. The police unit had initiated a pursuit, and that chase culminated in the crashing of the suspects' vehicle and the recovery of the weapons that had been fired, one of which was the shotgun that was believed to be the one used in Marcus Roberts' killing.

Edwards then explained that Levi Johnson had participated in two separate murders that night: the first involving the killing of Marcus Roberts, which he'd just described, and the second a drive-by shooting that left two men dead, both members of the rival Latin Kings gang. He indicated the State of Michigan had successfully persuaded the two other suspects to take a plea deal on the second drive-by shooting after investigators showed that several of the bullets retrieved from the deceased's bodies belonged to the handguns used by Joseph Adams and James Turner. Levi Johnson, the driver of the car, had not shot either of the decedents—a fact corroborated by Turner and Adams—and had taken a plea deal as an accessory to the murders. Turner's and Adams' plea deals, meanwhile, included a lower-than-customary fifteen-year sentence and obligation to serve as State's witnesses in the trial of Levi Johnson for the murder of Marcus Roberts.

They're potentially conflicted, Paul thought to himself.

Edwards added, "While Mr. Adams' and Mr. Turner's testimony is arguably subject to attack on the grounds it was intended to mitigate the length of their incarceration, I believe you will find their testimony credible and consistent. Their testimony, the proximity of the two shootings, an almost-identical timestamp of events, shotgun shell identification, and the testimony of Ms. Martha Howard, Mr. Roberts' next-door neighbor who visually confirmed a dark sedan matching the type of vehicle driven by the suspects, are ample evidence to establish guilt."

"They were on a shooting spree," summarized Edwards, "and while we may not know all the reasons Levi Johnson walked up to the door and killed Marcus Roberts as he stood in the doorway, the evidence will show, beyond a reasonable doubt, that Levi Johnson did willfully and with full intent shoot and kill Marcus Roberts on the evening of February 23, 2019."

Edwards then rattled off a description of Marcus Roberts. Originally from the South, he was thirty years old at the time of his death, had moved to Detroit two years prior, and had two children—a three-year-old boy and five-year-old girl—both in the custody of his ex-wife.

Paul was shocked to hear Roberts had children and felt the bile rise in his throat as Edwards recounted the challenges he'd faced in his life, how he'd been a "good father," generally paid child support on time, and had recently found a new job. "What a shame," Mr. Edwards summarily stated, "that this man was getting his life in order just as it was about to be snuffed out." He looked over at the jurors and said: "Ladies and gentlemen of the jury, you must render justice…for Marcus Roberts' sake." He then looked at the judge to indicate he was finished.

Paul's stomach had been churning for the past 90 minutes, and suddenly, he felt like he was going to vomit. As if on cue, the judge said, "Why don't we break for ten minutes," and Paul made a quick exit to the bathroom and did just that.

Chapter 15

As soon as Paul got to his car, he dialed Tom's number. To his surprise and immense relief, he actually answered.

"Tom, I need to talk to you right away. Is there any way I can come in now?"

"I have someone coming in at four thirty, but only for thirty minutes. How about five o'clock? The office will be closed, but you can come in anyway."

"That's perfect, Tom, I can't tell you how much I appreciate it. See you in about an hour."

At the appointed time, Paul sat in a chair opposite Tom, eyes on the beige carpet beneath him, and stated in a shaky voice, "I think I really screwed up. I don't know what to do."

Tom's puzzled expression conveyed concern.

"We have a confidential relationship, correct? I mean, if I open up to you about something, it stays confidential…within this room and not shared with anyone, correct?"

Nodding, Tom said, "Yes, of course."

Paul took a deep breath. "I was selected for jury duty and went in today. Turns out it was a murder case." Paul rubbed his face, dreading what was next. "The Marcus Roberts murder."

"Good heavens," Tom said with astonishment, "You recused

yourself obviously…"

"No."

Tom's eyes widened. "What? Paul, you don't mean to tell me that you're on the *jury*?"

"Yes."

"This is a colossal mistake and a terrible idea on so many levels. You do understand that, don't you?"

"I do."

"Why didn't you recuse yourself?"

Paul's eyes shifted nervously back and forth as he processed how much to disclose.

"I sort of froze up. I didn't want to say Katherine was assaulted by Roberts and was afraid the defense team could wind up using that somehow—that I would have to actually *testify* about the sexual assault and provide the details despite Katherine's desire for privacy and her fear of the whole thing getting out."

"Paul, she's gone. It wouldn't be the same as if she were alive, would it?"

"I don't know." Paul sighed heavily and said, "There's more to it."

As Tom stared with mounting disbelief, Paul proceeded to explain about the call to Tony to learn Roberts' identity, the brick through the window, the chase, and the pickup truck crashing. "I was trying to process all of this while they were asking me questions, and almost before I realized it, I was there on the empaneled jury."

"The brick," Tom said. "Is there any way to trace that to *you*?"

"I have no idea. I don't even know if he ever reported it."

They stared at each other for a moment, neither saying anything.

Paul finally spoke up. "But if I had disclosed I knew him and *how* I knew him, can't you see how everything I just told you would come out in the questioning? Forget the promise I made to Katherine…hell, I might even be a suspect."

Tom still said nothing.

Paul continued, "So I'm supposed to process all this in the short window between the judge asking if we're conflicted and our subsequent responses? What should I have said, Tom? 'Excuse me judge? Yes, I am conflicted. You see, this guy raped my wife so I tracked him down and threw a brick through his car window, which led to a car chase and a crash. So, what do you think? Can I get off this particular jury?'"

Tom rubbed his hand through his hair and simply responded, "Oh Paul," trying to process the situation.

Paul wasn't done. "The longer things went, the harder it was for me to say anything. I started asking myself if I could be objective, and I concluded that yes, I could. I could simply look at the suspect, who I have no feelings about, and make a call of guilt or innocence. I still think I can do that."

Tom said, "Paul, I think you have a very serious problem on your hands here with legal implications…You could find yourself in big trouble. I'd suggest you call an attorney for advice."

Paul thought about Tony but shook his head no.

"I'm not going to do that. At least not now."

"I don't know what to tell you, Paul. I think the longer this goes, the worse it gets."

Neither spoke for a moment.

Tom asked, "When does the trial start?"

Paul responded, "It started today. We heard opening statements."

Tom's mind searched through likely outcomes. "No one knows about this but you and me?"

"Right."

Tom shook his head, saying, "I still think you should talk to an attorney."

Paul responded, "The fewer who know, the better. This is only supposed to take two or three weeks. If no one ever finds out, and I can render a fair opinion, what's the harm?"

"Paul, you don't get it. *You* know, and the court *should* be informed. The whole system is based on fairness and impartiality."

Paul sat motionless, thinking.

Sensing Paul was resolute in his position, Tom stood and said, "I don't know what else to say. I advise against this path you're following and think it has a lot of risk to it, much more so than going to the court or authorities or whomever."

Paul stood as well to leave. "I understand your position, Tom."

He took a couple of steps towards the closed door and said, "Tom, look, you have been very helpful to me. Even though I'm not doing what you're suggesting, can I still come see you?"

"Yes, Paul. Nothing changes from that standpoint. I'm here if you need me."

"Thank you, Tom. I suspect I'll need you even more now than before. Court will likely keep me tied up during most of the next several days. Can we schedule something for next Friday at this time, but can I perhaps call you for an impromptu conference if I need to in the meantime?"

"Of course." Standing and facing Paul, Tom added, "I'm sorry you're going through this, and sorry if it seems I'm minimizing how difficult disclosing this to the court would be. I suspect you're trying to do the right thing in your own way."

The comment hit an emotional trigger and caused Paul to start weeping. He put his face in his hands.

"We'll get through this," Tom said, and put his hand on Paul's shoulder.

Paul took a deep breath, shook his head, and said, "Sorry about that. I don't know where that came from."

When Paul got home, he opened the door and called for Daniel, who was in the den watching television.

"Hey, Dad, I'm in here. How did the jury thing go?"

When Daniel saw Paul walk into the den, he said, "Wow, Pop, you look spent."

Paul rubbed his eyes and said, "Yeah, it was a long day."

"Did you actually get selected?"

"Yeah, but I can't talk about it."

Paul fell into his favorite chair. The local news was on, so he said, "Hey, can we see if there's a ball game on or something?

"Sure," Daniel replied, flipping over to ESPN.

Paul rested his eyes for a moment, and the next thing he knew, it was eight forty-five that evening. Daniel had left a note saying he was out with Darla, so Paul watched some of a baseball game before heading to bed at ten. Knowing sleep would be difficult that night, he thought about taking an Ambien but decided against it and opted for Benadryl instead. He was fast asleep by ten forty-five.

Chapter 16

Tuesday, July 16, 2019

Paul's stomach was unsettled as he made his way into the courthouse the next morning. He was dreading the day, set to include testimony from one of Roberts' neighbors and a policeman among the first to arrive at Roberts' home. Paul walked into the jury assembly room about eight-forty, saw Rebecca, and greeted her with a "Good morning."

She smiled back at him. "Grab some coffee. It's not so bad today," she said, taking a second sip.

"Great idea. I'll be right back."

Paul poured a cup and glanced over at Rebecca before adding sweetener and cream. He guessed she was in her fifties, making her a few years younger than him, and her brown ponytail made her look younger than she had the prior day. He was glad to have another jury member to talk to.

He sat in a chair beside her and took a tentative sip from the steaming cup. "It *is* pretty good today. You don't expect that from the government."

She laughed. "No."

Paul noticed a thick paperback in her lap. "What are you

reading?"

She picked up the book and handed it to Paul.

"*Pillars of the Earth* by Ken Follett. It's a tome but a great read and one of few books I've read where I actually whispered to myself, 'Oh no!' without realizing it…so, so good." She looked at him and their eyes met, and in that one moment, Paul felt mesmerized—much like when he was young and saw a beautiful girl.

As Rebecca began talking about one of the characters in the book, Paul was busy picking up cues just like any good writer: a ring finger adorned with an emerald not a diamond, a build that suggested an active, energetic lifestyle, and still-youthful skin with enough color to hint she spent time outdoors.

Paul noticed her scent too, and he instantly took a liking to it simply due to its association with her. "I like your perfume," he said.

"Oh," she said, laughing softly. "It's nothing special and actually something pretty inexpensive I picked up from a department store. Sunflowers by Elizabeth Arden, in case you ever want to get some for your wife."

"Actually, I'm a widower."

"Oh, I'm so sorry."

"It's okay. I'm getting along all right."

Changing the subject, Rebecca quickly said, "Anyway, I'll lend you the book when I'm done with it if you'd like. Do you read much?"

"I do. It helps with my writing."

"Oh, that's right, I remember you saying you were a writer during jury selection. So that's what you do professionally?"

"I try," Paul laughed. "I told someone once I was in the annuity business. These things become annuities at some point, if you write enough of them. If a few people buy them, you can make a living."

Rebecca smiled. "Nice way to look at it, I guess."

Paul went on, "Honestly, most of my books write themselves. The story kind of comes to my head and makes me feel like a transcriber. I'm not sure if what I write is even any good." Paul chuckled and said, "My imposter complex balances the hubris of thinking anything I have to say is important enough for someone to pay for."

Rebecca grabbed her book and pointed to it. "You kidding? Books are one of the best 'bangs for the buck' out there. I spent three dollars on this used paperback, and it's given me hours and hours of enjoyment. That's a pretty good investment." She smiled.

The court bailiff walked past them and said, "Time to head in, folks."

"Well, here we go," Rebecca said, stashing her book in her bag.

"Yep, here we go," Paul echoed. With the visual distraction of a beautiful woman no longer in front of him, he was reminded of the stark reality he was facing and wondered how he'd allowed himself to get into this situation.

The jury members filed into the courtroom, and Paul took a seat in the second row, behind and down a few chairs from Rebecca. He looked at her high cheekbones and the side of her neck, wondering if that's where she'd applied her perfume. For the first time since Katherine's death, Paul felt a twinge of romantic attraction to someone.

Judge Mayer, having completed a few introductory remarks, tapped his gavel and stated, "The State of Michigan may proceed."

Mike Edwards stood and said, "Your Honor, the State of Michigan calls Martha J. Howard to the stand."

Ms. Howard, a grey-haired, bespectacled woman who looked about seventy years old, slowly made her way to the front of the room and paused to support herself as she took the witness stand. She looked nervous while being sworn in, and Paul wondered what she would testify about.

Edwards asked her to confirm her name and address.

Ah, thought Paul after the woman responded. *Roberts' next-door neighbor.*

She said slowly, "I was in the bathroom, getting ready for bed. I heard what sounded like a loud gunshot and so rushed to the front window and saw a car pulling away."

Edwards asked, "How long after you heard the shot did you get up and look outside?"

"Less than a minute," she replied. "I'm not sure. I called 9-1-1 right after that."

Edwards asked her to describe the car.

"It was a dark car and therefore hard to see. There's a streetlight in front of my house, so it wasn't totally dark but still enough to prevent me from seeing any sort of detail," she replied.

Edwards moved to a line of questions about weather conditions that night, seemingly of little significance, but then asked a question that commanded Paul's attention: "Ms. Howard, what kind of man was Marcus Roberts? I mean, as a neighbor...Did you have an opinion of him as a person?"

Liam Olsen immediately stood and said, "Objection. Relevance?"

Edwards, as if he'd anticipated the objection, responded, "Your Honor, we are trying to establish that Marcus Roberts was a good neighbor to Ms. Howard and that there is no evidence he was in a rival gang or participated in illegal activities that could have been an aggravating factor contributing to his murder."

The judge nodded and said, "Overruled."

"Go ahead, Ms. Howard," Edwards instructed her.

"Well, Marcus was a nice young man, I can tell you that."

Is she serious? A nice young man? Paul's mind thundered. He tried to contain his incredulity as he listened to her recount a story about Roberts bringing groceries into her home and how he once helped her remove a black snake from her garage. Edwards seemed pleased with her response, less so though when she then started questioning aloud how the snake had even gotten into her garage as she "didn't even know black snakes lived in the area or why some people liked to protect them." Paul could tell from Edwards's demeanor she'd ultimately redeemed herself, though, wrapping up her comments by expressing how it was such a "shame" that he was gone.

Paul recalled the night of Katherine's sexual assault, of her rushing through the back door and falling into his arms, sobbing. He closed his eyes for a moment and tried to get the image of Marcus assaulting her out of his mind. There were so many details Katherine had never disclosed, and he felt his face flush as his brain became hyperactive. *What exactly had he done to her?*

Listening to Katherine's rapist be aggrandized, he imagined himself there in the car with them, watching the event take place with no ability to do anything about it. Tears of anger filled his eyes. If he didn't pull himself together, someone would notice. He closed his eyes and pinched the side of his thigh, the pain momentarily distracting him and bringing his attention back to Ms. Howard just as she was finishing her direct testimony.

On cross examination, Liam Olsen peppered Ms. Howard with questions about her visual acuity—or lack thereof—regarding the distance between herself and the car in question and the make of the car, none of which she had much idea about. "Like I said, all I know is it was a dark car, a 'sedan,' I think they call it," she finally admitted.

Olsen countered, "And how many dark cars go down your street on any given night?"

She looked at Edwards, who blankly stared back, and she responded, "I really have no idea."

Olsen looked to the judge and said, "Nothing further, Your Honor."

Ms. Howard, looking less confident than she had while discussing the snake, seemed relieved to be stepping down.

Edwards stood, thanked Ms. Howard, and called Sergeant Jeremy Tyndall—the lead officer who had apprehended the suspects—to the stand. He was sworn in while Edwards placed a map of the Chavis Heights area on an easel.

Edwards began by asking several questions about Tyndall's background and years on the force.

"Now, Officer Tyndall," he began, "can you tell me, or take me through, the events on the evening of February 23, 2019?"

Officer Tyndall responded, "Sure, we…that is, myself and my partner Officer Lucy Bolin…were patrolling a couple of miles from Chavis Heights on the evening of February twenty third."

Edwards interrupted, "Officer Tyndall, would you mind stepping down and showing us where on the map you were traveling?"

Tyndall looked to the judge—who nodded affirmatively—and stepped down, pointing to a major artery a few blocks from Pineview Street. "We were patrolling along here, on East Jefferson Avenue and driving south, when we received a radio call to check out an area around Pineview Street at around ten-fifteen p.m. in response to a possible gunshot. We didn't turn on the siren or lights since we were just checking things out and made a couple of turns to get on Franklin Avenue to make our way towards the Chavis Heights area."

Edwards clarified, "Chavis Heights is where Pineview Street is located?"

Officer Tyndall, still at the map, responded, "Yes." He continued, "Now, Franklin Avenue is a long, straight road, as you can see here," he said, his hand moving across a long narrow line down the center of the map. "We use it sometimes because it has very few stoplights and good visibility. It's a good shortcut."

Paul looked at the line on the map and remembered how he'd in fact used Franklin himself to return home the morning he drove by Marcus Roberts' house.

Tyndall went on, "So, right after turning onto Franklin Avenue, we looked down the street and saw—approximately four to five hundred feet ahead of us—the suspects firing into a parking lot from the passenger side of the vehicle. We immediately turned on our siren and lights and radioed that shots had been fired from a dark sedan, identified our position, and requested backup. The suspects' car was approaching ours at a high rate of speed, and as soon as they saw our patrol unit with our lights on, they quickly turned down Academy Street." Tyndall's finger traced the route of the suspects' car on the map, and he went on for several more minutes: explaining their attempted getaway and the crash at a high rate of speed.

"We radioed for medical personnel to be sent to the general location where we'd seen the shooting and stayed in pursuit until the crash. We also called in medical personnel for the suspects, who were pretty banged up. Once their vehicle crashed at the intersection of Davis Street and Route 301, Officer Bolin and I, along with several other patrol units, converged on the suspects." He paused, still standing at the map, and looked over at Levi Johnson who was watching him with an expressionless face.

Edwards stated, "So, just to make sure the Court heard you right, before the pursuit, the suspects' car was facing you, and you saw shots fired out the passenger-side window?"

"Yes, sir. That's correct."

"Thank you, Officer Tyndall." Edwards said. "I think we're done with the map for the time being, if you'd like to return to the stand."

Edwards then asked him a series of questions related to the chase and the weapons recovered from the car after the three suspects (Johnson, Adams, and Turner) were taken to the hospital. They included a Smith & Wesson nine-millimeter automatic pistol with an extended magazine, a forty-caliber Glock—also an automatic—and a Savage Arms short-barrel, twelve-gauge shotgun. Ballistics tests indicated all three had recently been fired.

Paul listened and took some notes, wondering how the State would ultimately connect Levi to the Roberts killing—not even specifically discussed yet.

A few minutes before noon, Judge Mayer suggested the court recess for lunch with Tyndall still on the stand. Paul walked out and saw Rebecca leaving with another female juror. He had about an hour and a half to eat something and perhaps sit in his car or drive somewhere to get his mind off things. He grabbed a sandwich and made a couple of calls from his car, one to Tom in the hopes that simply hearing his voice would quell a growing anxiety about being on the jury. He got his voicemail.

Paul returned to the courtroom at one-fifteen, hoping evidence tying Levi to the Marcus Roberts shooting would be forthcoming and compelling. Tyndall testified for another forty-five minutes about the details of the chase and subsequent crash, at one point saying, "While we were still on the accident scene and coordinating with emergency medical personnel, another call came in that there had been a shooting and a man down at his home at the Pineview address."

Paul's attention heightened.

Edwards asked, "Marcus Roberts?"

"Yes."

"Did you leave to investigate the matter?"

"No, as it's standard procedure for us to stay on the scene in cases like this so we can communicate with other units within our department and other law enforcement agencies."

Edwards asked, "Were the suspects able to talk and communicative when you came upon them at the accident scene?"

Tyndall responded, "Yes, all three were able to communicate. We read them their Miranda rights, but they volunteered they didn't know anything about any shootings."

"Can you please identify the driver of the vehicle for the court?" Edwards asked.

Tyndall replied, "Levi Johnson."

Edwards continued, "Was your dash cam, the camera affixed to the front of the police car, operating when all of this took place?"

Tyndall responded, "Well, technically the dash cam is always on, but it doesn't begin to record until we activate the lights and/or siren. When we saw the suspects firing out of their car, we flipped on the lights and so have a recording from that point through the time of the crash."

"I see," Edwards said. "So you didn't actually capture the shots fired from the suspects' car?"

"That's correct."

"Your Honor, the State would like to introduce into evidence the video recording from Officer Tyndall's police unit, marked as Plaintiff's Exhibit 8," Edwards said, looking at the judge.

Judge Mayer glanced over at Olsen, who acknowledged—as he had in all previous evidence submissions—that he had no objection to the admission into evidence.

The judge looked back at Edwards and said, "You may proceed."

The jury then watched the video of the events unfolding exactly as Tyndall had described them.

His cross-examination by Olsen and the redirect from Edwards lasted the rest of the day, although no major challenges were successfully mounted against Tyndall's testimony.

The court recessed at five after five p.m., with the jury dismissed and the judge issuing his admonitions and reminders. Paul got up to leave, and his eyes met Rebecca's. She gave him a look seemingly equivalent to a "Whew!" and he smiled and mouthed back, "See you tomorrow."

Paul thought about what the prosecution had presented thus far: credible testimony from the police indicating Levi had participated (albeit only as the driver) in the gang-related shooting, the weapons found in the suspects' car, and the admission (or at least plea deal) among Levi and the other two suspects with respect to the drive-by shooting.

No evidence specifically tying Levi Johnson to the Roberts murder yet, Paul thought, *though the timing did match, as did the location.* Nothing had been presented regarding a possible motive.

He started to call Tom on the drive home but hesitated, wanting to think through what he'd say, what he'd ask, and whether he should even make the call in the first place. It was after hours after all, and Tom would probably be on the way home. He went ahead and dialed anyway.

"Hi, Paul. How are you?" Tom asked upon answering.

"I'm okay, tired but okay. I'd love to talk but know you're probably heading out the door."

"It's okay. I was trying to get some billing and other things done and wasn't planning on leaving for a little while. I've been wondering how things are going. Do you want to swing by now for a few minutes?'

"Oh, wow, absolutely. I didn't expect you to be available. I'm on the way."

Fifteen minutes later, Paul was sitting in Tom's office. "I only threw up once," he said, shaking his head. "The prosecution actually tried to evoke sympathy for Marcus Roberts, and I literally got sick right after the judge called a recess."

"I can't imagine what this is like for you, Paul," Tom said. "Have they given you any idea as to timing? How long this whole thing will take?"

"Somewhat. They told us not to discuss the case with anyone, and my intent is to comply with their wishes so I'm not planning on talking to you about the evidence or my opinions of guilt or innocence. However, I do want to talk to you, if nothing else, to keep a line of communication open and have a sounding board if any issues come up. Is that alright?"

Tom smiled reassuringly. "Of course, Paul. I'll help any way I can."

"Guys usually don't tell other guys this, but honestly, Tom, I'm not sure what I'd do if I didn't have you in my life right now. I appreciate your availability more than you know."

"Don't think anything of it, Paul. Again, I'm here to help."

Tom went on, "What can I do right now?"

"Nothing at the moment, thanks. I was actually thinking about what has been presented so far on the way over here and am feeling more and more that I'll be able to get through it from an objectivity standpoint. I think I can be impartial."

"That's good to hear," Tom responded. "How's your sleep, by the way?"

"Fair," Paul responded. "I take the Benadryl you suggested every now and then when I need one, and the depression has gotten better I think. I'm still anxious as hell, but to tell you the truth, I think that's justified given the circumstances."

"Yeah, I agree," Tom responded. "The other good thing is that the trial, at least based on what you've indicated, shouldn't last a long time. Maybe it'll even wrap up earlier than they thought."

"That's certainly something to hope for," Paul said, rising from his chair. "Tom, is there any way I can schedule some brief meetings with you on a more regular schedule after hours like this? We could keep them short, even fifteen minutes. When I'm sitting there in the trial and begin to feel my anxieties grow, it would be helpful to know I have the ability to come over here and talk things through afterwards."

"Sure," Tom said. "Just plan on getting over here by five-thirty or so any day while the trial is underway, and I can meet you. Try to give me a heads up by lunch if you plan on coming though."

"Great," Paul responded. "Let's schedule our next meeting for the day after tomorrow unless I let you know otherwise." Walking to the door, he paused and said, "You know, I've wished Marcus Roberts was dead ever since he attacked Katherine. Now that he actually is, though, I don't feel nearly the relief I thought I would."

Chapter 17

As the jurors began filing back in, Paul reassumed his assigned jury seat and looked over at Rebecca. *No ponytail today,* he thought, seeing her wavy brown hair cascading down around her shoulders. By the end of the trial, he figured to have her profile memorized.

Edwards called his first witness for the day, George Petty, a twenty-three-year veteran of the force and one of the first officers to arrive on scene at Marcus Roberts' home. Petty took the stand and was sworn in.

Predictably, Edwards proceeded to ask questions about his years as a policeman and where he was when he'd received the radio call to make his way over to Pineview Street. Following about ten minutes of background information, Edwards moved on to questions about Petty's arrival at the house.

"Officer Petty," Edwards said, "Can you tell us what happened once you turned down Pineview Street?"

Officer Petty responded, "Well, our unit...I was with my partner Officer Jennings...approached Pineview fairly slowly as we were on high alert given the confirmation from the radio transmissions about a shooting in the area. We proceeded onto Pineview from Holly Street, on the other end from Forsyth, and drove toward 233 Pineview. That's where Ms. Howard, the woman who made the call about the gunshot, lives. As we drove by her house, we noticed the front door of 231 Pineview—Marcus Roberts' house—was wide open. Stopping in front, we saw a body on the floor in the hallway."

He paused and looked at Edwards, who said, "Yes, please proceed."

"Jennings and I reported this on the radio and exited the vehicle with weapons drawn, which is standard operating procedure, and approached the front of the house. As we got to the front door, we were able to see that the man on the floor— the victim—had a gunshot wound to his chest. We asked for immediate backup and EMTs. I didn't get a pulse and was pretty much certain based on the wounds and blood loss that the subject was deceased. Jennings and I then began searching the house, which was about the time two additional police units showed up. Two officers joined us inside the house while the other two searched its perimeter."

Edwards said, "I see. Were there signs of any type of struggle?"

"No, there were no indications of that."

"What was the condition of the house?"

"It generally looked to be in order, a fairly small house with two bedrooms. Other than the obvious homicide, nothing seemed out of the ordinary."

Petty was on the stand for about two hours total, answering Edwards's questions and then cross-examined by Olsen. When the court recessed around four o'clock, the bailiff collected notes from several jurors—as he did at the close of each day—and the judge thanked them, confirming with Edwards that Officer Petty would resume his testimony Thursday morning.

Paul walked out of the courtroom just ahead of Rebecca and

turned back and smiled at her at the building's exit, waiting for her to catch up.

"Hi!" she said. "Glad that's over with for the day."

Paul smiled, excited she'd initiated a conversation. "I know. It's been an interesting case so far, but I have to confess, I was ready for a break."

They took turns heading into the revolving door that spit them out into the late-afternoon hustle and bustle of downtown Detroit. Paul and Rebecca stood there in front of the building, neither knowing exactly what to say beyond the natural course of conversation about the trial that wasn't in fact allowed. Those circumstances alone almost teased them, challenging them to think of something else to talk about.

They stood there a moment longer and watched the people whiz by.

"Ever wonder who they are and where they're all going?" Paul finally asked.

"Who?"

"Them," Paul said, nodding towards the plaza bursting at the seams with passersby.

Rebecca smiled. "Not really. Do you?"

And just like that, Paul felt that pang of regret every kid feels when he asks a girl he likes a question and she responds in some way implying it was a seemingly stupid query.

"I guess that's just the writer coming out in me is all," Paul said, trying to redeem himself.

He figured the conversation was over until she said, "Speaking of! I meant to mention to you that I bought one of your books." She reached into her bag and pulled out *A Generation of Heroes*, his first book and one about the struggles of a family living on a Southern plantation in the late 1800s.

"I just started it, Paul," she said, her eyes shifting from the book to his own. He felt his heart flutter at the prospect of her having more than a mere passing interest in him. Her eyes sparkled in a way that mesmerized him, and it took extra effort to focus on saying something that wasn't foolish.

"It was my first book, so temper your expectations," Paul said with a chuckle.

"Tell you what. After I finish, maybe we grab a cup of coffee so we can discuss it. That would be fun," Rebecca said, smiling and putting the book back in her bag.

"It's a date," Paul confirmed.

"Well, I better go. See ya, Paul!"

Paul felt regret sinking in again. *It's a date?* he excoriated himself. *That was the best I could do?*

* * *

Court began promptly at nine o'clock the next day. After the judge made some introductory remarks, Edwards recalled Officer Petty who then finished his direct testimony. Liam Olsen mounted what Paul considered a weak cross examination, though there wasn't much to contest about Petty's testimony. After the judge declared a recess at lunch and reconvened at one-thirty, Edwards prepared to call his next witness.

He stood, turned to the judge, and said, "The State calls Detective Henry Barton of the Detroit Police Department."

Edwards began his line of questioning by asking, "Detective Barton, can you please explain your role with the Detroit Police Department?"

"Sure. I'm in the Investigations Division, a branch within the department that oversees the accumulation, protection, and management of evidence that may be relevant in the disposition of a case. We often work with initial responders to help secure the area where the crime was committed as well as document details about it, sometimes also obtaining statements from any witnesses."

"So, you're a crime scene investigator. Sometimes referred to as a CSI?"

"Correct."

"On the evening of February 23, 2019, were you on duty? Is that the right term…on duty?"

"Technically, no, but I was on call. We always have someone on call in case a serious crime such as a murder occurs. Time is of the essence in those situations, and we try to get there as quickly as possible. So, when the call came in about a homicide, I headed over to secure the area."

"Part of your job is to make sure nothing at the crime scene is tampered with before you have the chance to investigate, is that right?"

"Sure. One of the very first things we do is secure the perimeter around the crime site."

Paul felt a shudder as he recalled driving down Pineview Street on the morning after the shooting and seeing the police car and the yellow tape.

"I see," Edwards said. "What is the general procedure in a crime scene investigation like this?" he asked, glancing over at the jury.

"Well, there are certain things the initial responding officer, Officer Petty, had already done when I arrived on scene. Things like securing the location and neutralizing any remaining threats to safety, none in this case. Also calling medical personnel and guiding them to the victim in order to minimize any contamination of evidence and instructing them not to…uh, clean up…the scene. I got there just as Officer Petty was finishing up his preliminary documentation, evaluation, and securing of the location. So, I corroborated the details of his preliminary report and took over as investigator in charge—the term for the lead investigator—and began processing the scene."

"What does that mean, exactly? Processing?"

"There's a litany of items, like calling in the coroner and a pathologist to analyze the body in place before taking it to the morgue for a full postmortem. It also includes overseeing dusting for prints on the door, doorbell, and interior space, taking photographs and videos of the victim, his position, and blood spatter patterns, making sketches for areas not easily captured by photographs, and logging items possibly relevant to the motive or suspect identification. I also search for any evidence that might otherwise go unnoticed."

"Such as?"

"Shell casings, signs of a struggle, items inadvertently left behind by the perpetrator...things like that."

"Did you in fact find any shell casings at this scene in particular?

"No, we did not."

"How long does everything you just mentioned take?"

"I think we were there for about four hours before we secured the location for the night. We returned with the ballistics, blood pattern, and other experts the next day."

"How do you secure a location like that?"

"In addition to the police tape, we often station an officer at the location and use tamper-resistant tape to learn if any doors or windows are breached when he or she isn't present. We also leave a few lights on so local units can patrol during their rounds and keep an eye on the place."

"I see."

"Detective Barton, how was Marcus Roberts killed...scratch that...what type of weapon was used to shoot Mr. Roberts?"

"A shotgun."

"In your experience, are shotguns typically used in homicides?"

"Not often. They're very bulky and thus practically impossible to conceal, an obvious problem for criminals with respect to alerting the victim and getting caught. As most homicides have an element of surprise, pulling out a concealed pistol is often an easier way for the perpetrator to carry out his or her crime."

"I see. What are the implications of a shotgun being used in the case of Marcus Roberts?"

"Well, as a shotgun was found in the car Levi Johnson was riding in…one with his prints on it, I might add…This is obviously compatible with evidence of him as the shooter in this case."

"Thank you. Now, we often hear a lot about ballistics in shootings. Any chance ballistics can be used to positively identify which shotgun was used to kill Mr. Roberts?"

"They can't, unfortunately. Ballistics analysis is somewhat limited in a case like this, as the pellets—when exiting a shotgun barrel—never come into contact with the barrel itself as they're encased in a plastic sleeve. It'd be different with a single bullet without the sleeve, but in this case, ballistics can't positively tie the shotgun in Levi Johnson's possession to the precise one used to kill Roberts."

Edwards went on, "Detective Barton, what else can you tell us about the type of weapon used on Marcus Roberts?"

"Well, Roberts died from a single shot to the chest at close range…two to three feet, we believe. When a shotgun is fired, the spread of the pellets can sometimes be used to determine the length of the barrel; but the shotgun in Levi Johnson's possession was a sawed-off shotgun that typically produces a wider spray of pellets than a long-barrel shotgun—one that, say, might be used for hunting—and so the close proximity of the shot doesn't really help us identify the length of the barrel in this case."

Edwards asked, "Do any other aspects lead you to conclude the gun used to kill Marcus Roberts was the same one found in Levi Johnson's possession?"

"Yes. The medical examiner recovered nine large-caliber shotgun pellets from the body, all of which matched the size and weight of the type of shotgun shells found in the suspects' car. It's basically what's called 'double-aught shot,' commonly used for deer hunting and (to a lesser degree) self-defense against home invasions and that sort of thing."

"Could other types of shot have been used?"

"Yes, many loads. There's triple-aught shot that has eight pellets, the double aught that has nine pellets as the type used here, and single-aught shell that has twelve pellets. There's also number-one, number-two, number-three, and number-four buckshot that have, in the case of number four buckshot, twenty-seven pellets."

Edwards asked, "Detective Barton, can you explain for the jury what is meant by the shotgun 'gauge'?"

"It refers to the width of the barrel."

"Different gauges exist, correct?"

Detective Barton said, "Yes, there's ten-gauge, twelve-gauge, sixteen-gauge, twenty-gauge, and twenty-eight-gauge shotguns and even one small one called a four-ten."

"What gauge of shotgun was used in the Marcus Roberts killing?"

"Based on the double-aught load and penetration of the pellets, we determined it to be a twelve-gauge."

"You are fairly certain about that?"

"Yes."

Edwards continued. "So, while there is no conclusive ballistics match, the shotgun gauge just happened to be a twelve-gauge despite all of the aforementioned types; and while multiple types of shot could have been used as mentioned, double-aught was used here. The same as in Mr. Johnson's possession, correct?"

"Yes."

"Detective Barton, would you say that, in your professional opinion, you believe the gun found in the presence of Levi Johnson matched the type used to murder Marcus Roberts?"

"Yes, I would say that."

"Thank you, Detective Barton."

Edwards grabbed some notes from his table and then asked, "Now, Detective Barton, you indicated one of your job responsibilities is to conduct a complete inspection of the scene…essentially to take inventory of the house and its contents and look for pieces of evidence and perhaps even clues that might shed some light on a motive, right?"

"That's correct."

Edwards continued. "Let me ask this then, Detective. As you conducted this investigation, did you notice anything in particular perhaps relevant to the case?"

"I did."

"Can you elaborate?"

"Well, as you probably know, Mr. Edwards, racial tensions have escalated in the city over the past few months. A Confederate flag hung on the wall of Marcus Roberts' house."

Liam Olsen stood, irate. "Objection, Your Honor! That is highly prejudicial to this case, and you ruled in your *motion in limine* that such evidence would not be allowed. Mr. Edwards knows that full well as well as where the witness was headed with his testimony."

"Sustained." The judge looked squarely at Edwards. "Mr. Edwards, would you approach?"

Both attorneys walked up to the bench, and Paul watched the judge—whose expression conveyed both anger and incredulity—reprimand Edwards in a hushed but urgent tone, punctuating points with a thick index finger that alternated between wagging and pointing toward Edwards's face before sending them away. *Quite entertaining,* Paul thought.

The judge turned to the jurors, all of whom were now more attentive than they had been at any other time that day, and said, "Ladies and gentlemen, this is a tricky situation because I am going to ask that you forget what you just heard. This most recent statement that was made by Detective Barton can't be considered in your deliberations. The State is making the case that this murder was possibly racially motivated. That may or may not be the case. They may make arguments supporting that position later in this court, but that argument will not be based on what you just heard."

The judge looked back at Edwards, nodding for him to proceed.

"Of course, Your Honor." Turning back to the detective, Edwards said, "Let me instead ask this question: Detective Barton, is it, or is it not the case, that one theory your department advanced with respect to a motive was this might have been, in fact, a racially motivated killing?"

"Yes."

"Thank you."

"You know…" Detective Barton began but then hesitated.

"Yes?" Edwards asked. The judge was watching the witness carefully.

"I was just going to say that, in my years on the job, I've worked on a lot of homicides. The thing that keeps coming back to me is that this was some type of planned execution."

"You're saying Levi Johnson planned this in advance?"

"Yes, or perhaps someone planned it with him—maybe the other suspects or someone else."

Paul thought about that for a moment. *A man like Marcus Roberts probably had a lot of enemies.*

Olsen stood and objected, this time with more restraint. "Your Honor, again, I object. There is no evidence whatsoever suggesting this was a murder-for-hire situation. The State's witness is going off on wild suppositions that are totally unsupported by fact or even circumstantial evidence."

The judge looked at Detective Barton and asked, "Do you actually have evidence that someone hired Mr. Johnson?"

The detective said, "No."

Judge Mayer thought for a moment before turning to the jury. "I'm going to allow it but want to point out that, again, this is simply a theory. You must consider in your decision that there is apparently little evidence to support the idea."

Disappointed, the public defender shook his head and sat

down.

The court recessed for lunch. Walking out, Paul caught up to Rebecca. It was an unusually chilly day, and she was wearing a fur jacket—whether real or faux—that gave her a classy look. He also picked up the faint aroma of Sunflowers.

"Rebecca," he said, reaching out and touching her arm as she was almost at the revolving door.

She turned, "Oh, Paul, hi!"

"You got plans for lunch?" Paul asked.

"Not really. There's a sandwich shop a couple blocks away, so I was just gonna head there to get takeout. Care to join me?"

"Sure. I like sandwiches. Sounds good."

They walked side by side, and Paul wondered if passersby presumed they were a couple. He held the door to the shop open for Rebecca before sitting at an available booth. "Can You Feel It" by The Jacksons was playing in the background. "I love this song. Do you know it?" Paul asked her.

He gazed at her beautiful smile. *Her parents must have invested heavily in her teeth, or she otherwise takes incredible care of them*, he thought to himself. Sliding into the other side of the booth, she said, "Are you kidding me? How could anyone *not* know it? It's such a great song, and the beat makes me want to stand up and dance."

Paul took a mental note—she likes to dance—and watched as she closed her eyes, her head playfully rocking back and forth to the music. He sat there staring at her for a few moments, inhaling the faint scent of Sunflowers and listening to "Can You Feel It." *Yes, I CAN feel it.* He was moving on and falling fast. As she opened her eyes and returned his gaze, anticipation and ache converged as he recalled staring into Katherine's eyes when they had just begun courting.

They ordered their sandwiches, and the conversation flowed easily between them. He asked where she grew up. "Chelsea," she said, "near Ann Arbor. Do you know it? Our only claims to fame are that Jiffy Mix is made there and that Jeff Daniels grew up there.

In fact, Jeff went to the high school I went to. He finished several years ahead of me...maybe class of seventy-three or something. I was eighty-three." Paul did the corresponding math and came up with an age in the low 50s.

He asked, "Do you have family here?" although he feared she'd know the motive behind the question.

"I have a sister and brother and two children, a son and daughter."

"I see," said Paul, "Where are your children now?"

"My son's in Ann Arbor—he's an engineer—and my daughter's in New York. Her husband is in investments."

Paul decided to be direct. "So are you married or still breaking hearts?"

Rebecca laughed. "Neither," she responded, reaching out and playfully slapping at Paul's arm across the table.

Paul sensed her flirtation, and his heart jumped a beat. He felt like a teenager.

Her response emboldened him. "So, what would a guy like me have to do to persuade a woman like you to go to dinner sometime?" he asked.

"Probably ask," she responded coyly.

"How about this Saturday night?"

"I could do that, Paul."

Paul wrote down her address, and they agreed he'd pick her up for dinner at seven o'clock.

"By the way, Paul, I'm really enjoying your book! You write really well."

"Oh...well...thank you. I was hoping you'd like it but was afraid to ask."

"Only a third of the way into it, but..."

Paul watched as she spoke, and he noticed something to her left seemingly distracting her.

She completed her thought. "Sorry...I like the character development. What inspires you to come up with such details in your stories?"

"Everyday sorts of things, maybe a conversation I overhear or an observation I find provocatively noteworthy in some way. I try to write them down and have a collection of those types of things in a file on my computer, probably a hundred pages' worth." Paul smiled and added, "Each one of them is a scene or line in search of a story."

"I'd love to see them."

She again glanced to the left and said, "Don't look now, but that woman over there is staring at you."

"Tell me when I can look."

After a moment, Rebecca said, "Now."

Paul glanced quickly at a woman sitting alone several booths away. "Hmmm. I don't know her. Does it bother you that she's looking at me?"

"*Should* it bother me?"

"Yes, it should…but then you'd tell me it did, and I'd say you're the only person I want to be looking at right now." Paul smiled.

Rebecca reached out and gave his hand a squeeze. "That's the sweetest thing anyone has said to me this week."

Paul looked at his watch, "Wow, where did the time go? I guess we need to head back."

As Rebecca rose from the booth, Paul picked up the single receipt left on the table. Rebecca said, "Oh, no, Paul. I'll get mine."

"I've got it," Paul said.

As he made his way past the woman who'd been staring at him, she said, "Excuse me. Aren't you Paul Nelms?"

He and Rebecca stopped at the booth and Paul said, "Yes. Sorry, have we met?"

"No, but I'm reading your book," she said, pulling out *A Generation of Heroes*. He figured she recognized him from his photo on the back cover. "Would you mind autographing this copy for me?" she asked.

"Of course," he said, pulling out a pen and asking, "What's your name?"

"Emily."

Paul provided a personalized autograph and handed the book back to her, thinking he would have paid her if he could have; her timing could not have been better with respect to impressing Rebecca.

Rebecca thanked Paul after he took care of their bill at the register, and he placed his hand on the small of her back while ushering her toward the exit. It was the highlight of his day.

Along the way, she stopped for a moment and turned to him. "Hey, do you think they'd care if two jurors went on a date?"

Paul winked at her and responded, "Not if they don't know about it."

"Great minds think alike," she said and resumed walking.

Court picked back up at one-thirty, and Detective Barton returned to the stand. Edwards quickly finished up with his line of questioning before Liam Olsen began his cross-examination.

After a few introductory softball questions, he asked, "Detective Barton, you implied in your testimony that since there are so many different types of shotguns and the one used to kill Marcus Roberts was the same type in my client's possession—a twelve-gauge—this implicated him in the shooting, is that correct?"

"Well, I said the pathologist report indicated the gauge of the shotgun matched, as did the type of shell used: consistent with the State's position that Levi Johnson was the perpetrator."

"I see. Well, Detective Barton, based on your experience, what percentage of the time, would you estimate, is a shotgun used in a crime something *other than* a twelve-gauge?"

"I have no idea."

"Detective Barton, surely you must have some type of general idea. Let me try this a different way. How many homicide cases would you guess you've investigated over your..." Olsen paused to look down at his notes, "…twenty-two years on the force?"

"Several hundreds of cases."

"And roughly…I don't need an exact figure…what percentage involved a shotgun? Would you say ten percent…thirty percent…eighty percent…or something else?"

"Maybe ten percent."

"Okay, so of those times—and keep in mind ten percent of several hundred implies at least thirty or forty cases—how many would you say involved something other than a twelve-gauge shotgun?"

Detective Barton hesitated as if thinking back through the years and said, "Only a handful."

"The fact that it was a twelve-gauge shotgun really isn't that strong a connection, is it? I mean, you essentially just said that a twelve-gauge is almost always the one used, presumably because it's one of the more powerful shotguns, isn't that correct?"

"Generally, yes."

"And can't the same argument be made of the fact that double aught buckshot was used? Isn't that a very common type of shot used in a twelve-gauge shotgun?"

"It depends on the purpose. I believe the most common type of shot used for twelve-gauge shotguns is probably bird shot—small pellets—but for larger game or when used in a homicide, the double aught is probably a pretty common load, along with slugs."

"Thank you. No further questions."

The judge looked at Edwards. "Anything on redirect?"

"No, Your Honor."

"You may step down. Thank you," Judge Mayer told the detective.

Court was dismissed for the day, and Rebecca waited for Paul at the revolving door before they headed out into twilight under an overcast sky.

"Can I walk you to your car?" Paul asked.

"Sure, I'm in the garage around the corner."

"Great, same as me."

They walked, mostly in silence, then rode the elevator up to the fifth level of the parking garage.

"This is me," Rebecca said, pointing to a gray Volvo S60.

Paul opened the door for her, and she stopped before getting in. "Paul, thank you for walking me." She leaned forward and gave him a kiss on the cheek.

He blushed slightly and then said, "I'd have done it before had I known what the payment was."

They laughed, and she closed the door and drove away. Paul touched his cheek once she was out of sight. For the first time in a long time, he looked forward to the day ahead.

Tom called as Paul was pulling out of the garage. "Paul, hi. It's Tom," he said. "You still planning to come in for your check-in this evening?"

"I can, Tom, but honestly, I'm feeling okay. Not much to report today."

"No problem. Reason I ask is that my wife asked me to do something for her tonight...You sure you're okay with holding off?"

"That works fine, Tom. Sure thing."

On the way home, Paul called Daniel. "Hey, buddy, what are you doing?"

"Not much. Was just looking online at some jobs. I've been thinking a bit about getting a different one. Working at the Cineplex is getting to be a drag."

"I hear ya. Want to grab dinner out tonight, maybe the Ale House? We can grab a beer and a burger?"

"That sounds great, Dad. We haven't done that in a long time. How about I meet you in thirty minutes?"

"Sure," said Paul. "I need to fill up and stop a couple of places so that's perfect."

When Paul arrived at the Ale House, Daniel was already in a booth sipping an amber beer with a soft blanket of foam on top.

"Hey," Paul said, smiling and sitting down across from him.

A server walked over with two waters. "Hi! I have no idea what he's drinking but it looks good, so I'll have the same thing," Paul told her.

"You got it," she said.

"How was court today?" Daniel asked.

"It was fine. I think we'll hear testimony tomorrow and the beginning of next week and then probably begin deliberations thereafter—or at least that's what people are saying."

"Is it interesting?"

"Sort of. I'm not really supposed to say much about it but am increasingly coming to appreciate the role of a juror. It's an odd thing, Daniel, sitting on a jury and deciding the fate of someone else's life. Having that responsibility is pretty..." Paul found himself at a loss for words, a rarity. "I don't know. Humbling? Scary? Intimidating? Especially when you look over at the defendant and think about all the people affected by the outcome."

"I can imagine."

"I wasn't sure if it was the right thing for me, to agree to serve, but I'm glad I went ahead with it. It's like I'm right where I'm supposed to be."

"I'm glad to hear that, Dad."

The waitress walked up and placed the beer in front of Paul. After they'd both ordered burgers, Daniel asked, "What kind of case is it?"

"Believe it or not, it's a murder case; but I honestly probably shouldn't say much more than that."

"Wow."

"I've had one interesting development though," Paul continued.

"What's that?"

"I've gotten to know once of the jurors, a woman named Rebecca, and we're going on a date this Saturday."

Daniel burst out laughing, practically spraying beer out of his mouth, and said, "Oh my gosh, Dad. That's great…seriously. Sorry I laughed. The news just caught me off guard is all."

They enjoyed a moment of shared laughter before Daniel said, "Maybe we should double," chuckling.

"Hey, I'm game."

"I'm serious. There's a new tapas bar that just opened up near Chelsea. I've been wanting to take Darla there."

"Daniel!" Paul exclaimed incredulously. "You want to take her to a *topless* bar?!"

"Tapas! Dad, tapas…Spanish food." Daniel laughed.

"Oh…Well, that's a relief. Sure, that sounds good."

"So tell me about her. How old is she?" Daniel asked.

Paul described Rebecca to Daniel and how he looked forward to going to court just to see her.

"I get that, Dad."

"I think about her more than I probably should," Paul said.

"Is she pretty?"

"Daniel, there is more to a person than that."

"Sorry."

"But yes, very much so. More important, I just enjoy being around her."

"Well, I think that's great. Whatever helps is what's important."

"I think it does help."

Paul held up his glass and said, "Hey, here's to you and me getting out and having a beer."

"Cheers," Daniel responded, clinking his glass against his dad's.

Daniel looked away for a moment, as if staring at something in the distance, and swallowed hard. Paul wondered what was going through his mind, if he was thinking about his mom and whether she'd be hurt by his decision to date and move into a potential romance too quickly.

They spent much of the rest of dinner talking about the house: Paul's ongoing thoughts about selling it and his recent research into new condos being built downtown.

He got in bed by about ten o'clock, hoping to read to settle his mind. He closed his eyes, but most of his thoughts were of Rebecca.

Chapter 18

Friday, July 19, 2019

When Paul walked into the jury assembly room, he immediately looked for Rebecca. "Ready for another day?" she asked with a smile after seeing him and walking over.

"I don't know. I think I need extra coffee this morning," he laughed, adding, "We have the pathologist today, right?"

"I think so," she said, "I believe he is showing some photographic evidence today. I guess they want to establish a chain of events or at least have a theory, based on the body position and that sort of thing."

"Who told you that?"

"I actually overheard Mike Edwards talking to his team in the hallway," she said, adding, "They didn't even seem to notice I was there."

"Interesting," Paul responded.

Court began promptly at nine o'clock, like on all other mornings. Bud Peterson, a pathologist for seventeen years with the State of Michigan, was on the stand shortly thereafter. Edwards began his typical line of questioning, establishing

Peterson's background, years on the job and the procedures in analyzing a crime scene. Edwards then moved to admit the photographic evidence, which Edwards identified by State's Exhibits 25, 26, 27, 28, and 29.

First up was Exhibit 25. Paul's eyes narrowed, focusing on the details as he scanned the image of Marcus Roberts lying on his back, arms flung over his head in a blood-soaked T-shirt and shorts with a large amount of blood on the floor next to him. His face was only partly visible based on the camera angle as the photo had been taken from the porch.

I know that porch. I stood right there the night I threw the brick. Paul's breathing became shallow and rapid and he looked away to calm himself, taking a couple of slow, deep breaths.

Edwards resumed his questioning. "Mr. Peterson, what is your belief, based on the position of the body as it's seen here, with respect to the events that transpired on the evening of February 23, 2019?"

Peterson responded, "The body was close to the door, his left foot approximately thirty-four inches from the threshold. What is not shown but I will attest to is that the front door was a solid wooden door with no screen door attached. When the door opens inwards as most doors do, the person inside the house would be about twelve to twenty-four inches away from the threshold.

Edwards said, "Okay, please continue."

"The fact that there was no sign of struggle leads us to conclude that the victim did not suspect he was in danger when he initially opened the door and saw the suspect." Peterson pulled out a laser pointer and shined it on part of the exhibit, saying, "Also, if you look down the hallway, you see an opening to the left and to the right. To the left is the den area where a television was playing." Edwards flipped a button on his remote to call up a photo of the den and said, "Your Honor, we submit State's Exhibit 26."

The exhibit displayed a chair next to a long brown sofa, the sofa being under a window looking out the front yard and a coffee table with a few magazines on top of it. On the worn beige rug under the table was an empty candy bar wrapper. Paul remembered staring at Marcus' profile as he sat on that sofa and was only vaguely aware that Pathologist Peterson was saying something to the effect that nothing appeared particularly out of the ordinary in the room.

He tore his attention away from the photograph and directed it to Peterson, who said, "There was a half-empty soda can on the end table and a bag of chips on the sofa, so our conclusion is that Marcus Roberts was simply watching TV when someone either rang the doorbell or knocked on the door and he answered it."

Edwards said, "And then?"

Peterson said, "When he opened the door, the suspect was standing there with a shotgun, perhaps behind his back or perhaps in plain sight, but in any event, we believe the suspect quickly brought the shotgun to waist level and shot Mr. Roberts before he had a chance to react."

Edwards sought clarification. "So your contention is Marcus Roberts opened the door, and the shot was fired as soon as the door opened enough to fully expose his body."

"Correct. The door was undamaged, so we believe it was fully opened. There were no signs that anything was stolen from the home and in fact no evidence that the perpetrator (or perpetrators) spent much time in the house, supported by Ms. Howard's claim of seeing the sedan drive away a minute or so after she heard the gunshot."

Edwards asked, "Did your department dust for fingerprints?"

"We did but found nothing useful for a positive identification," Peterson responded.

Peterson then discussed three more photos Edwards displayed to the jury—one taken the evening after the shooting from the street with the front door ajar, another taken the next morning at an angle showing the front of the house and its proximity to Ms. Howard's house, and another of the hallway and body taken in the galley kitchen and shot from the other direction—before court adjourned for a brief break.

* * *

Peterson was cross-examined later that afternoon, the culmination of which occurred when Olsen summarily asked if there was any evidence positively linking Levi Johnson to the scene. "No," the pathologist concluded.

Court recessed. As the jurors stood to file out of the courtroom, Rebecca looked back at Paul and smiled. She paused at the door of the courtroom, waiting for him, and they walked out together.

"Walk you to the car again?" Paul asked, spent from the day's proceedings.

"I was hoping you would," she said. "I'm parked in the same spot."

On the way, she asked, "Paul, do you think we should be careful about being seen together? I mean, I wonder if people will catch on to us?"

"I have no idea," Paul said, "but it can't hurt to be discreet."

Rebecca looked around and, not seeing anyone from the courtroom, took his arm as they approached the garage. When she opened the car door and sat in the front seat, Paul said, "Hey, no kiss this time?"

She laughed and stood back up, planting a kiss on him. "I could get used to this, you know," he said in response.

"That's fine with me, Paul."

Loving the sound of his name on her lips, he watched her drive away.

Chapter 19

Paul began his Saturday early and enjoyed a leisurely morning making coffee, sweeping the kitchen, and reading the paper. When Daniel came into the kitchen to get breakfast, Paul said, "Morning, Daniel. What have you got on tap for the day?"

"Well, I'm heading over to Michael's in a little while and then going to pick up Darla to meet some people at Orchard Lake. It's supposed to be a nice day."

"Sounds nice, taking a woman on a picnic…or whatever you want to call it." He laughed.

"It is, Dad. We're not staying all day so I'll probably be back home by about four o'clock since I have to work tonight."

"Bummer," Paul said.

Daniel laughed. "Yeah. Bummer."

Daniel scarfed down a bagel and bounded up the stairs two-at-a-time into his room. Paul heard him grabbing some things to take with him, and several moments later, Daniel headed toward the front door carrying a Frisbee and football. Paul opened the front door for him and said, "Be careful, son."

Paul watched as Daniel gunned the engine and pulled away

from his house, nearly clipping the mailbox as he backed out of the driveway. Paul almost called him on the phone to tell him to slow down, but as soon as he thought about it, he considered the risk of Daniel taking a call while driving and driving too fast to boot. He sometimes worried about Daniel. He recalled one thing his friends had told him before his son was born: once you have kids, nothing will be the same.

Paul finished reading the paper, stretched, and thought about the day ahead. He planned on picking up Rebecca around seven o'clock, giving him the whole day to catch up on a few things. He primarily wanted to go through the attic to start getting rid of the junk that had accumulated over so many years, knowing many things would be impossible to discard given the strong emotional ties to Katherine and Daniel.

He remembered taping up a box years earlier of photos and materials from a trip to New England ten years prior when they drove to Maine and explored its rocky shores. He smiled, recalling the shot he'd taken of Katherine as she basked on some rocks so he could snap a photo of her. *How could I ever get rid of that?* he thought to himself. *I'll focus on the boxes of old clothes, old toys, and small appliances that had stopped working but we saved for apparently no reason. Maybe it'll actually be a healthy thing.* He looked forward to the feeling of letting go.

He finished his last sip of coffee and went upstairs to throw on some jeans and his favorite Outer Banks T-shirt from another trip he and Katherine once took. He walked up the stairs past his bedroom and climbed the pull-down ladder into the attic on the third floor. At least fifty boxes were scattered randomly over the entire floor. It was hard to know where to begin.

"You begin," he murmured to himself, "with the first box." He grabbed the nearest one, which was unmarked, and found sweaters and sweatshirts inside. They were Katherine's clothes, things she'd apparently put in there for storage a year or two ago. He pulled out a black and white pullover with dots and vaguely recalled seeing her in it but felt no sadness as he held it up and then returned it to the box, moving it to an area of the attic he'd mentally designated as the donate pile. The second box was filled with Daniel's childhood clothes. "Why we kept all this, I will never know," Paul said to himself. He worked for a couple of hours and was able to make it through about fifteen boxes, most of which ended up in the donate area of the attic.

Paul took a break at lunch and watched a golf tournament for a couple of hours. About three-thirty, he headed back up to make a little more progress. Daniel walked in about thirty minutes later, yelling, "Dad, I'm back," to which Paul responded, "I'm up in the attic trying to get rid of a few things."

"Sounds good. I'll be heading to work in about thirty minutes."

Nearly an hour later, Paul looked at his watch, which said four-twenty. It was about time to stop for the day. He reached for a small box, one that was not taped shut. He sat down on the floor and pulled the box between his legs, unfolding the top and expecting books, or perhaps some old bank statements. He barely noticed the bunched-up sweater in the bottom of the box because his attention was drawn to the handwritten letter addressed to Katherine lying on top.

The first thing that struck Paul was the handwriting. It was a style of writing with few of the elegant flairs and loops so characteristic of a woman's penmanship. To the contrary, the style seemed much more rooted in efficiency of stroke. *Did a man write this?*

He slowly opened the envelope. It read:

My dearest Katherine:

I don't know exactly why I am writing this to you, or whether I will eventually even send it, but I find myself wanting to express some things to you, and I wanted you to be able to hear them and not have to react, but simply to listen. Letters are good for that. I hope you understand.

What we have had together over the past year has changed my life. You are an amazing woman: beautiful, both inside and out; sensitive; artistic; engaging; provocative; sexy.

Sexy. Paul stopped reading, his eyes stuck on the smiley face accompanying a word that conveyed so much. He immediately flipped the letter over in search of its author and found it signed, "With love, Tony." *Tony Leone,* he thought. *Katherine's co-worker.* He thought of the night when she was in her red dress at her surprise birthday celebration and she'd danced several dances with him. *The very same Tony Leone I reached out to when I was trying to figure out who attacked Katherine.*

Paul sat frozen on the floor, trying to make sense of the words and finding it impossible. The date on the letter—August 1, 2018—was roughly a year ago and a couple weeks before Katherine's suicide. He returned to the letter.

Katherine, I know these past few months have been terrible. I can only imagine, after all you've been through, how you must feel completely lost. As I've told you before, if you ever want me to set things straight with Marcus Roberts, all you would have to do is ask.

Paul stopped reading and said incredulously, "You *told* him?" He said again, louder this time, "You *told* him?" His voice was shaking, tears of rage beginning to pool in his eyes. He stood up, clenching the letter tightly and yelled, "You tell me I can't tell anyone, even the police, and then you have an affair with *him*, and you *tell* him?" Paul felt the paper crumple within his hand.

"Dad, you okay?!" Daniel yelled from downstairs, having returned earlier on.

Paul tried to catch his breath. "Yeah, I'm okay. Sorry, Daniel. It's nothing."

"Need me to come up?" Daniel asked from the pulldown ladder stairs.

"No, don't come up, I'm just going through some stuff. I'm okay."

"Okay, Dad. Down here if you need me."

Paul realized he needed to regain his composure, his attention returning to where he'd left off reading.

Katherine, I know people that can get things done. You'd never have to worry about him again. The thought of another man offering to protect his wife and "set things straight" in a way he never had turned Paul's stomach.

When we talked that time about running away together, I was serious. You didn't think I was, but I want you to know I am ready to leave Betsy when you are ready to come with me. The main thing I want for you is happiness. I know you aren't happy now, and I think getting away from our lives is a way to start out anew. There is no one I would rather do that with than you.

I love you, Katherine. Let me know when you are ready, as I am already there.

He numbly stared at the letter. *How could I not have known? How long had this been going on?* He looked back at the wording. Tony mentioning "the past year" and the postmark of August 1, 2018 implied they'd been having an affair since before August 2017. Paul thought about her birthday celebration: the woman dancing so gaily in her red dress was dancing with her lover. *Where* had it been going on? Question after question relentlessly pinged his brain.

Suddenly, an idea hit Paul: *Could Tony have killed Marcus Roberts?* His mind began crafting elaborate explanations of what could have happened. *What if Levi had been hired to do it? What if there had been some connection between Levi and Tony? But how would Tony know Levi? And would Tony have actually carried this out after Katherine's death?*

Theories began to emerge: *Maybe Tony had gotten Levi out of a jam and Levi had implied he owed Tony a favor? And maybe Tony, knowing Levi to be a gang member who had the ability to carry something like this out, called in the favor?*

But wait, Paul thought, *Levi would never have the money to hire someone like Tony to get him out of a jam. So how would they have come to know one another in the first place?* Then again, Paul recalled that Katherine occasionally helped Tony on court-appointed work.

What if Tony had taken Levi's case? What if Katherine had helped in the case? What if she and Levi knew each other? Could Tony have explained to Levi that the woman who had helped in his case had been raped and that the guy needed to be dealt with? The money, assuming Tony paid him, could probably set a guy like Levi up for a long time; Tony was no doubt very well off. His mind reeled with possible scenarios.

Paul's eyes stung and he realized he had not blinked for several minutes while his mind spun. He was only vaguely aware that he was sitting there mesmerized. He blinked and shook his head, as if that would clear his mind.

He pulled out the sweater but found nothing else in the box. He put the sweater and box in the "Donate" stack, went downstairs and reread the letter one more time, word by agonizing word, before placing it in the bottom of his sock drawer. He half stumbled down the steps, his eyes not looking at the steps as he descended. He walked into the den where he sat down in front of the television. He stayed there, staring at the screen, for an hour, past the time that Daniel walked out on his way to work.

* * *

It was five-thirty when Paul remembered his date with Rebecca. "Damn!" He considered canceling. How could he go on a date in a total fog as he was? He couldn't think of a good excuse, but one thing was certain: he would not be good company and would kill his chances to see her again in his current mental state.

He dialed the number she'd given him several days before.

She picked up. "Oh, hi, Paul!"

"Rebecca," he began, "I don't know how to say this, but I think I'm going to need to reschedule our date."

There was a pause. She said, "Oh. I'm sorry. Are you okay?"

"To be honest, I'm not."

"Paul, what's wrong?"

"Rebecca, if I could talk to you about this, I would. I found out something today that literally knocked the wind out of me. I'm afraid I wouldn't be good company tonight anyway; it wouldn't be fair to you."

"Want to just come over to my place? We can have a drink, I can throw a pizza in the oven, and you can stay as long as you'd like and take off anytime. We don't have to go to a restaurant."

"That's actually tempting. I think, though, that I just need to be by myself tonight. Is there any way we can set something up for next week, maybe Saturday night?"

"Of course, but if you change your mind, just come on over. We could rent a movie or just talk. You'd have a good time, I promise."

"I'll call before coming over if I change my mind, okay?"

"Sounds great, Paul, and I hope you feel better. Can't have my favorite author upset."

Rebecca's words brought a smile to Paul's face, something that had seemed impossible just moments before.

"Thanks, Rebecca. Good night."

"Night."

Paul hung up and could kick himself for breaking the date but knew he'd do the same for going through with it as well. He retrieved the letter and read it again.

Why in the world did she leave the letter where it could be found? If she knew she was going to kill herself, why not destroy it and save everyone the pain? What if Daniel had discovered it? One thing was certain: he did not intend to tell their son about this.

Paul went to the study, sat at the computer and typed "Michigan court cases" into the browser. Google made seventy-two million suggestions. After viewing the top twenty, about half of which allowed for search capability, Paul began to realize finding the answer to whether there had been a connection between Levi and the McGee and Crampton law firm might not be so easy.

He spent the rest of the evening poring over sites that allowed for case searches by legal team and defendant names but consistently received "No records found" messages while searching for Michigan cases involving "Tony Leone" and "Levi Johnson."

Upon seeing that it was almost eleven o'clock and not feeling sleepy, he decided he had earned the right to take an Ambien. Since he hadn't taken one in several months, he figured he would take a half dose to be on the safe side. He came back downstairs and, tired of searching to no avail, switched on the TV to watch the end of a ball game.

Daniel came home soon thereafter, grabbed some chips and sat down with a beer next to his dad.

Paul looked at Daniel through haggard eyes and asked, "How was your day with Darla?"

"Good. Um, how was your day?"

"Fine."

"Dad, I hate to tell you this, but I got a speeding ticket today."

"Where, and how fast were you going?"

"On the way to the lake and going 75 in a 55; but, Dad, I think his radar was off."

"You should know better than that, Daniel. You know you'll need to pay for that, right? Plus, your premiums will go up."

"I'm sorry, Dad. It was stupid, and I wasn't being careful. It won't happen again."

Paul said nothing and stared at the TV before breaking the silence. "I'll try to call Mark Emerson next week to see if there's a way out of it. A good attorney can get you out of a lot of things; maybe he can help."

"That would be awesome, Dad. Thanks so much."

"Hey, didn't you tell me you had a date tonight?" Daniel asked Paul.

"I didn't go."

"How come?"

"I just didn't feel well. I think we're going to try again next weekend."

"Make any headway in the attic?"

"Yeah. Daniel, you sure you wouldn't mind if I decide to sell the house?" Paul asked, changing the subject.

"That'd be fine, Dad," Daniel responded. "Where would you want to move?"

"No idea."

"That makes sense, Dad, it really does."

Paul was finally getting sleepy. "I think I'll turn in. Been a long day. Night, son."

"Night, Pop."

Chapter 20

When Paul awoke at nine o'clock the next morning, he stared at the ceiling for several moments, his brain trying to process what had transpired over the past twenty-four hours. It had been a restless night, his mind never disengaging from Katherine's infidelity, from Tony and his possible role in Marcus Roberts' murder. Had it been a weekday, he would have called Tom.

"Holy cow, you're starting to remind me of *me*, sleeping in like that," Daniel said as his dad walked past his bedroom.

Paul mustered a smile. "Late night and didn't sleep well."

"Sorry to hear that."

Paul went downstairs, looked at the paper and had breakfast. He then returned to the attic, halfway worrying what he might find, but he only came across the additional clothes, artwork and toys that he expected. The "Donate" area was getting pretty cluttered with boxes. There was a nonprofit that was open on Sundays; he would try to get rid of the boxes later if he had time.

It was an unseasonably warm day, one that invited outdoor activity, so he headed out for a long walk around ten-thirty; but it failed to distract him from the growing sense of anger and betrayal he felt. He entered his garage and saw his old bicycle, filled the tires with air, and rode down his street.

He peddled faster and faster, his legs pumping up and down like pistons fired by some unstoppable energy. As he watched the scenery accelerate past his field of view, he peddled even faster and tightened his grip on the handlebars. He lowered his head, peddling all out now and gulping in air as the lactic acid built up in his legs to the point of pain. His eyes stared without focus at the road as it whizzed by underneath him, and he felt relief as his mind shifted from his adulterous wife to the blur of the asphalt, the rush of the wind, and the surge of adrenaline powering his body.

He looked up just in time to see he was approaching an intersection at a dangerous rate of speed. Two cars were approaching from the left. He slammed on his brakes just as the driver of the first car, apparently seeing Paul's rapid approach, did the same. Over the thirty or so feet between Paul and the intersection, the bike came to a halt.

Paul put his feet on the street and straddled the bike, his face grimaced and chest heaving. The two cars continued past him, the driver of the first car staring at him with an incredulous look. And then Paul found himself alone at the edge of that intersection, with no cars to the right or left or in front or behind him. He needed the release. He put his face in his hands and wept.

It only took moments for him to calm down and to reassure himself that he was okay. He turned the bike around and hopped back on, peddling slowly back toward his house. He rode into the garage and walked back into the house as Daniel was about to leave.

"Where you headed?" Paul asked him.

"Darla and I are going to hang out."

Daniel walked out the front door, and Paul watched as his son waved when he drove off. The sense of betrayal and anger that had so controlled his mind for the past twenty-four hours relented. Daniel, who would probably never achieve great success professionally, had given Paul a flashback with that wave—back to days when Daniel was in elementary school and would wave to him from the school bus.

That memory led to more recollections of building soapbox derby cars together and Katherine throwing her arms around Paul when Daniel finally won the race, of late-night Christmas Eves assembling kits and cars and toys and laying them out just so and Katherine and he reclining after all of it on the couch—her head on Paul's shoulder as they shared a cup of eggnog before turning in.

Daniel wouldn't graduate from Yale, Harvard, Wharton, Stanford, or any of those Ivy League schools so many of Paul's friends boasted about when the subject of children came up. It had been a pet peeve of Katherine's, hearing about all those achievements: record high academic scores and posh job offers. Paul, always trying to elicit a laugh from her, crafted a Christmas card letter one year mocking the "let me tell you how great life is" message a few people invariably sent. Paul's mock letter relayed how Daniel had just graduated first in his class at Harvard Medical School and was set to take over Johns Hopkins Medical Center, how Katherine had recently been selected to become Oprah Winfrey's partner in a new television series about achieving balance in life, and how Paul had just won the Hawaii Iron Man Triathlon—stopping at one point to revive a man who'd had a heart attack on the out and back section of the final leg of the race.

Paul smiled at that recollection, but that smile faded as he watched the rear of Daniel's car disappear. Those were simpler times. There was no point in telling him. Daniel was the only family he had now. Maybe he was the only real family he'd had for some time now.

Paul returned to the attic, looked at the stack of boxes in the "Donate" area, and found the one he was looking for, which was labeled "Daniel – Elem. Sch." He opened it up, looked through a few yearbooks and photos, and moved it from the donate stack to the set of boxes neatly arranged with "Do Not Throw Away" written on the sides.

Paul walked downstairs, showered, threw a pizza in the oven and sat down in front of the television. He flipped across a number of channels, not finding anything satisfactory to distract his mind. He turned it back off and closed his eyes, resting his head on the back of his chair.

It was incredible how quickly life could turn. Only a year ago, Katherine was with him and seemed to be adjusting, albeit gradually, to the trauma she had experienced; he was working on his book; Daniel had just gotten a job at the Cineplex; evenings were gloriously boring, punctuated by decisions of what kind of take-out to get and what to watch on television. And yet now…

His mind filtered through memories of times when she had mentioned Tony's name, seemingly subtle comments like, "I have to work late on a deposition for Tony…"

"Yeah, I bet," Paul whispered.

Chapter 21

Monday, July 22, 2019

The sounds of Daniel moving about stirred Paul from his sleep. He sat up, looked at his bedside clock and saw it was seven forty-five, a bit late to be getting a start on the day. He jumped in the shower and dressed, made his way downstairs, and told Daniel goodbye. Paul arrived at court, saw Rebecca in the jury assembly room, and walked up to her.

"Good morning," he said.

"Paul," she said, "how are you feeling?"

"Better, thanks. Hey, I'm so sorry about—"

"Don't worry about it, Paul. I understood and stayed in and caught up on some laundry. It's fine, really."

"Can I get you some coffee?" Paul asked.

"No, no. I have some at my chair already, but thanks."

As Rebecca turned and walked back to her seat, Paul wondered how much damage he'd done by breaking their date.

When court was called into session, Edwards called Joseph Adams to the stand. Adams, wearing an orange jumpsuit and handcuffs, walked with what seemed a confident air to the witness stand and sat down.

He was pushing six feet tall, Paul guessed, with the build of a running back: lean, quick, athletic. Paul looked at the closely shaved head, the several days-old stubble on a chiseled jawline, and the scar over his right eye. *From a battle in the streets, perhaps?*

Edwards started by asking a series of background questions about where Mr. Adams had lived, where he'd grown up, and whether he had a job. "No" was the response.

He then asked, "Mr. Adams, do you know Levi Johnson?"

Adams replied, "Yeah. We've known each other about five years."

"And are you two affiliated, connected through membership in a gang?"

"Yeah. We're Bloods."

Edwards went on, "And the Bloods…this is a fairly large and organized gang that has a presence in many cities throughout the United States, and a strong presence in Detroit as well?"

"Right."

Edwards asked a series of questions about gang activities before focusing on his primary interest. "Now, Mr. Adams, can you please tell the court your whereabouts and who you were with on the evening of February 23, 2019 at approximately ten p.m.?"

"Jimmy and Levi and me was on our way to do a drive-by on Franklin Avenue."

"Okay, hold on a second, Mr. Adams. So that we get this on record, can you confirm you were speaking of James Turner and Levi Johnson?"

"Yeah, that's right."

"And when you say you were on your way to a 'drive-by,' can you explain what that means for the jury?"

Adams nonchalantly responded, "A drive-by shooting. We'd had some run-ins with the Latin Kings. They jumped a couple of our guys and roughed one of 'em up good so he was in a coma for a week and then died. We knew who did it and agreed a few of us would settle it."

"Can you tell me the names of these individuals who allegedly jumped some of your members?"

"Yeah, the two we knew was involved was Mateo Pasquez and Jose Garcia. We seen them hanging out with another couple gang members earlier that night and heard from some friends that they was going to Club 66 that night. So we had a good idea where they was going to be and so we each—I mean the three of us, me, Levi Johnson, and Jimmy Turner—we headed out to pop 'em."

"Shoot them? You were going to shoot them?"

"Yeah."

"What weapons did you have with you?"

"I had a Springfield nine-mil, and Jimmy had a Glock nine-mil. Both automatics. Levi picked up a shotgun."

"Did the three of you plan this together, each knowing you were going out as a group intending to shoot Mr. Pasquez and Mr. Garcia?"

"Yeah."

"Whose car did you take?"

"It's my brother's car. Navy blue 2003 Nissan Altima."

"So, Mr. Adams, your plan was to get into the car, drive to this Club 66, and hopefully find Pasquez and Garcia and shoot them?

"Yeah, we planned on casing it out first. You drive by, see if they outside in the parking lot talking, or maybe working the crowd. Sometimes they selling drugs in the back of the parking lot."

"Did you get in the car and start driving in the direction of the club?"

"We did."

"Now, Mr. Adams, did you end up making it straight to the club?"

"No, sir, we didn't."

"What happened?"

"Well, we was on the way. Levi was driving, heading down

72nd Street, and he turns down this road. I say, 'No, Levi, that ain't the way, we ain't got time, we got to go.' But Levi said, 'No, it will just take a second,' and he turn down Fifth. So, we driving down Fifth Avenue, and I say to Levi, 'Where we going?' He says, 'Pineview.' Jimmy and I both start saying, 'Levi, we ain't got time for this,' but he just keeps on saying how it will just take a second."

Adams paused and looked at Edwards, who said, "Okay. Please continue."

"So sure enough, about four blocks up is Pineview Street, and we turn down that street and Levi slows down. I wondered if it had to do with picking up somebody, but there wasn't nobody out. So, we come up on this house and Levi stops. Levi grabs the shotgun next to him and hops out and walks up to the house. The window in front of the house don't have curtains, and you could see part of the TV screen, which was on." Adams rubbed his unshaven chin and paused, looking up at Edwards.

Edwards said, "And then?"

"Well, then Levi go up and knock on the door, holding the shotgun behind his back. Jimmy and I are asking each other, 'What he doing?' It's ten at night, and he's knocking at some door. I almost decided to leave him, but then the door opened, and this guy stood there looking at Levi."

Edwards interjected, "Did it look like they exchanged words? Was there anything you saw or noticed indicating why Mr. Johnson had stopped at the house?"

"No, just the guy opening the door and standing there. Quick as a flash, Levi flip the gun from behind his back and shoot him in the chest, and it blows him back a couple feet. Levi ran back to the car and got in. We're screaming at him because the gunshot set off a bunch of dogs barking, so we figure people will be looking out windows and call the police and everything. We start yelling at him, 'What the hell you doing, Levi? Who was that? That ain't right, that ain't part of what we're doing.' Now Levi don't say a word. He just starts driving fast outta there, not saying a thing.

He makes a couple of right turns to get us heading back out to the main road."

Edwards interjected, "Mr. Adams, let me ask you a couple of things. Were you all under the influence of any narcotics?"

"We smoked some weed earlier. I don't know what else Jimmy and Levi done. Levi act like he be on something strong, crack maybe, I don't know."

Paul watched as Joseph's and Levi's eyes met for the first time, or at least the first time Paul noticed it and saw the icy stare rooted in the betrayed loyalty of a former brother.

Edwards said, "Okay, thank you, Mr. Adams. Now, taking us back to that night, Levi Johnson has just shot Mr. Roberts in his doorway, and he gets back in the car and you all speed off. You said Mr. Johnson didn't say anything at all?"

"No. It was strange, like he in a trance or something. We like, 'Levi, what'd you do that for? Who was that?' and he just sits there and don't say nothing." Adams added, almost as an afterthought, "Sometimes that kind of thing can happen, though, when the adrenaline kicks in and you space out, especially if you be on something."

Edwards said, "Okay, and then what happened?"

"Well, like I say earlier, we had business to take care of, and I figure the police would probably be checking out the sound of a gunshot so we speed over toward the club."

"And all the while, Mr. Johnson is still silent?"

"Well at one point he say, 'It was something I had to do' or something to that effect, but that's all. We left it alone because we was coming up on the club."

"And so now," Edwards continued, "the three of you are driving toward the club and looking for Pasquez and Garcia?"

"Right."

"Please go on."

"Okay, so we driving along, and come up to the Club 66 parking lot and slow down. We don't see nobody at first, but then after we drive on past, we park down the street just to watch for a while. We sit there about five minutes, not long, and we see Pasquez come out. Garcia walk out after him, but he have a girl with him, none of us knew who she be. They start walking toward the street. It don't look like they was heading to a car in the parking lot, so we start the car and try to get over to them before they cross the street."

Edwards nodded.

"So we driving toward them, and almost like right on cue, Garcia stops to light a joint or a cigarette or something right on the sidewalk. We tell Levi to make sure there are no police around and he say, 'No, it looks clear,' and so Levi guns it and heads right toward them."

Edwards asked, "Did they look up at your car?"

"No, they just was talking there, sort of doing their own thing. We don't squeal off or nothing, but we come up to them pretty quick and stop right beside them. Our passenger-side windows are down. I tell Jimmy and Levi I like to get in close so we stop, like we was just going to ask them directions or something. As soon as Garcia see us, he say something like, 'Oh no,' and start to turn to run as Jimmy and I start shooting at them."

Edwards asked, "And you are aware that forensics determined several of the bullets fired from your gun were, in fact, recovered from Garcia's and Pasquez's bodies?"

"Yes, sir."

"And you and Mr. Turner…Jimmy, as you call him…the two of you were shooting at all three of them?"

"No, sir, just Garcia and Pasquez."

Edwards said, "I see."

"So we start shooting from about ten feet away, and Jimmy empty his magazine and slip in another and fire a few more rounds. The girl is screaming and run off, and both Garcia and Pasquez are down, so we knows they hit but not sure how bad. I tell Levi to take off, and about that time we look down the street and sees a police car flip its lights on."

Edwards said, "Officer's Tyndall's unit? The one that pursued the three of you?"

"I think so, yes, sir."

Edwards continued asking questions, with Adams responding quite credibly—at least in Paul's mind—describing the events up until the crash, the trip to the hospital, and subsequent arrest.

Edwards seemed to be almost finished with his questioning but then asked, "Mr. Adams, you agreed to plead guilty to the murder of Pasquez and Garcia, is that correct?"

"Yes, sir."

"And in return for the testimony you have provided today, you agreed to plead guilty to the lesser charge of involuntary manslaughter in the murder of Marcus Roberts, rather than being charged with first-degree murder, is that correct?"

"Yes, sir."

"Thank you, Mr. Adams." Edwards returned to his table, while Adams looked over at the judge.

The judge looked at Liam Olsen. "Cross?"

Olsen stood and said, "Thank you Judge Mayer."

He walked in front of Adams and said, "Mr. Adams, can you tell me how the decision was made to execute Mr. Garcia and Mr. Pasquez?"

"Objection. Relevance?" said Edwards.

The judge said, "I'll allow it."

"Go ahead, Mr. Adams," Olsen said.

"Well, a group of us was over at my apartment when we hear that a couple of guys from our group had been beat up. We go over to the hospital where Reggie, one of the guys, is in a coma. We was sitting there looking at him and I think the idea come to all of us that we need to set things straight, you know? When we left the hospital in the car, somebody brought up going after the guys that did it. I don't remember who, but there was general agreement that it was something we needed to do."

"Is this how a lot of gang-related killings occur, meaning that if a gang member is hurt or killed, a group retaliates after discussing it?"

Adams nodded slowly and said, "Sometimes, yeah."

"Did it not strike you as strange, Mr. Adams, that my client didn't tell you anything about his intentions when he, according to you, shot Mr. Roberts?"

"Oh, yes sir, it definitely struck us as strange; I say as much earlier."

"So, you're asking us to believe that the three of you, on the way to what must have been a somewhat planned-out...uh...mission, totally go off track, and you knew nothing about it?"

"Look, this wasn't that big a deal. I mean, yeah, we was planning on being careful, and it's true we was going to scope out the situation first. So I guess there was some planning in a way, but the whole thing kind of came together without much planning."

"I see. Okay. Mr. Adams, you just said you agreed to testify for the State in return for a reduced sentence of involuntary manslaughter, is that correct?

"Yes, sir."

"So, you benefit by coming in here and testifying, likely avoiding some additional prison time by testifying against my client, isn't that true?"

"Yes, sir."

Irritation in his voice, Olsen asked, "Isn't it true, Mr. Adams, that you realized a strong case could be made against you as a shooter in this drive-by shooting of Garcia and Pasquez, and that you fabricated this story about Levi Johnson shooting Marcus Roberts in order to achieve a reduced sentence?"

"No, sir. It happened as I say."

Olsen shook his head and asked, "What proof do you have that the three of you even drove to Mr. Roberts' home?"

"Excuse me?"

"How do we even know you were there?"

"I am telling you that."

"Sure you are, and the prosecution cut a deal with you to get a conviction in the Roberts case."

Edwards stood and said, "Objection!"

The judge responded, "Sustained."

"Okay," Olsen said, "let me go about this a different way. When Mr. Johnson got out of the car and walked to the house, do you have a pretty strong recollection of that? I mean, it seems to me that the image of him walking to the house would be pretty clear in your mind…like you could picture that in your head even today, is that true?"

"Yes, sir. That's true."

"Well, when you stopped, did the car stop right in front of the house, or was it just past the house or just short of the house?"

"Um…I would say it was just short of the house."

"Roughly how many feet?"

"How many feet? I don't know…maybe ten?"

"So you stopped short of the house by about ten feet and Mr. Johnson gets out the car and walks at a forward angle toward the front door, is that correct?"

"Yes."

"What did the house look like that night? You said a moment ago that it was pretty dark."

"Yes, sir, it be dark."

"How well could you see Mr. Johnson as he was walking to the house?"

"We could see him pretty well. I think there was a streetlight not far away."

"What about inside the house, were the lights on?"

"Maybe just one or two, but you could see the TV on because you could see the flickering on the inside walls as the TV picture changed."

"I see. So, it was dark enough inside the house that you could see a TV was on."

"Yes, sir."

"Let me ask you this. Could you see the television screen from the car as you looked into the window?"

"Um, no sir, at least I don't think so. I'm not sure."

"Was there anything else you remember about that night you can tell the court, any detail that comes to mind?"

"None I remember, no, sir."

Returning to his chair and with audible frustration, Liam Olsen stated, "No, I didn't think there would be. No further questions, Your Honor."

The judge looked at Edwards. "Any redirect?"

Edwards answered, "No, Your Honor."

When Adams was excused, Paul thought about his examination—seemingly credible notwithstanding the fact that he'd reduced his sentence in return for testifying.

The judge declared a ten-minute recess, after which James Turner entered through the same doorway where Adams had exited.

* * *

Turner was called to the witness stand and sworn in. Not surprisingly, most of his account matched up with Adams' testimony. As he appeared to wrap up his questioning, however, Edwards asked, "Mr. Turner, we know from another witness's testimony that, relative to Roberts' house, the car in which you were driving stopped just short—"

Liam Olsen stood and exclaimed "Objection! Your Honor, if I know where this going, counsel is leading the witness and thus directly compromising his testimony."

The judge looked sternly at Edwards and said, "Sustained. Mr. Edwards, I would think you'd know better than that."

The prosecutor said, "Yes, Your Honor. Strike that. I think we're good on our side."

Judge Mayer looked at the table where Levi Johnson's defense team sat and said, "Your witness, Mr. Olsen."

Olsen asked a few questions to clarify points Turner had made under direct examination and then went through the same questions he'd asked Adams about the agreement to plead guilty to a lesser charge in the Marcus Roberts murder case in return for testifying against Levi Johnson and receiving a reduced sentence. He glanced every now and then at the jury members to try to gauge their expressions.

"Mr. Turner, Mr. Edwards was about to bring up the location of the car when it stopped near the house. I would like to ask you, where in relation to the house did the car stop?"

Mr. Turner thought for a minute and said, "We was right in front of the house. Maybe a little past it, I think."

"A little past it."

"Yes, I think a little past it."

"Okay, Mr. Turner, which house lights were on that night?"

"I don't remember."

"Well, surely you must remember some aspect of that scene. You were on high alert that night so surely paying close attention. Was the front porch light on?"

"Yes, I think so."

"Okay, how about lights inside the house?"

"Just a light in what must have been the living room, which you could see cause of the large window in front of the house."

"Was it a fairly bright light?"

"Yeah, pretty bright, I guess."

"Bright enough that you could see into the house and see things on the wall if you walked up and looked into the window?"

Turner looked at Edwards, who was expressionless, and then back at Olsen. "Uh, yeah, I think so."

"Could you tell if a television was on inside the house?"

"No."

"Was the room too bright to see, say, the flickering of a television?"

"Right, it was too bright for that."

"Let's talk a minute about the ride from this house to Club 66. Did Mr. Johnson say anything during that car ride?"

"No, he didn't say anything. He just say he needed to do something."

"Mr. Turner, have you and Mr. Adams discussed this case at all?"

"Not directly, no."

"Not directly. What does that mean?"

"I meant to say no, we didn't discuss it."

"So to summarize, you drove up to the house, stopped just past the house or right in front of it, the front porch light was on you believe, the lights inside of the house were pretty bright, and you couldn't tell if a TV was on or not. Is that right?"

"That's how I remember it."

"Thank you, Mr. Turner. No further questions, Your Honor."

The judge declared a recess for the day, and Rebecca and Paul walked out together as per usual. A female juror looked back at them and said something to another female juror walking beside her, the other looking back and laughing. It was clear they'd been talking about Paul and Rebecca.

As Paul thought about Levi and the testimony that day, his initial leanings were towards Levi's innocence. However, the notion that Tony may have hired Levi to kill Roberts caused him to doubt that inclination. After all, he knew something that none of the other jurors knew: a potential motive.

Rebecca and Paul, saying little, made it to the outside door and walked into the evening air.

Rebecca said, "I think those women ahead of us were talking about us."

"So, you noticed it too?" Paul confirmed.

Approaching the garage, Rebecca stopped and said, "I guess we have closing arguments tomorrow, right?"

"I think so."

"Do you think it'll be a hotly contested verdict?" she asked.

"I don't know. Maybe."

"What makes you say that?"

Paul responded, "Because I don't know myself."

Rebecca gave an acknowledgement that was neither an agreement nor disagreement.

"The one missing piece is motive," Rebecca said.

"I know," Paul said, feeling the urge to tell her about Tony and the nagging question that so vexed him: was Levi *hired* to kill Marcus Roberts?

Rebecca turned towards him and said, "Oh, by the way, I finished your book. I liked it," she said. There was no smile in her voice.

"Thanks," Paul answered in a similar unenthusiastic tone, feeling irritated—or maybe disappointed—in her reaction.

"Well, I guess I'll see you in the morning" she said before turning away and walking briskly to her car.

"Good night, Rebecca," he called after her, thinking how difficult it was to be angry with a face that pretty.

* * *

Paul headed to Tom's office. Walking into the reception area, he saw Margie and said, "Surprised you're still here."

"Yeah, just trying to wrap up some paperwork tonight. Tom is ready for you."

Tom stuck his head out of his office and said, "Paul, hi. Come in."

"How are things?" Tom asked.

"Katherine was having an affair."

"What? With whom? How do you know?"

"I was cleaning out the attic and came across a letter from a man in her office…I know him…It was a love letter from him."

Paul reached into his pocket, pulled out the letter, and said, "Here, I brought it with me. Feel free to read it."

Tom stared at Paul for a moment, unsure if he was serious.

"Really…Go ahead, I don't care," Paul said.

Tom pulled the letter out and read it, then said, "Paul, I am so sorry. Where did you say you found it?"

"Inside a box in the attic. I was getting rid of things and came across it."

"Did you have any suspicion that something was going on between Katherine and this…" he looked at the letter again, "Tony?"

"No. They danced several times at her birthday party, the one I told you about with the red dress. He's the attorney I called to find out Marcus' name."

Tom asked, "Wait…this is the same guy who you gave the license plate to and asked if he could tell you who owned the car?"

Paul nodded.

Tom had a look of shock in his eyes, and asked, "So he figures out the name Marcus Roberts for you based on you telling him about the suspicious vehicle driving around the neighborhood, and we don't know if Katherine had told him at that point about the rape or not, correct?"

Paul nodded, adding, "At some point though, she clearly did."

Tom asked, "Paul, what's this Tony guy like?"

Paul, looking down at the floor and recalling the evening of the red dress, replied, "He's everything that an overweight, balding man like me would hate: good looking, full head of wavy, jet-black hair, broad shoulders, self-assured…just head-turningly good looking. I've watched women's eyes." The image of Tony removing his jacket that night, putting his muscular torso on full display beneath a custom-tailored shirt, came to Paul's mind.

As Tom processed it all, Paul imagined Katherine confiding

in Tony about the assault and collapsing into his powerful, protective arms as she wrapped hers around that chiseled back of his. Her looking into his damned eyes any female writer worth her salt would describe as "engaging yet mysterious."

Paul's galloping imagination began to play the scene out to its logical conclusion, picturing Katherine kissing him deeply before clothing was shed and glistening bodies moved together rhythmically—just as they had in front of everyone on that dance floor that night, their minds oblivious to anyone or anything else.

Paul screamed, "Aggh!!!" and felt tears sting his eyes. He was breathing hard and looked at Tom. "I'm sorry."

"Don't apologize, Paul."

Paul took a sip of water from a bottle he'd brought along and closed his eyes, as if concentrating.

Tom looked levelly at Paul and said, "I guess I'm wondering if Tony could have been involved in the murder somehow."

Paul replied, "I've wondered the same thing."

They were silent for a few moments before Paul said, "What I don't understand, Tom, is all the 'whys.' I mean, I knew things between us weren't perfect, but I thought we were working it out. So why did she go outside the marriage? Why did she keep the letter and not destroy it? Why didn't she get rid of it before she committed suicide so it would never be found? I mean, she left it right on top of one of her sweaters in a box in the attic." Paul hesitated and then added, "How could she have thought it would go undiscovered?"

"Maybe she didn't," Tom said calmly.

Paul became defensive and snapped, "Well, if that's her idea of a confession, she won't get absolution from me."

Tom didn't say anything.

Paul tried to calm down. "I think I could have forgiven her had she come to me and explained it all, explained how she'd made a mistake and had somehow allowed herself to get pulled into a relationship…but she didn't. Instead, she was essentially lying to me every moment we were together."

Tom stayed silent, listening patiently.

Paul stared off into the distance, his face suggesting his mind was wrestling with something.

"What is it?" asked Tom.

"I was just thinking about our intimacy, pretty much shot over the last year. I'd never pushed it, thinking it was due to the assault, but now I wonder…was that due to the assault…or that she was in love with Tony Leone?"

"It may have been both the assault and the affair, Paul."

As Paul processed the thought, Tom asked, "What are you thinking you should do with this information?"

"What *can* I do with it? I know I'm not telling Daniel, which would have no point."

Tom nodded.

Paul looked squarely at Tom and asked, "What do you do when you suddenly discover the life you've been living has been one big lie?"

"Well, Paul, parts of your life weren't."

"I guess. I'll tell you one thing, Tom. For the first time in a long time, I don't feel the crushing sadness. I feel mad as hell, betrayed as hell, stupid as hell…but not the devastating sadness I've been feeling."

Tom nodded.

"Maybe I actually didn't lose her on August 15th but instead a long time before that."

Paul rubbed his forehead and then both eyes and said, "Yesterday, I came across a picture of a young couple in a wedding photograph. What struck me was the look of uncontained joy on their blissfully naïve and expectant faces, each looking forward to spending their lives together until they eventually said their earthly goodbyes."

Paul's voice sounded resigned and weary. "I wanted to step into that photograph, shake them, and tell them to stop smiling as

171

if everything would be just perfect; life doesn't happen that way." He shook his head in disbelief. "They looked as if they'd stay in love forever and that nothing could shake that."

Tom said, "How do you know they didn't?"

"Because the wife killed herself and the husband is sitting in his therapist's office trying to figure out what the hell happened."

Tom said, "I'm sorry, Paul."

"No, the apology is mine. I didn't mean to take it out on you."

"Paul, you ever try some deep-breathing exercises?" Tom asked, testing a different approach.

"No."

"Humor me for a minute."

"When you breathe deeply, it sends a message to your brain to calm down and relax. The brain then sends this message back to your body; so it starts with the body, affects the mind, and then reinforces the body. It's all part of the mind/body connection."

"I don't feel differently," Paul said after trying it a few times.

"Well, give it a try when you feel stressed out. You'll get better at it with practice."

Tom stood up and pulled a book from his shelf and handed it to Paul. "If you're interested, read this. A lot is about meditation. It's pretty good."

Paul agreed.

"So, how are you feeling about the trial?" Tom asked.

"As good as I can, I guess," said Paul.

Tom nodded.

"I really don't know if he did it or not. Sometimes during the testimony, I'll just stare at Levi, wondering what the hell is going through his head, playing back the night of February 23rd, wondering if he actually did pull the trigger, and trying to figure out a motive and now whether Tony was involved or not."

Tom nodded and said, "I still think it's a mistake for you to be on the jury, Paul. You know that, so I won't harp on it. It's probably not too late to back out. There are alternate jurors, aren't there?"

"Two."

"Why not disclose, Paul? You could leave out the brick incident and just say you didn't initially do so because you were protecting Katherine's desire for privacy but now know she told someone else, someone she was having an affair with."

Paul rose from his chair and started for the door, "I'm already in this too deep." He shook Tom's hand. "Can I come back in a couple of days, maybe Wednesday, at the same time?"

"Sure. You can come back sooner if you need it."

Paul stopped at the drug store on the way home to pick up a few items: more Benadryl, as his supply was dwindling and he wanted to avoid the Ambien if possible, plus some Extra Strength Tylenol. He saw Mark Emerson on the way in, a friend who worked at Katherine's law office. Paul had always been very comfortable with him, the pair always having some good chats about books at the firm's social functions.

"Mark!" Paul said as soon as he saw him.

"Paul, how are you?" Mark asked, his tone one of real interest.

"Okay, I guess," he said. "I'm adjusting and actually thinking about selling my house. It's just too big. Know anybody who wants a two-story colonial in a good section of town?"

"Does it come with your book collection?" Mark asked, smiling.

"Hey, those aren't for sale at any price," Paul said. "Well, maybe a few." He laughed.

Mark said, "Paul, I'm sure sorry about Katherine. Everyone at the firm was so shocked. She was such a wonderful person."

"Thank you, Mark."

"You know, I didn't have a chance to speak to you at the visitation due to a conflict. I've regretted that and feel bad for not checking in with you."

"Don't give it another thought," Paul said and patted him on the shoulder.

They chatted for a moment about Mark's family, and Paul asked, "Hey, Mark, I'm glad I ran into you. I actually have two questions for you. First, Daniel picked up a traffic ticket. Any idea who can handle that for me?"

"Easy. Ben Sutton. He knows the traffic court folks and will get him off with a slap on the wrist unless he has a lot of prior citations. I'll have him call you."

"Thanks. Next question. If I were trying to find out some information about a case your law firm might have worked on, how exactly could I do that?"

"Depends. What exactly are you trying to find out?"

Paul wasn't totally prepared for the question, and his mind searched for an appropriate response. "Research for a book I'm doing, just trying to find out who handled a particular person's case," he said as naturally as if it were the truth.

"Well, probably the best option is to simply look it up online if you need the details of a case. There may be a charge, but if you're simply trying to find out who represented someone in a case, you can find it that way. Heck, you could even buy the entire transcript if you wanted."

"Got it," Paul said.

"I can help you if you'd like."

"Oh no, that's not necessary. I probably will just let it go; I just thought I'd ask since I saw you."

They chatted a few more minutes about the latest book Mark was reading, shook hands, and before leaving, Mark pulled out one of his business cards and said, "Look, here's my direct number. If you need any help on the transcript thing, give me a call, and I can probably steer you in the right direction."

Chapter 22

When court began promptly at nine o'clock, it struck Paul as odd that the defense had not called any witnesses—hardly surprising, though, considering Levi's attorneys were court appointed and defense witnesses often involve a cost.

Judge Mayer looked at the jury and said, "Ladies and gentlemen of the jury, at this time, you will receive a copy of your final instructions, which I will read aloud to you. We will then proceed to closing arguments. Before I begin, let me first discuss procedure with respect to closing arguments. Because the prosecution has the burden of proof, it will present closing arguments first, followed by the defense. After the defense presents its final arguments, the prosecution has a final opportunity to make a rebuttal argument."

Paul looked at the multipage instructions and then his watch, betting on a long day.

The judge continued, reading verbatim from the page.

"Members of the jury, irrespective of your opinion about what the law is or what the law should be, your verdict *must* be based on the law I give you in these instructions, and you must apply that law to the facts in the case which you determine to have been proven by the evidence. Let me speak a moment about what evidence is and what it's not.

"Anything, whether that is something you saw on TV, something you read in the paper, something you heard someone say, or anything else outside the courtroom is not evidence. You must decide this case solely on the evidence offered and received at trial. Any theory you come up with that relies upon any information obtained outside this court is inapplicable to your decision."

I know a possible motive; how can I not consider it?

The judge then went on to define, as he had at the opening of the trial, what constituted the words "cause," "intent," and differentiated intent and motive, as he had done before, reminding the jurors that a motive was not necessary to secure a verdict of guilty.

The judge went on to say that the jurors should not consider any evidence that was objected to and "not received" by the court, that the burden of proof was with the State, and that the defendant was presumed innocent until proven guilty beyond a reasonable doubt, from the State's presentation of evidence.

Finally, the judge said, "You will not have a copy of the written transcript of the trial testimony available for use during your deliberations, although you may request to see exhibits that were admitted. You must continue to rely primarily on your memory of the evidence and the testimony introduced during the trial. Before you can find the defendant guilty, the evidence, whether it is direct or circumstantial, must satisfy you, beyond a reasonable doubt, that the defendant committed the offense."

Paul thought about the case made against Levi. There was the direct testimony of his fellow gang members, but they may have been coerced into testifying as a result of the plea deal. Much of the other evidence was circumstantial, certainly the timing of the shooting, the shotgun being the same type of weapon, the exact same type of shot used. Taken alone, he was not sure the evidence was adequate for a guilty verdict. But when he added in a possible motive and the nagging feeling that Tony was involved, it became a tougher call.

He heard the judge say, "The weight of evidence does not depend on the number of witnesses on each side."

Good thing for Levi, Paul thought, *since his attorney had presented none.* He was a little surprised Levi himself hadn't testified.

The judge then listed factors to weigh in deciding the credibility of each witness such as whether they had any interest in the case, clarity in their recollections, consistency or lack thereof with other testimony, possible motives for falsifying testimony, and other facts and circumstances supporting or discrediting it.

Several of these might compromise the Adams and Turner testimony, Paul thought to himself.

The judge summed up by saying, "A defendant in a criminal case does not have to testify, and it's his or her constitutional right not to do so. Lack of the defendant's testimony may not be considered in assessing guilt or innocence. Ladies and gentlemen of the jury, these are your instructions. There will be additional closing instructions, but those will be made after the completion of closing arguments."

Wrapping up, Judge Mayer announced a recess to allow each side to make any last-minute preparations for closing arguments.

Paul walked out to use the restroom. As he was walking back out, he saw the little boy, presumably Levi's son, trying to peer over the water fountain edge to fill a water bottle with water. He was pressing the button to release the water, but his inability to see where the stream of water flowed led to most of the water missing the top of the bottle. Paul looked around and, not seeing anyone close by, walked up to him and said, "Need some help?" The boy looked up and handed Paul the bottle, staring at him. Paul filled it and handed it back.

"Thank you," the little boy said, and he started to turn toward the entrance of the women's rest room, where his mother presumably was. He stopped and turned back, saying, "He didn't do it, you know. My dad…He didn't do it. They told him not to testify, so he won't, but he didn't do it."

Paul said, "Thank you, son," and watched as the lad walked back to wait for his mother to come out of the ladies' room.

Paul walked back into the courtroom and sat down, and the judge looked at the prosecuting attorney and said, "Mr. Edwards, you may begin."

Edwards stood and said, "Ladies and gentlemen, let me start by thanking you for the time and attention you've given to this case. I know many of you are busy and have taken time away from jobs and daily lives to fulfill this important duty. In this closing argument, I will discuss some of the facts the State believes are important. As you know, as far as the State goes, all the evidence in this case points to one person who could have committed this murder: Levi Johnson.

"That opinion is based on facts. Facts are truth, and the truth doesn't change. I plan to review some of the important facts of this case and why we think we have proved the case, beyond a reasonable doubt, against Levi Johnson.

"Let's go back over what was presented. We have three men driving in a car together, members of the Bloods gang who've admitted to being on their way to murder two rival gang members and thus already in the mindset of killing. Two admitted to taking mind-altering drugs that evening, the same two indicating they were in a car driven by Levi Johnson and taken to Pineview Street where they stopped at Marcus Roberts' home. Both indicate Johnson got out of the car with his shotgun and killed Marcus Roberts, both describing the situation and mannerisms of Mr. Johnson in some detail.

"We also have the report of Bud Peterson, the pathologist, who indicated a shotgun was in fact used to kill Marcus Roberts and fired at close range, just as Mr. Adams and Mr. Turner testified. Not only that, but the double aught shell used to kill Mr. Roberts was the same type of ammunition found in the car and in Mr. Johnson's possession after the chase and accident.

"And finally, we have Ms. Howard, a neighbor who heard the gunshot and looked out her window to see a dark sedan driving down the street that matches the vehicle in which Mr. Johnson was riding. Ladies and gentlemen of the jury, I only wish all of my criminal cases were this open and shut.

"The one thing we don't really have here, however, is a stated motive; but as the judge instructed, a finding of guilt beyond a reasonable doubt does not require you to explain motive or even consider it. We may never know why Levi Johnson killed Marcus Roberts. Perhaps it was racially motivated. There had certainly been racial tensions within the city. Or maybe a random act of violence? We'll likely never know, nor do we have to.

"Your job, ladies and gentlemen of the jury, is to simply answer the question: Did Levi Johnson, with full intent, exit the vehicle on Pineview Street with shotgun in hand, walk up to the house located at 231 Pineview, and shoot Marcus Roberts in cold blood? Marcus Roberts, a man who Ms. Howard described as a good neighbor, a man who helped her carry groceries and a man who was innocent. Marcus Roberts is gone, and nothing we can do will bring him back. Let's not ignore our responsibility, however, to render justice for the person responsible: Levi Johnson."

Edwards paused, looking at the faces of the jury, and smiled before returning to his seat.

The judge looked over at Liam Olsen. "Mr. Olsen?"

Mr. Olsen stood and walked in front of the jury. "Reasonable doubt. Reasonable doubt...That is the problem, isn't it? Ladies and gentlemen, there is reasonable doubt throughout this case. Here we have a man accused of a crime by two people who are known murderers, both of whom have agreed to testify and plead guilty to a charge of involuntary manslaughter that carries a sentence of somewhere between ten and sixteen months in prison rather than being tried for first-degree murder. Now, you might say, what does that matter since Mr. Adams and Mr. Turner are already sentenced to life in prison? In other words, why would they care if they had an extra life sentence since their *original* conviction was for life? Well, it matters for this reason. Should the sentence for the Pasquez and Garcia murders ever be vacated—due to new evidence clearing Mr. Adams and Mr. Turner—or their sentence commuted for some reason, it would make a difference in prison time. Bottom line, they have a conflict of interest in this case as their testimony reduces their potential time behind bars.

"Allow me to back up and discuss witness credibility for a moment. I just mentioned one factor, whether there are any conflicts. Another is consistency with other testimony. In this case, we have two witnesses, both of whom were purportedly in the vehicle when it stopped at 231 Pineview. Ladies and gentlemen, I want you to think about one's likely state of mind at that moment. These men were on their way to murder other gang members. Their adrenaline would have been pumping and they would have been on high alert, paying close attention to every detail. In this case, we have inconsistencies in those details. True, some of it matched up, but how do we know that the witnesses—who knew each other well—didn't agree ahead of time to make parts of their stories consistent? They could certainly take a guess at likely questions involving Levi Johnson's demeanor or what he said, things of that nature.

"Other things involving the car's movement and lights in the house, for example, probably don't fit that mold. Did their accounts match up with respect to these? No, not very well. Why not? Because the three were never there, and Mr. Adams and Mr. Turner believe that their best interest is served by taking a slap on the wrist for something they didn't do rather than to risk receiving a harsher sentence if they didn't cooperate.

"How about the matching pellets? You heard Detective Barton himself testify that double aught buckshot is one of the most common types of shot used in a shotgun among just a few choices, the match here likewise not as significant as the State implied. How about Ms. Howard saying she saw a dark sedan driving down the street? Ladies and gentlemen, it was dark that night. Mrs. Howard, with all due respect, is elderly and wears glasses.

"And finally, we have the issue of motive: never brought up by the State because they have none to offer. There is no reason to believe Levi Johnson had any reason to kill Marcus Roberts. If this indeed existed, don't you think the State would have presented it? True, you don't need to have motive to convict, but without it, the State has very little to tie Levi Johnson to this murder."

Paul's mind went instinctively to Tony.

Olsen went on, "In fact, the only real thing that ties my client to the scene is a parallel timeline; but that isn't sufficient evidence to prove guilt and *especially* not guilt beyond a reasonable doubt. Ladies and gentlemen, as you prepare to engage in your deliberations, I hope you will keep in mind that the burden of proof—and I want you to think about that word proof—rests with the State. Every person is assumed innocent until proven guilty. The State has not done this. Thank you for your careful attention during the trial; I trust your consciences and judgments will guide you in your deliberations."

With no rebuttal from the prosecution, the judge looked at the jury and said, "Ladies and gentlemen, the time has now come for you to make your decision in this case based on all the evidence presented. Arriving at a verdict is obviously your most important duty, and in rendering your verdict, you must be very careful and deliberate in weighing the evidence. Your duty is to render a just and true verdict.

"This being a criminal—not civil—case, the jury's verdict must be unanimous. One of your first responsibilities when you return to the jury room will be to select a foreman, one of your members who will preside over your deliberations. That person's opinion of guilt or innocence has no greater significance than any other juror's. When a verdict has been arrived at unanimously, have it signed and dated by the person you have selected to be foreman. Please return the unsigned verdict forms as well. At this time, the bailiff will usher you to the jury room. The jury is excused."

* * *

The group, which included seven men and five women, but not the alternates, moved to Room 723 down the hall from the courtroom. The room was stark, although someone had put snacks, sodas and coffee in the corner. Paul looked at the large, imposing table, its heavy weight matching the weightiness of the negotiations that regularly occurred around it. He studied the finish, which bore countless mars of indentations, scratches and scrapes where fists with rings had no doubt been brought down in frustration and anger as the search for justice was pursued. He wondered what new marks would be added to the table this week.

A man who looked to be about seventy years old spoke up. "Hi, my name is Nathan Cashwell. The judge asked that I get things started this morning and suggested we first elect a foreman. I thought maybe we could start by going around the table and introducing ourselves, saying something about who we are. That might help us choose a foreman."

Several people nodded affirmatively, relieved to have someone in charge.

Mr. Cashwell said, "I'll begin. I'm a retired attorney who practiced in Detroit most of my career. I grew up just outside the city and have been here pretty much all my life."

Others followed. There was Jim, a church custodian; Julia, a retired woman and "very religious person"; Wilson, an Army veteran; Maggie, a social worker and recovering substance abuser; Rick, a county tax office clerk; John, an unemployed man; Meredith, a disabled woman; Mac, a truck driver; Nancy, an accounts receivable clerk for a doctor's office, and finally, Paul and Rebecca.

Mr. Cashwell was unanimously elected foreman, not surprising given how the deliberations had started.

"Well," he began, "as Judge Mayer indicated, we have a verdict to render. One thing we may want to do is have a brief discussion about the expectations we each have in this room. I'm not making the rules here, and any rules are those we decide on as a group. It's important for us to reach a unanimous decision on the verdict, but that's probably not how we'll start off."

"Please each express your opinion," he added. "If you disagree with someone, you need to say so and say why. Disagreeing is fine, but let's not be 'disagreeable' in disagreeing. Everyone's opinion in this room deserves respect. If someone is a holdout, that juror has the right to do that, and we must honor it. I've had cases I've argued where a lone juror swung the case the other way."

Mr. Cashwell handed out name tags and a marker. "I want us to be able to call one another by name so we can communicate more easily."

After everyone complied, he asked, "Would anyone like to say anything or ask any questions before we begin?" He looked around as the jurors looked at each other, several shaking their heads no. "Okay. One thing that sometimes helps in getting started is to take an initial vote to see where we're at. Does anyone object to this?"

Seeing no objections, he handed out twelve strips of paper and placed some pencils on the center of the table. "Please mark your slip of paper with 'guilty,' 'not guilty,' or 'undecided' and return it to me. Try not to use 'undecided' unless you are absolutely not leaning one way or the other. This won't be our official vote; it's simply to gauge where we are as a group."

Paul felt a growing discomfort at having to decide, particularly based on the information that was uniquely his. *What do I believe? What would I believe if I lacked any sort of connection to the case and was unaware of a possible relationship between Tony and Levi?* Most people scribbled something down immediately and gave Mr. Cashwell their slips.

He looked down at the sheet, wrote "Guilty," and folded it up and handed it down the table.

Mr. Cashwell pulled out a legal pad, wrote the date at the top of the page, and tallied the responses. "On our first vote, we have seven 'guilty' verdicts, four 'not guilty' verdicts, and one 'undecided.' That actually isn't too bad for a first vote."

Paul felt some relief that he was among the majority. It lessened the probability that he would have to contribute as much to the discussion, which was a welcome thought.

Mr. Cashwell said, "Let me remind each of you at this stage that our goal here is to arrive at a verdict we can all agree to, and again, everyone's opinion is valid. It would be helpful to go around the table and get some feel for why each person voted the way they did. Anyone object to that?"

Given the silence that ensued, Mr. Cashwell said, "Great. Anyone want to start?"

The retired veteran seated next to Paul spoke up. "Hi, again. My name is Wilson, and I will be happy to begin. I voted guilty. I think it's clear that Levi Johnson was the killer. He was driving the car that night and was in the same neighborhood. When you look at all the circumstantial evidence and the fact that the police don't even have another suspect, how can you conclude he didn't do it?"

No one responded, but there were a few nods.

Maggie went next. "I don't see it that way and think there's a burden of proof that the prosecution didn't meet. I realize there are no other suspects, but honestly, how do we know that the police even tried to look for anyone else? And can we really trust the testimony of Adams and Turner? They were trying to save their own skins by becoming witnesses."

Wilson interjected, "Yeah, but they weren't guaranteed a lower sentence, were they?"

Maggie responded, "I thought they were…"

Mr. Cashwell said, "Hang on a second, let's not get into that debate right now and simply give everyone a chance to say where they are in their thinking."

"Okay, sorry. Sure," Wilson answered.

A man named Rick, a clerk in the tax department of the county government, went next, saying, "Guilty, same reasons as expressed before."

The next juror, John, who was unemployed, indicated not guilty but did not give a reason why, while the next three jurors, Meredith, a disabled female, Rebecca and Mac, a truck driver, all indicated guilty and gave brief reasons that were variations of what had been said before.

The eighth juror, Nancy, an accounts receivable clerk for a physician's office, said, "Honestly, I don't get it. You have nothing actually tying the guy to the crime other than the type of shells that were used and the testimony of two criminals who want reduced sentences."

Maggie nodded in agreement.

Nathan Cashwell was the ninth juror to speak as they made their way around the table, and he said, "I marked my slip 'guilty.'"

Jim, a church custodian, the tenth juror, said he had marked the ballot "undecided" but that he leaned towards not guilty, saying, "I agree with Nancy. Also, I'm a hunter. I use double aught shot all the time, in fact, it's the main shell I use."

The eleventh juror was Julia, the retired woman who was religious. She said "God bless him. I don't think he's guilty."

Finally, it came to Paul, who simply said, "Well, to me, it seemed like the circumstantial evidence was enough to convict."

Mr. Cashwell spoke up. "So just to be sure, our 'not guilty' votes are from Julia, Maggie, Nancy, and John, is that right?"

They all nodded, Jim chiming in and saying, "Actually, you can probably list me as 'not guilty'. I said undecided, but if I had to vote one way or the other, it would be 'not guilty' at this point."

"Okay, that's fine then." Mr. Cashwell said. "Including my guilty verdict, we're starting with seven guilty and five not guilty. Let's open it up then, and maybe we can get some headway on building a consensus."

Maggie spoke first. "One of the things that bothers me is the lack of a motive. There is nothing that explains to me *why* he would have done it."

Rick said, "Yeah, but like the judge said, we don't have to come up with a motive. All we have to do is determine whether or not he did it."

"True," Maggie responded. "I understand that, but when you're trying to rationally justify a verdict beyond a reasonable doubt and the State fails to explain why someone may have done something, that's a problem."

"It's not a problem for me, and the judge said it shouldn't be one either," said Mac, the trucker, who looked at Rick, who was nodding.

Rebecca said, "Well, they were all drugged up anyway, right? I mean, couldn't that lead to some irrational behaviors? Do we know what sort of behaviors can result when you're on…what was it…crack?"

Mr. Cashwell said, "Well, I think Adams testified they'd all smoked marijuana but that he thought Levi Johnson might have taken something like crack."

Maggie said, "I'll tell you one thing. I used crack when I was younger. It can scramble your brain and make you feel invincible, like you can do all sorts of things no one can explain. I don't think he's guilty, but a lack of motive isn't the main reason."

Nancy asked, "So, how do we know Adams and Turner aren't

lying?

"Why would they lie?" asked Mac.

"To save their skins," Nancy replied.

Mac said, "The State didn't require they receive a conviction, just that they testify."

Maggie said, "Oh, come on. The State wants a conviction, and that's all they want. I guarantee you they've got sworn statements they took weeks ago and knew exactly what they had and that it would help them get a conviction."

Mac replied, "Well, going back to motive, what about the argument that it was racially based? I think we're all familiar with the tensions in the city,"

Paul noticed Julia and Wilson, African Americans, nodding.

"I thought the evidence that it was racially motivated was very weak," Jim opined.

Mac said, "Again, folks, they don't have to prove motive for us to get a conviction. All they have to do is to satisfy twelve people that he is guilty. Those are two different things. Proving racism has nothing to do with it."

Maggie retorted, "Motive is absolutely relevant in this case. It may not technically be required, but it's relevant for proving beyond a reasonable doubt…at least in my opinion, anyway."

Paul watched Maggie as she spoke. *If she knew what I know*, he thought, *I bet she'd vote guilty.*

"What about the Confederate flag? Are you saying that was made up?" asked Mac.

A thought suddenly struck Paul. "Wait a minute," he said. "This just occurred to me…Wasn't there a Confederate rifle, also?"

"I don't remember that," someone said.

"Neither do I," said another.

Paul said, "I feel like I remember there being one."

Mr. Cashwell said, "Paul, I believe you're mistaken. I think I would have remembered that."

Wilson nodded. "I agree."

Someone said, "If it helps, we can have the photos brought in to see for ourselves."

"Sure, we can request that, but let's figure out if there is anything else we want to see at the same time. Anybody have anything else they want brought in?" Mr. Cashwell asked.

Mac said, "We're already way down a rabbit hole here. I don't think we need to even bother with it."

Several jurors nodded.

Mr. Cashwell, sensing some frustration among the panel, said, "Let's ask for it and get it out of the way. Tell you what, let's also ask for the inventory of items from the house. They referred to that in the trial, and it might show a rifle as well."

He stood and walked outside to request from the bailiff the photos showing the interior of the house as well as the inventory. The bailiff returned a few minutes later with an easel holding two blown-up photos, one of Marcus Roberts' body lying prone in the hallway and the other of the living room where Roberts had presumably been watching television. He also handed the extensive list of inventoried items to Mr. Cashwell before exiting the room.

Mr. Cashwell skimmed the pages. "Hmm, I'll be darned! Sure enough, it says replica Civil War musket rifle. You're right, Paul. I just don't remember it in the photos." Frowning, he put the pages down and walked up to the easel. "That's odd…no rifle in these photos. Paul, do you recall where you saw it?"

Paul's mind began to spin. *Did I see it that night when I was on the porch looking at Roberts through the living room window? Surely that must be it?* He searched his mind through the photographic evidence, wondering if he recalled seeing the rifle in one of the photos. He did not.

With a mounting sense of panic, Paul responded, "No. No, I don't. Maybe I was just thinking I had seen one. I could have sworn I saw one in one of the photos but maybe I was mistaken."

Mr. Cashwell looked over to Maggie and said, "Maggie, would you mind asking the bailiff to bring in the rest of the photos that were introduced as evidence?"

Paul swallowed. Mr. Cashwell passed the list around the room for the others to look it over. A few moments later, the bailiff and another man brought in about ten interior and exterior shots of the house and lined them up, side by side, around the perimeter of the wall.

Paul tried to stay calm while thinking through how he'd explain knowing about the rifle when no evidence had been presented showing its presence. He stood and peered at each photo with great scrutiny while desperately hoping to see the rifle or even part of it depicted.

The other jurors began looking at the photos as well.

They were all high-resolution photos showing minute details, but it quickly became clear no rifle was visible.

"See? No rifle," Wilson said.

Paul said, "That's strange. I'm sorry, I could have sworn I saw one."

Someone asked, "Hey, does the inventory show which room it was in?"

Mr. Cashwell looked back at the page.

"Living room," he said, giving Paul a puzzled expression, "but I still don't see any picture that shows it."

Paul tried to conceal his mounting anxiety. He walked up to the photo of the living room and studied it closely. The photo evoked a strong sense of déjà vu in Paul, as if he were being transported into that living room. Another juror said something else, then another, but what was said, Paul never heard.

He kept staring at the image with ever-growing uneasiness and recalled more details, like the table and the two magazines lying on top of it. He felt certain one of them was *Sports Illustrated*. The cover was a man holding a football. He remembered that cover clearly but couldn't quite place it...and then he recalled, yes, I know that cover: it's Andy Reid, the Kansas City Chiefs' coach. He stared at the beige rug under the table…That was familiar as well. The feeling of having been there, of having been present at that very scene, *of seeing the room from the inside*, was overwhelming.

Paul felt the blood draining from his face, and as he walked back and sat down in his chair, the jurors rambled on, none of whom he heard because his mind was reeling. *Am I losing my mind? Was I actually inside the house?*

Did I shoot Marcus Roberts?

His mind jumped to the shotgun Daniel had used the year before to go deer hunting with some buddies in Montana. *In the basement…Could I have used it? But how could I not remember…*

Then it hit him: the sleepwalking. He suppressed a gasp. The timing matched pretty closely. He vaguely remembered thinking his car had been moved one morning. The night he knew he had sleepwalked, Daniel had said he had looked totally awake, in fact he'd had a conversation with him, and yet, he had been totally unaware of his doings. Could he have driven to the Roberts home? It seemed a stretch in some ways, and yet, it explained his recollection of things and his overpowering sense of having been in the room.

He looked at the other jurors, none sensing his eyes darting back and forth.

He began hyperventilating. Rebecca said, "Paul? Paul?"

Paul closed his eyes and breathed heavily, his chest heaving up and down and sweat beads forming on his forehead.

Mr. Cashwell stood and rushed over to Paul, instructed someone to call 9-1-1 and said, "I think he's having a heart attack," and told Paul to try to lie down on the floor. Paul leaned over in the chair and half sat, half fell onto the floor, continuing to gasp.

Nancy, the accounts receivable clerk for the doctor's office, said, "This doesn't look like a heart attack. Paul, what are you feeling? Can you hear me?"

Paul attempted to get words out and found it difficult to

speak, but uttered, "Give me a…gasp, gasp…minute."

Several of the jurors were beside him now, and the bailiff rushed in, having been summoned by one of the other members of the jury. "What's going on?" he asked.

Mr. Cashwell responded, "We have a medical situation, not sure what exactly."

The bailiff asked, "Has someone called 9-1-1?" Several jurors nodded. Seeing Paul's breathing starting to slow, the bailiff said, "He seems to be recovering a bit. You all sit tight with him a minute, and let me tell the judge." He exited the room.

Paul, lying prone on the floor now, stared at the rectangular ceiling tiles and tried to calm his mind. He closed his eyes and imagined lying on his bed, doing some of the deep breathing Tom had taught him. His breaths gradually began to moderate.

He opened his eyes and saw several heads surrounding his. Rebecca was holding his hand, her brow furrowed with concern. He gave her a weak smile. "I think I'm okay. I have no idea what just happened."

Mr. Cashwell said, "Just stay still, Paul. An ambulance is on the way."

As if on cue, Paul heard the distant sound of a siren and focused on the undulating sounds as it gradually got closer. With each inhale, he felt the pounding of his heart beginning to slow down.

He started to rise, but Maggie gently pressed his upper body back down to the floor and said, "No, Paul, stay down until the medics get here."

"Okay."

When the medics arrived, the bailiff returned and told Mr. Cashwell court had recessed for the day. All the jurors left except for Mr. Cashwell, Maggie, and Rebecca, all three huddled in the corner talking.

The medics asked Paul a series of questions, took his vitals, and inquired about his medical history and what he'd eaten that morning. He answered calmly and cogently, and after several minutes, one of them said, "Everything seems to check out okay. Your heart rate is a bit elevated but not so high that it's a concern. Do you want us to take you to the hospital?"

"No, I don't think so. I think I'm fine. Sorry for causing so much of a problem."

"It's no problem. This is what we're here for."

Mr. Cashwell chimed in. "Paul, why don't you go on in, just to get checked out?"

"I just want to go home," Paul replied. He sat up and gradually inched himself into his chair. "Did I hear someone say we're recessed for the day?"

Mr. Cashwell said, "That's correct. You'll need someone to drive you home. Is there a relative we can call?"

Rebecca spoke up and said, "I can give him a ride."

"That would be great. You're sure you don't mind, Rebecca?" Mr. Cashwell inquired.

The medics asked Paul, "Do you feel like you can stand up?"

"Yes, I think so." He was a bit shaky but rose to a standing position.

"Want a wheelchair?" Rebecca asked.

"No thanks, but I could use some water."

The bailiff, standing just out of view, left the room and came back with a cup.

Paul took a sip and immediately felt better. His body was calming down, but his mind was another matter. He didn't know exactly what to think, but he did know one thing: he knew details of that room no one else did. He started trying to remember any other events from that night but felt panic rising in him once again and so stopped thinking and focused on Rebecca: her face and eyes, the soft brown curls of hair cascading around her shoulders, and the youthful curve of her body.

She put her arm around his waist to steady him, and he thanked her as they started towards the door to leave the courthouse.

"Why don't you wait here, and I'll drive up?" Rebecca suggested.

"Are you sure?"

"Yes, I'll be right back."

As soon as she walked away, Paul pulled out his cell phone and dialed Tom. Margie answered.

"Hi, Margie," Paul said, "It's Paul Nelms. Thank goodness you picked up. Is Tom free?"

"He's with someone. Can I give him a message?"

"I need to see him right away. It's a bit of an emergency. I'm sorry to ask and wouldn't do so unless it were absolutely necessary."

"Okay, Paul. Let me talk to him as soon as his appointment leaves in about forty-five minutes. I'm guessing he'll be free around five-thirty. How about if he calls you then?"

"Great. Thank you."

Chapter 23

Paul stood there alone, feeling numb, as people filed in and out past him. He didn't like being alone with his thoughts and welcomed the sight of Rebecca's Volvo S60 as she pulled up.

"Thank you for doing this," he said, getting in.

Rebecca said, "Oh, gosh, Paul, you're welcome. How are you feeling?"

"Better," he said, and with as convincing an expression as he could muster, added, "I really don't know what happened."

"It almost looked like an anxiety attack."

"It felt a little like that, though I've never actually had one of those so don't know what one is really supposed to feel like," he laughed.

They made their way through the downtown area and into the suburbs, with Paul directing her where to turn. When they reached his street, she remarked, "Goodness, Paul, this is a beautiful neighborhood."

"Thank you. There are nice people here."

Reaching the driveway a minute later, Rebecca gasped. "What

a gorgeous home." She pulled in front of the house, turned off the car, and opened her door. "Let me make sure you get in okay."

"Sure."

Paul fished out his keys and walked up the steps with Rebecca beside him.

He opened the door. "Daniel?" he yelled. Silence.

"Come on in," Paul said, "Can I get you something?" he asked, immediately regretting the question with his mind totally focused on whether Daniel's shotgun was in its usual place. He also wanted desperately to speak to Tom.

"What do you have?"

"Most anything you'd want. Wine, cocktails, sodas, water."

"Maybe a white wine?"

"Sure." Paul showed her to the living room and returned a few moments later with white wine for them both.

"You have a stunning house," Rebecca said, her eyes perusing the spacious rooms and ornate accessories.

"Thank you," Paul said. "Hey, would you mind if I excused myself for a minute?"

"Of course," Rebecca said. "In fact, I may use the restroom myself. Is there one nearby?"

Paul led her to the bathroom around the corner, gulped down his drink, refilled it, and walked down the stairs to the basement. Daniel kept his shotgun in a safe in the storage room. Paul knew the combination and desperately hoped to see the shotgun there as Daniel had left it after his last hunting trip.

Empty.

Paul's heart began pounding. Worried about another panic attack, he tried to catch his breath and began rummaging through cabinets and in corners and other areas he could've placed it if he'd grabbed it while sleepwalking. It was nowhere to be found.

He went back to the safe and looked over the ammunition. There was a box of number one and BB shot—bird shot—and then, as expected, double aught buckshot. He looked in the box and found it half full.

Paul heard Rebecca walking around upstairs. He closed the safe door, spun the dial, and headed back up to join her—finding her in the living room holding a family photo she'd picked up from a table. "Was this your wife?" she asked, studying the photo.

"Yes, and my son Daniel. He must be out."

"She was pretty."

"Yeah. You want to see the house?"

"Oh, I'd love to. It really is lovely."

"I'm actually thinking of selling it; it's too big for Daniel and me. Please don't mind the bare spots on the wall. We had some art that I...well...sold."

They walked into the kitchen, through the large dining room, into the den, then through the music room with the player piano. "Do you play?" Rebecca asked.

"No, but my wife did. This one is a player piano." He paused, and with partly concealed bitterness, asked, "You want it?"

She laughed. "Why would you say that?"

"I have no idea anymore."

They walked upstairs, and he showed her several of the bedrooms—glad he'd made his bed that morning. Being in his bedroom with her suddenly felt very awkward and personal. She gazed around the room, and he watched her eyes while trying to decipher her thoughts.

"Where do you write?" she asked.

"Oh, down in the den. The big desk down there is my favorite spot, though sometimes I go out on that porch." He pointed to doors leading from his bedroom to a second-story screened-in lanai.

"Oh, how lovely," she said, walking over to the opening and looking out.

She stayed there a moment. Paul felt ill prepared to have a beautiful woman in his bedroom, notwithstanding the fact that he had no intention of anything happening with her up here. Daniel could walk in at any moment, after all.

He looked at his watch: almost five o'clock. "Rebecca, you were really nice to bring me home, but I do have an appointment I need to get to by five-thirty."

Rebecca said, "Oh gosh, I'm sorry. It was presumptive of me to come in like this. I should get going anyway." She smiled at him while making her way toward the bedroom door.

But as she passed, he reached and touched her arm, and she stopped and looked at him. He pulled her to him and kissed her, a long, drawn-out kiss like those that mesmerize audiences in a love story movie. They were standing beside a dresser, and she broke from the kiss long enough to set the drink down and then pulled his lips back to hers and wrapped both her arms around his neck.

For the briefest of moments, Paul forgot about the trial and was only aware of the scent of Sunflowers, the velvet touch of her lips on his, the softly audible sound of her breathing, and the welcome stirrings of a fifty-six-year-old body that suddenly felt awakened.

They stopped to look at each other. "You know," Rebecca said, "I could stay here with you tonight if you wanted me to."

Paul would have typically been elated at the prospect, but his mind went to Daniel and the need to talk to Tom.

"Thank you, Rebecca," Paul said. "I'm definitely tempted to ask you to stay, but Daniel will be home soon…and I think I'll be okay."

She nodded, saying, "Are you sure?" and slightly tightened her embrace.

This is killing me, thought Paul. "No," he whispered, "I'm not sure at all." He took a deep breath and studied her face for one last moment.

He smiled. "We're still on for dinner this weekend though, right?"

"Absolutely."

"Rebecca?" Paul started but couldn't finish the sentence, not knowing exactly what he even wanted to say.

She finished the sentence for him. "I'd better go," she said. "If you change your mind about tonight, you'll call me?"

"Of course."

They walked out of the bedroom and down the stairs toward the front door.

"Hey, I have a question for you," Paul said.

"What's that?" she said.

"Have you ever been to the Greek Isles?"

"No. When do we go?" she piped back playfully.

"I don't know yet."

He opened the front door and took her hand.

"Rebecca, thank you…" he started.

"Shh," she said, leaning in and giving him a brief kiss on the lips. "You don't need to say thanks."

She walked to her Volvo, stopped, and asked, "How will you get your car?"

"Daniel will be here soon; he can help me get it."

"Will you be there tomorrow?"

"I think so."

"And you're sure you're okay?"

"Yeah."

She extended her thumb and pinky in a mock telephone gesture, mouthed the words, "Call me," and winked before getting in the car and driving off.

He closed the door and looked at his watch. It was five-fifteen, and Tom hadn't called yet. He dialed Daniel, who picked up. "Hey, Dad."

"Hi, Son. Hey, where are you right now?"

"Best Buy. I'm working at the Cineplex tonight but don't have to be there until six."

"Would you be able to head home and give me a ride somewhere?"

"Sure. Your car messed up?"

"Not really. I'll explain later."

"Okay. How about I get home in about twenty minutes?"

"Great. Thanks, Daniel."

Paul sat down at his computer, trying to process the very real possibility that he had killed Marcus Roberts. He closed his eyes and tried to recall any other images, coming up short, and then typed "sleepwalking crimes" into his browser. Less than a second later, Google spit out 444,000 suggestions for further reading—the first one titled "Eight Criminal Cases That Invoked a Sleepwalking Defense" by a national publication.

Paul clicked on the link and began reading. He glanced at the first case, which involved a man named Boshears who was a U.S. serviceman in the UK in 1961 and had strangled a local woman—purportedly in his sleep—and disposed of the body the next day. He was arrested days later but subsequently acquitted.

The second case, involving a man named Parks, was somewhat more interesting. Paul skimmed the article...*a Canadian man developed a gambling problem...got in his car and drove to his in-laws' and bludgeoned his mother-in-law to death with a tire iron and then turned on the father-in-law...then drove to the police and said he thought he had just killed two people.*

The case referred to the man's "parasomnia" and had a hyperlink Paul clicked on to find it defined as sleep disorders involving abnormal actions, dreams, emotions, and perceptions that occur during sleep. He clicked back to the case and read Parks had highly unusual EEG readings—measures of brain activity—an abnormality consistent with a sleepwalking defense. The trial court had acquitted him, the Canadian Supreme Court upholding the verdict in 1992.

There were other cases, some dating back to the 1800s, the perpetrators convicted in about half. His situation was unlike many of them in that he had a prescribing psychiatrist who could attest that Paul was a sleepwalker; but it was also different in that

Paul clearly had a motive to kill Marcus Roberts.

He had just clicked back to another of Google's 444,000 suggestions when his cell phone rang.

"Tom, thank goodness," Paul said after picking up.

"Hi Paul. You okay? Margie made it sound like you were in some distress."

"Yes. Tom, I don't want to impose, but is there any way you could see me tonight, like maybe in forty-five minutes?"

"Sure, Tom, come on over. I can be here."

Paul exhaled. "Thank you, Tom, thank you. I'll leave in just a few minutes."

He heard Daniel drive up and walked downstairs to meet him at the door. "Thanks for coming home," Paul said. "My car is downtown. Can you drive me down there?"

"Sure, hop in," Daniel said.

Along the way, Paul explained he'd had a panic attack during jury deliberations. Daniel asked if he was capable of driving home by himself, and Paul assured him of such but that he needed to stop to see Tom first.

"Okay," Daniel said, "but let me know if you feel another one coming on, okay?"

Paul thanked Daniel again and headed to Tom's, his heart was pounding as he walked into the reception area.

"Paul," Tom said, standing up and coming to the door, "Come in."

"Um…" Paul said and suddenly broke down crying.

"Why…What in the world?" Tom said. "Paul, what happened?"

Paul composed himself and glanced up at Tom through tear-filled eyes. "I'm wondering if I killed Marcus Roberts."

Tom's face was frozen yet confused. "What? I don't understand."

"Neither do I."

"Stop for a minute and tell me what you're talking about."

Paul recounted what happened with the evidence from earlier that day. "Tom, I'm remembering things I simply would have no way of knowing without actually being in the house."

"Paul, stop a minute, this makes no sense. If you were there, how would you not know?"

Paul's face was filled with fear and despair, "Because I was sleepwalking."

Tom was trying to understand and asked, "Tell me again what it was you remember being there?"

"A rifle, one of those old timey ones with the flintlock or whatever, that fired muskets." Paul stopped midsentence and said, "Oh, my…" as if recalling a distant memory. "The night Daniel came into the bathroom when I was sleepwalking that night."

"What about it?"

"I just now remember saying I had a musket ball caught in my throat."

"Do you think you did?"

"No, Tom, of course I didn't. But it seemed like such a random thing for me to have said, and I wondered where the notion of a musket ball had even come from. Now I'm wondering if somehow I saw a musket in the house and that I started dreaming I had a musket ball in my throat after I saw it." Paul held his head in his hands. "I don't know what I think."

"Can you somehow figure out the date and see if it ties back to the date Marcus Roberts was killed?"

"That's a good thought. I don't know. I know it's close to the time."

"Wait a minute," Tom said, walking over to his desk and typing on his keyboard. "I keep records of our visits."

He studied the screen for a few moments. "Okay, I prescribed the Ambien on January seventeenth. On February twenty-sixth, you indicated you'd had a sleepwalking event three or four nights before, which would have been…around the twenty-second or twenty-third."

He looked up at Paul.

"Remind me what night Roberts was killed?"

Paul closed his eyes, not saying anything.

Tom asked again, "Was one of those the date?"

Paul nodded.

Neither spoke for several moments.

Tom came over and sat beside Paul, who was seated on the couch. "Look, we can get through this," he told him before pulling out his cell phone and calling his wife to say he'd be home late that night.

"Okay," Tom said, returning to the matter at hand. "Let's assume for a minute you shot him. You didn't know what you were doing…right?"

"Right."

"I can support you on that and have the records of when you came in. I can testify that Ambien has a side effect of somnam-bulance, or sleepwalking, and attest that I took you off it as soon as we realized it was becoming a problem. You do recall that, correct?"

Paul knew what he was getting at. "Tom, you're not responsible for any of this. You didn't do anything wrong."

"Sorry. I just think we both did what any reasonable people would do. I don't want there to be any question of recklessness on either of our parts."

"Neither of us were. The thing is, I don't recall anything specific about that night, not even talking to Daniel."

"Paul, what about the weapon? Do you own a shotgun?"

"No, but Daniel does. It's usually in the safe but wasn't there when I checked for it earlier."

"Have you said anything to Daniel about this?"

"No, I haven't told anyone but you."

"Do you think anyone suspects you?"

"No, not at all. No one has any inkling that I may have some involvement in this."

"Have you thought about what you're going to do?"

"I have no idea."

Tom stood and began slowly pacing the room, stroking his gray beard and immersed in thought.

He stopped and turned to Paul. "Let's play out the different scenarios. How do you see those from where you are right now?"

"Well, one scenario is I simply confess I may have killed him, and they do an investigation and possibly have a trial where I'm the one in the defendant's chair. Maybe they convict me for first-degree murder or a lesser charge, but whatever it is, I wind up in an orange jumpsuit."

"Yes, that seems like a possibility."

"Another...I guess," Paul said in a measured tone, "is that I confess and am not convicted due to a lack of direct evidence."

Tom listened, showing no expression.

"Another scenario....is I keep quiet about the whole thing."

Tom nodded slowly.

"Have you considered going to a lawyer? It seems like that would be a pretty good option. Maybe someone you know?"

"I don't know if I'm ready for that. If I were to decide to disclose this to anyone else, yes, that would be my next step, but I don't know if I want to do that yet."

"I understand," Tom said. "I know you aren't supposed to talk about the trial, but I think our need to figure out the best...or perhaps I should say 'least bad' solution... trumps that. Where do things stand in the trial?"

"The presentation of evidence is complete, and jury deliberations began today. We had our first vote, and the majority felt he was guilty. Seven guilty, five not guilty so far."

"How did you vote?"

"Guilty."

"Hmmm," Tom said. "If you voted now, would you vote 'not guilty'?"

"I would. I don't know how I would justify it, but I would

change my vote."

"Does that mean you're thinking about continuing on and not saying anything?"

Paul looked over at the bookshelf, then the artwork, and then at the floor as if searching for the answer somewhere in the room.

He looked back at Tom and said, "I guess I am."

"Paul, you know, if you came clean about all this right now—which I could help you do—they would possibly drop the charges against Levi. Who knows, they might not even try you. Even if they did, though, they may let you off with a mild sentence." He paused. "But if you go down this path and string things along and then the truth does indeed come out, I hope you realize the consequences for you will likely be a good deal worse, right?"

"I guess I just don't see how anyone else could find out about this. You and I are the only ones who know."

"Let me tell you something about…" Tom searched for the right word, "…truth. Truth has an intrinsic energy of its own. It's always trying to escape. It doesn't care if you are the only one who knows it or if *no one* knows. The energy to escape may drop to almost nothing, but rest assured, it never drops to zero. And it takes energy to contain it. A lie doesn't have that intrinsic energy because it isn't real. Do you understand what I am saying?"

"You make it sound like the truth has an actual identity."

"For me it does," Tom said, adding, "not in the same way as for you, but for me, yes, it does."

Paul simply acknowledged the comment with a nod.

"So, you're saying I need to confess and just take my chances?"

"No, I'm not telling you what you should do. I just want you to make a decision after weighing all the consequences of your actions. I would expect the stakes to become much higher if you try to conceal this."

"I realize that, but one thing I can tell you is that I *can* control whether Levi is convicted or not. I can vote not guilty, and I will.

He'll never be convicted while I'm on the jury."

"What are the mindsets of the other jurors who voted not guilty? Do you know?"

"Pretty much that there's reasonable doubt and no motive."

"At least that's a start."

Paul's facial expression changed, indicating something had suddenly occurred to him, and he said, "Oh my gosh, I forgot to even tell you, I had a panic attack in the jury deliberation room today when I realized I may have been in Marcus's house."

"Good heavens…a full-on panic attack? Did anyone notice?"

"Are you kidding? They thought I was having a heart attack. EMS came, and the jury was dismissed for the day."

"Paul, how could you forget to mention this earlier? I mean, doesn't that make you think twice about trying to conceal this?"

"There was a lot to update you on."

"Did you go to the hospital?"

"No, Rebecca drove me home."

"Ah, Rebecca. What about her? Will you tell her?"

"I doubt it."

"Well at this stage, maybe that's appropriate. I will say this though…Deception tends to build other deceptions and become toxic in relationships."

"I understand. Look, Tom, I think I'll be okay. I think it was the shock that caused the panic attack…at least I'm pretty sure."

"I could argue it was the truth seeking its outlet."

"Maybe," Paul offered, then added, "Tom, I do have one thing I want to ask you about. I think I need something to stay calm throughout this process, maybe some Xanax or something I could take to calm down in a given moment."

"You're still taking the Effexor, right, and not having any problems with that?"

"Still on it and no, I don't even notice I'm on it right now."

"Good. Xanax isn't a bad choice, but you should only take it if you feel another attack coming on. Taking it with Effexor can increase the chance of having a hard time concentrating and sometimes causes some dizziness, but I can write you a prescription."

"Thank you. So only use it if I feel unusually anxious?"

"Right, and don't take it when you need to drive somewhere because it can make you drowsy."

Paul nodded.

Tom said, "So are you supposed to report back for jury duty tomorrow?"

"Last I heard, yes. I'm assuming the foreman will call me tonight."

Tom handed Paul the prescription and then looked at his watch: six-forty-five. "Well, Paul, I don't know if there's a lot more we can do tonight. Anything else I can do?"

"No. Thanks, Tom. You've been a big help. I realize I've thrown a wrench into your schedule, and you've been quite accommodating. Thank you."

"That's okay, Paul. Why don't you call me tomorrow after court breaks and let me know how you're doing?"

"Will do."

Paul turned to walk out of the office, a small wall hanging catching his eye on his way out. It was a quote from Martin Luther King, Jr.: *The ultimate measure of a man is not where he stands in moments of comfort and convenience but where he stands at times of challenge and controversy.*

"Good quote," Paul remarked.

Tom nodded, "I think so too."

Arriving home after picking up his Xanax at the pharmacy, Paul walked into the den and found Daniel with a large pizza and ESPN on the television. "Got enough for us both," he said, looking up briefly. "How are you feeling??"

"Better thanks."

"Will the trial end soon?"

Paul responded, "I think so. Maybe a few days, I guess."

He went to the kitchen, poured himself a glass of wine, and grabbed a plate to share an uneventful dinner with Daniel. His phone rang a few minutes after they finished cleaning up. "Paul, hi. This is Nathan Cashwell from the jury. I was just calling to see how you're doing."

Paul walked into the kitchen and out of earshot of Daniel. "Ah, Mr. Cashwell, nice of you to call. I am much better, thank you. I don't have any idea what happened today. I think I just had some sort of spell or something, a random event of sorts."

"Do you think you'll be able to continue? We're supposed to resume deliberations in the morning."

"Absolutely. I think I can be there with no problems. Again, I am so sorry about this and really appreciate your help."

"You're sure?"

"I am."

"Okay, we'll see you in the morning."

"Thanks for calling."

Paul hung up the phone and walked back into the den. "Any games on tonight?"

"Not much of anything. I think I'm actually gonna head out to pick up Darla to go do something."

Paul wanted to ask if he'd removed his shotgun from the safe but concluded there was no way to do so without potentially arousing suspicion so just responded, "Okay, Son. Have a good time."

He refreshed his drink and sat down at his desk, trying to process the possibility that he was somehow a murderer. He closed his eyes and tried to recall any other images but was spent. He didn't want to think about the trial or Marcus Roberts anymore.

His cell phone rang again. He looked down and saw Rebecca's number.

"Hello?"

"Hi, Paul. I was just calling to check in on you…How are you doing?"

"Better, thanks. Hey, you were so nice to bring me home. I really appreciate it."

As Rebecca started to express her happiness to do it, Paul thought of how she'd called to check on him as something a girlfriend or wife would do—their relationship obviously now more intimate and her attention more focused. More than that, though, it was as if something had shifted in her head, and she decided it would be okay to be in a relationship with him. *Maybe I'm reading too much into it*, he thought. *Focus on what she's saying.*

"Will you be there tomorrow?" she asked.

"Yes, I don't think it'll be a problem. I still don't know what happened and am wondering if it was something I ate."

"Well, that's good. Just know I'm here if you need me or want me to come over."

Come over…see? Paul thought to himself. *This is new…something has definitely shifted.* He smiled and imagined her fragrance, her eyes, the feel of her body next to his, and the wavy brown hair that looked like it belonged to a younger woman. *Is this what it feels like to start falling in love again?*

"Are we still on for Friday night?" she asked.

"I was planning on it."

"Great. We could go out, or maybe I can come over and make dinner for us at your place. I love to cook. Just a thought, anyway."

"Really?" Paul chuckled. "Sure. You really don't have to, though."

"No, I'd love to, Paul."

"Well, why don't I help at least? Want me to grill something?"

"No, listen, leave everything to me. Is there anything you can't eat or don't like?"

Paul laughed again. "Nah, I'm pretty easy."

"Okay, I might do an Italian pasta with mahi-mahi. That okay?"

"Sounds great. I'll have some wines for us to try."

"Is it okay if I come over closer to five-thirty, since it'll take me some time to pull it all together?"

"Um...sure."

"I don't have to, Paul," Rebecca hesitated, concerned she'd pushed too hard. "We can just go out if you prefer."

"No, listen, five-thirty is great. We'll put on some music and open the wine and make it an evening."

"I can't wait," she said.

"Me too," Paul said, grinning broadly.

They talked for another twenty minutes about books, movies, and restaurants. Paul's book—which he'd given her earlier—came up. "I did really enjoy it, Paul. Can I keep it?"

"Of course," Paul said.

"Listen, I better go. I have some brownies in the oven I'm baking for a friend and need to take them out. I'll see you tomorrow."

"Sounds good, Rebecca. Thanks for calling."

Paul felt better than he had all day on the heels of the phone call. He walked up to his bedroom and mentally replayed the earlier scene with Rebecca, sitting on the bed and imagining her staying there with him. *That would be tough with Daniel here,* he thought.

His gaze wandered over to the travel brochure, and he thumbed to the page containing the cruise information about the Greek Isles—trying to read the itinerary but finding it difficult to focus given his restless energy. He flipped through each of the pages, looking at photos and imagining them as backdrops for him and Rebecca.

But moments later, mounting feelings of despair tempered those thoughts of Rebecca, as the reality of his legal predicament began to weigh upon him. He got in bed about ten-thirty, hoping to nod off, but it was difficult to sleep. He reached over and took a Benadryl and finally fell asleep about midnight.

Chapter 24

Walking into the kitchen to make some breakfast, Paul started to pour himself cereal but then decided against it—his anxiety wrecking his appetite and giving him heartburn—before returning upstairs to shave and shower.

Standing in front of the bathroom mirror, he lathered up his face. How would the other jurors react when he changed his vote to not guilty? *That is,* he thought to himself, *what I indeed plan to do, isn't it?* He wrestled with the question for a moment.

I mean, this Levi is a long-time criminal and gang member, there's no doubt about that. Even the defense had admitted as much. Just for the sake of argument, if Levi were convicted, how much additional time would he be given? And how much difference would that really make in the grand scheme of things when he'd spend the next twenty years of his life in prison anyway?

Twenty years. A long time, and all sorts of things could happen between now and then. Levi could have his sentence commuted, be released early for good behavior, the gang members could recant their stories…Anything was possible. If Levi were found guilty, Paul's life would likely proceed with very little interference. In fact, it might be a pretty good one: with Rebecca in it, filled with days of writing and travels to the Greek Isles. Maybe he'd own a small but upscale downtown penthouse and a second home in a warm place to winter.

The term "path of least resistance" came to Paul's head, seemingly from nowhere, and he wondered what made him think of it. When it came to getting the trial wrapped up, this particular path wasn't very clear. While it would only take convincing five "not guilty" jurors to vote "guilty," versus seven "guilty" jurors to vote "not guilty," he figured the more intractable positions might be the "not guilty" jurors. After all, many of them might feel worse about wrongfully convicting an innocent man than a juror who winds up letting a potential criminal go unpunished.

He stopped shaving for a moment and studied his face in the mirror. A question hit him: *What kind of man am I?* He searched the reflection of his eyes as if they held answers and whispered, "The real question is what kind of man will I *become?*"

Today's jury vote would likely take him down one of two paths. He could either cast a guilty verdict—which carried with it the expectation that those arguing for guilt would eventually prevail—or a not guilty verdict, greatly increasing the chance Levi would not be convicted, particularly if Paul was resolute in not changing his vote. After all, if Paul resolved to maintain a vote of not guilty, the worst case for Levi (at least in this trial) would be a hung jury.

He looked at the lines in his face, the blemishes and discolorations marking almost six decades of life, and wondered if recent worries had contributed to them. He dried his face.

Paul thought about Martin Luther King, Jr. and the quote he had read in Tom's office: "The ultimate measure of a man is not where he stands in moments of comfort and convenience but where he stands at times of challenge and controversy." He studied Levi sitting there in the defendant's chair, his former friends turning on him. He thought about the woman and young child he'd noticed sitting in the back of the courtroom, the little boy saying his father wasn't guilty. *It's funny how the question of right and wrong shifts when people's lives are inserted into the question.*

He said out loud, "Okay. I will vote not guilty." Getting dressed and putting his bottle of Xanax in his pocket, he added, "I *think*."

When Paul arrived at the jury room about eight-fifty, several people came up to him as soon as he entered and asked if he was all right. He answered in grateful and reassuring tones. He glanced around the room and took his seat at the table, noticing, with some relief, that the photograph of the Roberts house had been removed from the jury room.

Paul saw Rebecca talking to a Nancy in the corner of the room. As soon as she spotted him, she excused herself from the conversation and walked over to him. "You okay?" she whispered, placing her hand on his arm.

"Yeah. Doing fine, Rebecca."

Paul glanced over at Mr. Cashwell, who'd just entered the room, and noticed the man's gaze drop to Rebecca's hand on his arm before meeting Paul's eyes. Mr. Cashwell said with a grin, "Paul, good morning! How are we today?"

"Much better, thank you." Paul looked around the room at the jury members who were watching him and said, "In fact, thanks, everybody. I'm really sorry. I don't know what happened, but I feel fine today and am glad to be here. I would recommend, though, that you stay away from the cheeseburgers in the commissary." A few people chuckled.

Mr. Cashwell said, "Well, that's great to hear. We should get started in a minute after grabbing some coffee, for those who want it."

Mr. Cashwell poured himself a cup and took his usual spot at the head of the table as everyone followed suit around it, same seats as the day before. Paul was a little relieved not to be sitting beside Rebecca, worrying their exchanges and natural body language might give away their relationship.

Mr. Cashwell cleared his throat. "Yesterday, as you recall, we took a vote. The outcome was seven votes for guilty and five votes for not guilty. I'd like to begin by taking a new vote since you've all had a night to think about things." He handed out new slips of paper.

Paul looked down at the paper and rolled the pencil back and forth between his fingers. His instincts told him the easy solution was *not* to change his verdict. He scribbled on the paper, folded it, and turned it in.

Mr. Cashwell gathered the slips and began tabulating the anonymous votes. After a few minutes, he looked up. "Ah, so no one has changed their verdict."

"One moment," Jim piped up. "I changed my vote to guilty."

Mr. Cashwell started to recount just as Paul said, "And I changed my vote to not guilty."

"Interesting. So we're still at 7 to 5," the foreman announced.

Paul felt the need to explain himself and, concealing his true beliefs, said, "The more I thought about it last night, the more I couldn't get past the lack of a possible motive. I know it isn't a requirement, but there's no reason in the world—at least that the prosecutors talked about—explaining why Levi would have done it. It puts reasonable doubt in my mind."

When no one responded, he continued, "Also, I thought about Levi Johnson's life as it is. He's already going to jail. It isn't like he's going to be wandering the streets as part of a gang and getting into trouble. He'll be in jail for years as the driver in the drive-by shooting. So, this verdict doesn't really matter that much anyway."

"It actually matters a great deal, Paul," Mr. Cashwell stated, taken aback. "You're right about him going to jail in any event, but this verdict will indeed affect how much time he spends in prison."

Maggie added, "Plus, what about the victim's family? You think it doesn't matter to them?"

Paul glanced around the table in search of possible support from his peers but found none. "I understand. I still don't think he's guilty. Or rather, let me change that to, I don't think the State *proved* he is guilty beyond a reasonable doubt."

Nancy added, "He's exactly right. Our job is not to necessarily say if we think he did it or not. It's to determine if the State *proved* he did it. It goes back to the *presumption* of innocence; the default is that you are innocent."

Mac said, "Wait, so you all are saying that even if you thought someone committed a crime and that they were guilty but the court didn't prove it beyond a reasonable doubt, you'd still vote not guilty? Even though you truly believe the person did it?"

Several of the jurors with "not guilty" votes glanced at each other and nodded affirmatively.

Mac shook his head. "This is why so many murderers are still walking the streets."

"Wait a minute," Mr. Cashwell said. "They are actually right. It happens all the time, with guilty parties released because there simply isn't proof. Without proof, guilt can't be known. It's also about fairness. Look, there are mistrials frequently where there is very compelling evidence to convict someone. Ultimately, though, the concept of a fair trial trumps the suspect's guilt or innocence. If something about it isn't fair, the court can't convict. Fairness is the most important underpinning of our judicial system."

Mac said, "So, what was unfair about this particular trial? Are you saying something here wasn't fair to Johnson?"

Mr. Cashwell clarified, "No, I'm just saying that Paul and Nancy are right; the burden of proof is on the State."

Meredith jumped in. "Is anybody else here bothered by the fact that he didn't even testify on his own behalf?"

Rich said, "Yeah, I do wish we'd heard him at least deny it and tell his side of the story."

Mr. Cashwell said, "You can't consider that. Every suspect has the right to take the Fifth."

Wilson, in a militaristic, no-nonsense tone, forcefully tapped the table and said, "What about the fact that he was a known murderer? He probably has a rap sheet as long as this table."

Mr. Cashwell said, "You can't consider that either. Well, let me correct that…First, you don't *know* he has a long rap sheet. All you know is what the court presented. Don't forget the judge's instructions. The only thing you *know* is that he participated in the murder of Pasquez and Garcia in the drive-by shooting."

"That's enough for me," said Rich. "I don't want to be spending the rest of the week in here arguing over whether the guy is a murderer. He's a gang member and a killer; we know that. There is no way he is innocent."

Mr. Cashwell sought to correct him. "No one said he is innocent. A verdict of not guilty does not mean a verdict of *innocence*. In fact, there is no verdict of innocence. As we were just saying, it comes down to whether the State proved its case. Not guilty simply means the State didn't prove guilt beyond a reasonable doubt."

Paul, watching all of this unfold, was silent.

Mr. Cashwell said, "Let's hear from some others. How do *you* feel?"

Julia said, "Well, I understand what you're saying, Mr. Cashwell. I voted guilty, but honestly, I'm not that strongly convinced."

"Okay, well that raises an interesting question," Mr. Cashwell pointed out. "We know how everyone voted, guilty or not guilty. This is a little unconventional, but so that I can have a sense of where we are, let's go around the room and indicate how strongly convinced you are of your position. Let's say on a scale of one to ten, where one means you're absolutely convinced he's not guilty and ten means you're 100-percent sure he is guilty."

Rich said, "Eight, a guilty eight."

Julia said, "I am probably a six."

The next juror was Nancy, who said "Three."

Paul's turn was next. "Two," he said. The following jurors each indicated their numbers, which ranged from four to nine, with Mac being the only one indicating a ten.

An interesting approach, Paul thought, *probably so Mr. Cashwell knows whose positions are easiest to sway.* He wondered if he'd done it before.

For the next two and a half hours, the group rehashed the evidence of the case and the testimony of the detectives, gang members, and investigating officers.

At one point, Nancy said, "Let me ask you all a question: How would you feel if you were Levi Johnson? You're being tried by a group of people, most of whom probably grew up with many more chances in life than he's ever had."

Mac interjected, "Okay, there she goes. I knew it would happen eventually, the murderer as the victim. Let's all feel bad for the murderer who grew up poor and couldn't help it." Mac shook his head and muttered, "You people…" under his breath.

"Hang on," Mr. Cashwell said. "Let's try not to let this get personal. We may be in here a long time and need to show each other some respect."

Nancy stared at Mac, neither speaking.

Rebecca said, "I agree with part of what Mac said actually. This guy is a known killer. What percentage of the population could kill a person in cold blood?" No one answered. "Not very many, right? So, what are the chances that someone happens to drive down that particular area, at that particular time, with a shotgun…using buckshot I might add…and happens to kill this Roberts guy?" She looked around the room, a few heads nodding in agreement.

Nancy responded, "Well, the population that could do it may be higher than you think if you add in people who are on drugs. My kid sister is an addict. Two years before she became addicted, she was a great kid…straight A's in school, easy for my parents to control, came in on time, the whole nine yards. Then she starts using drugs and before long, she's caught in addiction. Mom and Dad cut her off financially, and she winds up stealing money from the register at a fast-food place where she worked. The cameras caught the whole thing. She ended up getting let off with what I consider a slap on the wrist…I still sort of disagree with that…but anyway, my point is that she did not fall into that portion of the population you're referring to as bad people." She paused. "There are good people who go down bad roads all the time. It's less rare than you think."

Paul showed no expression. Nancy could have been talking about *him*.

"I can attest to that as a recovering user," Maggie chimed in. "I haven't used for eight years, and one thing I've learned is that when someone is struggling, it often brings out a side of them that isn't the true person. What you're seeing is a result of something else. I don't even know if there really are 'bad' people."

"Are…you…*serious?*" Mac said incredulously, "*No* bad people? So, child molesters, cop killers…rapists…You're saying they aren't *bad* people?"

"All I'm saying is that in some cases, drugs and alcohol can change a person's mind. They may be fine when they aren't under the influence but completely different otherwise."

"That ain't what you were just saying," Mac scoffed.

"Well, that's what I'm saying *now*. Take Levi Johnson…Was he drugged up? Yes, he was. Nobody, not even his attorney, denies that."

"So what if he was?" Mac said.

Wilkson looked at Nancy and said, "Are you saying it's like being guilty at a different level? Kind of like, if someone isn't under the influence and kills somebody, that's more serious than someone in a drug-induced state and out of his head? Because if you are, I don't agree with that…Guilty is *guilty*."

Jim, who'd recently changed his verdict to guilty, said, "I may know what you mean. There are things people do where I can't comprehend why they'd want to do them. Thank goodness I don't have some of those desires to begin with, but here's the point: I doubt they knowingly chose to have those desires. I think genetics determines some of that stuff."

Nancy nodded and said, "My main point is that the brains of some of these people are *sick* rather than *bad*. We can label someone as either a good person or a bad person all we want, but so often, they're sick or hurt."

"I've heard everything," Mac said, and looking at Mr. Cashwell, said, "I don't know how we can possibly expect to get a conviction when we have people saying, 'Oh these poor people are just sick and need our help.'" He stood to get a cup of coffee. "Honestly, this pisses me off. This is what's wrong with our whole frigging country."

Mr. Cashwell interjected, "Look, I think we're getting a bit astray here. Let's take a ten-minute break and we meet back at ten-forty-five."

Paul filed out behind the other jurors to go to the restroom and noticed Mr. Cashwell walk over to Mac, put a hand on his shoulder, and say a few words to him before returning to the table and looking at some notes he'd been writing.

Paul found Rebecca waiting in the hall for him after he finished up in the bathroom. "Hi! How are you holding up?" she asked.

"Doing great. You okay?"

"Doing fine," she smiled. They walked back into the room together.

Mr. Cashwell looked up as they entered. Once Paul was about to take his seat, Mr. Cashwell said, "Paul, do you have a second?" and gestured for him to step out into the hallway.

Paul followed Mr. Cashwell out. "How are you feeling, Paul? You doing okay?"

"Yes, Mr. Cashwell. Doing fine, thanks. I'm feeling fine."

"Paul, I want to chat with you sometime when you have a few

minutes. Just about something I've been noticing is all."

Paul frowned. "Can you give me an idea of what it's about?"

Mr. Cashwell looked around and said in a lowered tone, "Look, Paul, I don't really know how to say this without just coming out and saying it…but it seems like there may be something going on between you and Rebecca. I don't know for sure, and I'm not asking. But let me just say that something like that could be grounds for throwing out our verdict if it were discovered that there had been a romance within the jury. There've been a number of cases where the jurors were sent home after a romance was discovered."

Paul nodded and said nothing.

"Again, I'm not asking if there is. All I'm asking is that if there is indeed something developing or something that *has* developed, please put that on hold until this is over, okay?"

"Sure," Paul said, knowing his lack of denial likely amounted to an admission of guilt and that Mr. Cashwell's hunch was correct.

"Fine, Paul," Mr. Cashwell said, "That was all I needed to say. Thanks for your discretion on this. I don't *think* this will be a lengthy process anyway."

Paul smiled, "Good."

Mr. Cashwell added, almost as if an afterthought, "Having said that, this deliberation process is like an evolution of the truth coming out…It can't be rushed."

Paul walked back into the jury room, and Rebecca looked at him and mouthed, "Everything okay?"

Paul nodded and quickly returned to his seat as Mr. Cashwell asked for the few conversations around the table to stop. "Folks, it's almost eleven o'clock, and we've had a few hours to talk. I want to take another vote to see where things are."

He pulled out a stack of slips to pass down the line before gathering them and tabulating as he did before.

"Eight to four, in favor of guilty," he said. Looking up, he asked, "Who changed?"

Julia, the retired teacher, raised her hand.

"About time," Mac said, making an exasperated sound, adding, "Can you talk some sense into the others?"

Chapter 25

The jury broke for lunch. Rebecca walked to the commissary with Maggie and Meredith while Paul headed to a nearby sandwich shop and ate in his car.

At two o'clock, the jury reconvened and debated into the afternoon, Paul mostly remaining silent. Frustrations rose about an hour into the process, Mac looking at Paul, Nancy, Maggie, and John and saying, "You people need to start seeing what all of us are seeing: that this is an open-and-shut case. We need to finish this up. We're wasting time and about to let a good man's life end without there being any consequence for it."

He looked around at the other jury members' faces and went on, saying, "I mean it. You four are sitting there feeling sorry for this Johnson. You know who I feel sorry for? Marcus Roberts. The guy minding his own business and watching TV peacefully like any one of us might do in the living room one night. Someone rings the doorbell or knocks at the door; he goes to see who it is and gets blown away. Who of you saying not guilty is thinking about *him?*"

"It has nothing to do with him," Paul said.

"Excuse me?!" Mac was incensed and repeated with mounting disbelief, "*Nothing* to do with him?" He looked around the room to see if others were as angry as he was. "How does it have nothing to do with him? Without him, there *is* no murder!" He was shaking with agitation. "I don't understand you people. God help us as a country if it's people like you making it up."

"Folks, let's settle down," Mr. Cashwell said. "Mac, I think what Paul is saying is that Mr. Roberts, and the kind of person he was and what he was doing, doesn't really affect whether Levi Johnson is guilty or not. Mr. Johnson's guilt is a function of the evidence."

"Which is plenty," Mac said.

Maggie interjected, "Let me ask you a question, Mr. Cashwell. What if we think this doesn't meet the definition of first-degree murder? First degree means it was planned. I'm not sure this was planned; I think Levi may have just snapped."

Mr. Cashwell responded, "Well, 'planning,' when it comes to first-degree murder, only means it was done with intent—which can happen mere moments before the act occurs. It's not as if the event must be planned out days in advance. For example, if Levi Johnson—upon seeing the house or a Confederate flag or maybe even simply recalling seeing it there one day—said to pull over, then the moment he told the driver to do so signifies full intent."

Maggie said, "I would still feel better if we at least had the option of a second-degree murder charge. Do we?"

"No. In some cases we would, but the prosecution decides that ahead of time. If they feel like they have a strong enough case, they may not want to give the jury that option. A sympathetic jury will often drop down to that lesser charge when it's an option. If it isn't an option, the jury must decide between guilt or innocence, and it forces their hands. That's basically where we find ourselves in this case."

She persisted, "And if we asked the judge if we could consider second-degree murder?"

"He couldn't grant it; it's just not the way the process works. The prosecution drives that."

"Leave it alone, Maggie," Mac said. "The man said it isn't an option."

Maggie said, "I have an idea. Can we put up a blackboard and write out and discuss each piece of evidence and how we should look at it?"

Meredith agreed, and for the next couple of hours, they pored over the testimony and evidence and assigned weights for the relevance of each. Not surprisingly, positions on evidence correlated with the side of the verdict, meaning that if a juror had voted guilty, he or she tended to believe all or most of the evidence was compelling, while someone voting not guilty tended to think the evidence less strong.

Late in the afternoon, the jury took a break, and everyone walked outside to use the restrooms. Rebecca waited in the hallway for Paul, who filed out directly ahead of Mr. Cashwell. Paul smiled at her as he walked right past. With a slight look of confusion on her face, she called out, "Paul?" Mr. Cashwell continued walking toward the restroom as Paul stopped and walked back over.

"Come over here with me for a second," he said softly to her, nodding toward the other side of the hallway.

Rebecca followed.

"Hey, Mr. Cashwell talked to me this morning and asked if there was something going on between us. Apparently, they can throw out the verdict if they think a relationship has developed between two of the jurors."

"I can't see how it's his business," she said but then added, "I guess it isn't his decision though."

"We just need to keep things on the down low while we're in the courthouse, okay?"

"You mean I can't come up to you and throw my arms around you and kiss you?" she asked with a mischievous smile Paul found pleasantly provocative.

"Sure you can! Just not here," he responded, winking at her. "Hey, I have to hit the head; let's talk later tonight."

"Okay. Call me later."

The jury met for an additional hour before Mr. Cashwell suggested they conclude that day's deliberations. They took one last vote, this one by a show of hands. When Nancy didn't raise her hand either time, Mr. Cashwell said, "Nancy, am I mistaken, or did you not vote?"

She replied, "You're not mistaken. I didn't. I think I've concluded that even if you're sick or have a mental disorder or whatever, it doesn't change the question of guilt; and there really isn't anyone else who could have done this, so I'm changing my vote to guilty. Count me as a guilty vote."

A relieved expression came to several jurors' faces, Mac's most notably.

Mr. Cashwell said, "I think we're making progress here. Our job is simply to get a consensus. It's Wednesday, and we've gone from seven guilty and five not guilty on the first day to nine guilty and three not guilty now. Let's see if we can all become comfortable with arriving at a unanimous verdict by the end of the week, which gives us tomorrow and Friday. I know many of you are away from work and other things you need to be doing."

Paul and Rebecca walked out separately, Paul heading straight to Tom's office.

* * *

He arrived at about five-thirty and walked in. Tom was on the phone and waved him in to sit down, as Margie had apparently left for the day. Tom hung up the phone and said, "Paul, hi, sorry. How are you today? How did things go in court?"

"It went okay. Lots of things whirling through my head. Tom, I know I'm not supposed to discuss the case, but I do need to talk about it…That's still okay, right?"

"Of course."

"There are three of us left now voting 'not guilty.'"

Tom nodded. "So, by 'us,' you mean you also, correct?"

"Yes, it wasn't as easy as I thought it would be."

"Are you glad you did?"

"I think so. I think I did the right thing," Paul said. "I don't know where this thing goes though. There are a couple of jurors who seem to have pretty intractable positions on the guilty side, one in particular."

"I see. Paul, do you have any more recollections of the events from that night? Can we talk again about your flashback with the images in the room…the recollection of the details…what you remember?"

"We can, but I can tell you it won't do any good. I've been doing that for the past two days and keep coming up short."

"I think trying to spend some time on this could help. I know that you believe you may have been there that night, that you killed Marcus Roberts. I wonder if that is necessarily the case. I know that you have a strong feeling of being in that room, and that the sleepwalking timing matches up, but still, I'm curious if there might be some way for you to recall any clear and concise events from that night."

"I really don't see how."

Paul's phone suddenly vibrated in his pocket, and he immediately pressed the button to silence it.

Tom asked, "Do you need to take that?"

"No. If it's important, it'll go to voicemail."

"Okay. Well anyway, I have a friend who specializes in something called EMDR. It stands for eye movement desensitization and reprocessing. It's usually used for recalling past trauma and for dealing with panic attacks. Based on what he's told me about it in the past, I'm wondering if it might help us with answering the question of whether you killed Marcus Roberts."

"Tom, I don't know if I *want* to know."

"It's your choice, of course."

"Let me think about it. The trial will be over by the time we'd even get into all that…I think."

Tom nodded. "How are things with you and Rebecca?"

"Well…interesting. The foreman figured out we're involved and warned me it could be grounds for throwing out a verdict. So, we have to put things on hold—at least in the courthouse—until this is over. It's interesting though…she seems to have developed much more interest in me after she came to my house."

"What do you make of that?"

"I'm not sure. I mean she came in, and I showed her around…I guess I'm just saying she seems to have gotten a lot more interested after she realized I'm pretty comfortable financially."

"Is that bad?"

"I'm not saying it's bad, it's just…I guess I just wish her interest was based on my rugged good looks and charming personality," Paul said, smiling.

Tom laughed and said, "Paul, I had a young woman in earlier this week who was describing a man she was interested in. When I asked her to describe him, do you know what she said? She said, 'Oh my gosh, he's a dream…His credit score is over 700.'"

Paul chuckled.

Tom added, "Don't get me wrong, I'm not saying Rebecca shouldn't care about your financial stability. The fact is, there are a lot of men out there who aren't responsible; if people can't manage their finances, they often have trouble managing other aspects of their lives including relationships. Women seem to have a sixth sense for those kinds of things. Some don't realize they have it, but many do."

"I'll take your word on that."

"If that was part of her motivation for being interested in you, would that affect your opinion of *her*?"

"I don't know," Paul responded.

Tom smiled, and for a moment, no one said anything. "Paul, is there anything I can do to help you as you go through this?"

"You're doing it, Tom," Paul said. "Just having someone to talk to so openly like this…I can't tell you what a relief it is."

"I'm glad to hear that," Tom said. "In some ways, you're allowing a little of the truth to get out, helping some of that intrinsic energy to escape."

Paul said, "Yeah, I hear you on that." Then, after reflecting a moment, added, "You know, five years ago, I was married to who I thought was a wonderful and devoted wife. Things were great, and I was getting ready to publish a new book. Had you told me then that within five years, my wife would have had an affair and committed suicide and I'd be on a jury trying to decide if I was actually guilty of murder, I would never have believed it."

"I still don't know if I can believe it myself, Paul," Tom said. He paused and then said, "Paul, do you really think you could have done it?"

Paul responded, "That's the thing. I don't know that I'll ever know. There is no way to go back to that night and record myself somehow, to go and see if my DNA is on the door where I may have knocked or rang the doorbell; there is no way to know anything. All I have is the evidence that points to me: I was sleepwalking at the time, I had a weird musket ball sleepwalking incident on the night he was killed, and I think he had a musket rifle in his house, my vague recollection of being in that room, my wanting him dead, maybe even my subconscious telling me I should have settled the score for Katherine, like Tony said he was willing to do. There is more evidence and motive pointing to me than there is to Levi. The hard part is knowing, and yet not knowing. That's the burden of evidence, of having some but not enough…wondering if you're a killer does strange things to your mind."

Tom nodded.

"In the meantime, I'm trying to figure this out, Tom...trying to be strong, trying to figure out a solution."

"Paul, do you know what Darwin said was the single-most important determinant of survival?"

"No, what?"

"It wasn't intellect or strength; it was the ability to *adapt*."

"I can see that," Paul said, "but understanding that and doing that are two different things." Paul looked at his watch and saw it was getting late. He stood. "See you tomorrow night, same time?"

"Sure."

Paul walked out and got into his car. When he pulled out his phone to check in with Daniel, he saw the missed call was from Rebecca and that she'd left him a voicemail:

"Paul, hi, it's Rebecca. I just wanted to call to say hey and make sure everything's okay. No big deal, just give me a call when you can. Okay? Thanks Paul. Bye!"

He smiled at her cheery "Bye!" and then continued listening when he realized she'd never actually hung up. He could hear a shuffling sound—perhaps the phone being returned to her purse—and then Rebecca's voice in the background. "Oh, it's just a guy I met on the jury. He has a gorgeous home he wants to sell."

Whoever she was speaking to—Paul couldn't tell if it was a man or woman—said something he couldn't understand in response, and then he heard Rebecca chuckle and say, "You don't think I thought of that?"

Paul's heart sank. Even he, who was so well schooled in the use of words, was amazed at the emotional punch that a single word such as "just" could harbor.

Rebecca stopped speaking at that point, the remaining two minutes of the recording filled with the swish and jiggle of her walking. Paul listened with such intensity that he nearly ran a red light and made sure to save the message when it eventually ceased playing.

He wondered, *Is this what it's like to date again?* He sighed, the term "just a guy" reverberating in his head. So, that was what he was to her: "Just a guy…with a gorgeous home."

"I'm a *sale*," he murmured though pursed lips.

He called Daniel.

"Hey, Dad."

"Hi. I'm on the way home. Need anything?"

"Nope, thanks."

"You in tonight?"

"No, going out in a minute with Freddie, Doug, and Lee. We're thinking about taking a weekend trip in the fall and we're going to plan it."

"Ah. Sounds good. Well, if you boys do any drinking, Uber home or call me. Actually, no, just Uber since it'll be past my bedtime." He laughed.

"Okay, Dad."

They hung up. Freddie, Lee and Doug were Daniel's hunting buddies, and Paul thought about the missing shotgun—something Daniel had apparently not discovered or otherwise said anything about if he had. *Could I have used it on Roberts and thrown it away? Did I put it somewhere else in the basement? What if Daniel discovered it missing?*

Another thought occurred to Paul: *If I can find the same model and replace it, Daniel might never know the difference.* After all, Daniel's gun was still new-looking, having been purchased only a few years earlier from a local outdoor equipment store as a Christmas present. Rather than head straight home, Paul turned around and drove there instead.

He headed straight for the gun section. The man behind the counter asked, "Can I help you?"

"Yeah, I'm looking for a Remington Model 870."

"Sure, that's a pretty good seller for us. Unfortunately, we don't have any in stock right now but might get some in a few weeks. Want me to order one for you?"

"Nah. I'll look around and see if I can find one somewhere else. Thanks."

Paul walked out to his car. Chances were good, he figured, that the new shotgun's appearance would be identical to the one he had bought Daniel—gun styles seldom changed from one year to the next, and Daniel had kept his gun in pristine condition.

Paul went to two other stores, the second of which had a Remington Model 870. He bought it.

He drove home, checked to make sure Daniel had indeed left, put the gun in the case in the basement, and then disposed of the box in a dumpster behind a nearby shopping center.

Chapter 26

The next morning, jury deliberations began at nine o'clock as usual. Mr. Cashwell started by saying they would stay late tonight if necessary. He began by reminding the jurors that they were not far from reaching a successful outcome, as nine to three was not *that* far from unanimity.

Mr. Cashwell opened up the discussion by asking, "Has anyone had any new thoughts since last night?"

Mac and Maggie began sparring.

Mac: "Yes, I want to know how anyone can have a reasonable doubt here?"

Maggie: "You're talking about a man's life."

Mac: "No, you aren't. His life is over anyway."

Maggie: "What about the life of his family? Have you seen the lady in the back with the little boy? I bet that's his family."

Mac: "That has nothing to do with anything."

Maggie: "Doesn't matter if it has anything to do with it or not, my point is that you seem to be minimizing the implications if we convict the wrong guy."

Mac: "I'm not wrong."

Maggie: "Three of us think you are."

Paul interjected. "Besides, even if I thought he did it, and I don't think he did, I don't think it was proven beyond a reasonable doubt."

Mac turned to Paul and said, "Can you please explain to me why Marcus Roberts' killer should be let go, scot-free, simply because Mike Edwards didn't do as good a job as he should have?"

"It's not about the job the prosecuting attorney did. In fact, he did a good job with what he had to work with."

Rebecca spoke, "I feel sorry for Levi Johnson, I do. But I also think about the probabilities. What is the probability that someone else was driving down that street at the same time, the chance that Ms. Howard would see a car that was similar?"

Nancy interrupted and said, "But what about Ms. Howard's vision?"

"Let me finish," Rebecca said. "What is the probability that a different killer would have used a shotgun, which seems impractical, and the same size and type of ammunition? When I take all those things together, yes, I guess it's possible it was someone else; but is that a reasonable probability?"

Paul said, "But if it's not one-hundred percent or at least close to it, shouldn't you be voting not guilty?"

Rebecca said, "Not necessarily. Paul, you voted guilty originally as I recall. Are you saying that you know with one-hundred percent certainty that he's not guilty?"

Rebecca turned to the other jurors. "Are you, Maggie? John? Certain at a one-hundred-percent level?"

Paul chimed in, "I am one-hundred-percent certain they didn't prove it to a one-hundred-percent certainty level."

Rebecca said, "I have no idea what you mean."

"Sure you do," he replied.

Rebecca stared at him, and Paul realized they were seeing new sides of one another.

"So you're saying I know what you mean but I'm just being

obstinate, is that it?"

Paul smirked.

"Yeah, that's right, laugh," she said defiantly. "He's a lifelong crook."

Mac said, "Damn right."

Paul said, "That's very judgmental."

Rebecca's eyes flashed with mounting anger, and she blurted out, "Here's a news flash Paul…We're a jury. We're *supposed* to be judgmental." A couple of people chuckled, and she shook her head in exasperated disbelief.

She went on, "I don't understand your change here, Paul. You started out 'guilty' and then suddenly, after you have your spell— or whatever it was—you change to 'not guilty.' What I worry about is whether something happened to your brain that compromised your mental capacity."

Now it was Paul's turn to stare at her. She went on, "And I know another thing: I am ready to get back to work and my job. I'm getting tired of being locked up in here with you people going around in circles."

Paul watched Rebecca as she spoke and began to consider how little he really knew her, having been so captivated by her beauty that he hadn't focused a great deal on what resided beneath it. He didn't understand her perspective nor care for the sarcasm, especially directed at him. Those thoughts begged even more nagging questions about the true source of her interest in him.

Mac added, "He even looks guilty."

Maggie asked, "Is that because he's *black*?"

Mac fired back, "No, it's not because he's black. It's because he looks guilty. You people act like everything is about race; it isn't."

John said, "If he was white, I bet you wouldn't be saying he looked guilty."

Mac shot back, "Don't be an idiot. Why do I have to be on a jury with a stinking idiot?"

John, who was over six feet tall and muscular, stood up—his presence quite imposing—and asked, "Who are you calling a stinking idiot?"

Mac, whose paunchy physique seemed to shrink behind the table, shook his head and said nothing.

Mr. Cashwell stood and said, "John, please sit down. Mac, I will ask you to restrain your remarks to those appropriate for this deliberation." He then turned to the group.

"Look, I know you all are tired of this. I am too. This isn't my first time serving as jury foreman. What I will tell you is that we are making progress, but you need to trust the process. There is wisdom in the way we arrive at a solution here, but it isn't fast, and it isn't always direct."

The testy exchanges seemed to alleviate some of the tension and suspended the tendency for many jurors to glance at the clock every few minutes. For the first time in several days, there seemed to be no one with the energy or desire to talk. The mood was restless, and people's frequent trips to the coffee pot only added to a caffeine-enhanced impatience.

When they broke for lunch, Rebecca walked briskly out of the courthouse by herself, and Paul returned to his car to eat another turkey club from his newly discovered sandwich shop.

The jurors returned at two o'clock, and for most of the afternoon, little was said that hadn't been said and littler still that didn't have an edge to it. Minutes ticked by in silence, with occasional observations that often went unanswered. At one point, someone attempted to lighten the mood by asking, "Anybody read *No Exit* by Sartre?"

Mac simply responded, "No, nobody has."

A little before five o'clock, Rich asked, "What do you think about letting us out a little early today? I mean, no one is saying anything. I think we're pretty much set where we are and just talked out at this point. I need to go do some things and didn't count on this taking me away from my job this long. I have to check in with my supervisor about missing work next week."

Mac said, "Yeah, do you know how much this is costing me? I mean personally? I'll tell you: one-thousand, one-hundred bucks per week. I get paid twenty-five dollars a *day* for being in here with you all, twenty-five dollars a day. That's three bucks an hour. I make twelve-hundred twenty-five dollars a week driving a truck for Walmart. Take the difference between that and the hundred twenty-five and there you have it: one-thousand, one-hundred dollars, all for having to put up with you all for a week. I'll be damned if I'm going to miss another week of pay."

A couple of other jurors nodded and looked to Mr. Cashwell, who found himself nodding as well. He looked at Mac. "We'll have a decision soon. Mac, your presence and perspective are important. I think one of two things will happen in the next few hours: Either we will arrive at a unanimous decision or, if we don't get any movement, we may have to go to the judge and say we couldn't reach a verdict."

"You mean a hung jury?" someone asked.

"Yes."

"What happens in that case?"

Mr. Cashwell responded, "Depends. Sometimes they empanel a new jury if the case is strong enough. Sometimes they just drop the charges. I'm guessing here they would retry."

"How often does a jury deadlock?"

Mr. Cashwell said, "Probably in about ten percent of cases. It isn't usual, but it happens more frequently than most people think."

Paul thought about the prospect of a hung jury and what that would mean for Levi. He figured a new jury would eventually find him guilty. After all, had Paul not known—or at least suspected—that he himself may be the killer, he would have maintained his original guilty verdict.

It was five-thirty, and eleven exhausted people were about ready to walk out of the jury room if Mr. Cashwell didn't allow them to recess. The judge sent the bailiff to check on the status of deliberations, and Mr. Cashwell advised him they were still not unanimous but would proceed to a final vote before breaking for the evening. As soon as the bailiff was gone, Mr. Cashwell looked around at the weary faces of the jury. His eyes lingered on the three who had voted not guilty. "Paul, Maggie, and John, any change?"

John, looking down at the table, said, "I give up...guilty."

He looked at Paul and Maggie. "Paul, Maggie, here's how I see it. We have one of two options. Either we stick it out and this becomes a hung jury, in which case the whole thing starts over with a new jury, and I have little doubt the new jury will convict him. Or we save some time and steps and money and aggravation and go ahead with it. The three of us aren't going to change things in the end."

"Finally, we have some sense," Mac said, "John, that is exactly right."

Mac looked at Paul and Maggie. "Can't you two see he's right? There is no way you will win this."

Maggie looked at Paul. "Paul, I'm sorry. I have to admit, I'm ready for this to be over. My kid is sick, and I'm tired of being insulted in here. Okay...guilty."

It was as if a shot of electricity surged throughout the room, everyone's attention suddenly glued on Paul. It was one of the things he'd feared most: being the lone holdout juror in favor of a not guilty verdict.

"Just a minute," Paul said. He went over to the credenza, poured some cold coffee into his empty cup, pulled the bottle of Xanax from his pocket and took one—washing it down with some grounds from the bottom of the carafe.

He sat back in his chair, wondering how long the Xanax would take to kick in, and felt a certain resignation: fearing he wouldn't be able to maintain his not guilty vote.

Mr. Cashwell's gaze was fixed on Paul, hopeful that he might acquiesce as a result of the prodding from the other jurors. Mr. Cashwell looked at the clock. "Paul, I don't want to put undue pressure on you, but if you can see it within the realm of possibility that you might be wrong about all this, that the rest of us are overwhelmingly in support of a guilty verdict, we could wrap this up here right now, all go home and get on with our lives."

Paul stared at a spot on the table, wishing the Xanax would kick in.

Mr. Cashwell continued, "As Rebecca said, it *was* sort of sudden how you changed your vote, you know? You were originally voting guilty. Doesn't that tell you something? Doesn't that imply something might have happened to you that caused you to no longer think about this in a reasonable way?"

Paul said nothing.

"Paul...Say something...What are you thinking?" Mr. Cashwell asked.

Paul shifted in his chair. "I don't know what to think. I'm exhausted, I'm stressed out, I'm ready to have this off my back."

Meredith said, "We all are, Paul. It's in your hands."

Paul looked up at their eleven faces, all transfixed on him.

He thought about Levi, the woman in the back of the courtroom, the little boy, the truth trying to get out, the consequences of living with the knowledge he'd probably convicted the wrong man, being able to go home and return to the life he knew.

"I don't know," he said.

Julia, the reserved woman who was a retired teacher, said, "Paul, what is *wrong* with you? How can you not see what we all now see?'

For the next twenty minutes, he was pressured, questioned, and challenged by every member of the jury. Even with the Xanax taking effect, it was difficult to endure. He looked at the clock; it said five after six.

Mac, noticing, said, "Yeah, that's right. It's after six o'clock, and it's time to go home."

"We don't want to have to go through all this tomorrow. Come on, Paul!" Wilson said harshly.

"I agree!" Rich said.

"Look, let's go, Paul," Mac said. "Do the right thing."

The right thing, Paul repeated in his mind. He looked down to avoid eye contact and swallowed.

He said, "Okay."

"Okay?" Mac said, "You said okay…Meaning guilty?"

Paul nodded.

A cheer erupted from several members of the jury.

Jury members patted each other on the back, a few coming over and assuring Paul that he'd done the right thing. That it was justice for Marcus Roberts and that somewhere, Roberts was probably smiling down on them that very minute.

Julia, eyes closed, whispered, "Praise be to God."

Paul looked at Rebecca, who smiled and mouthed, "Thank you."

Mr. Cashwell said in a loud voice, "Hold it down, folks, hold it down. We need to make this official. Let me hand out the slips of paper again. I want you to write down the verdict one last time so we can say we have a unanimous verdict here."

Paul took one of the slips and looked at it for a moment. The other eleven wrote their one-word responses on the slips and turned their attention to Paul, who was still holding his slip.

Paul turned it over in his fingers and took a deep breath. If Levi were found guilty, there was no way Paul could ever be prosecuted. He thought for a moment about his life, where he'd be in years to come, and how this week on the jury, even this moment, was placing him on a path that was one of the most important crossroads of his life.

How does one process so much at one juncture? He thought about Tom and what he'd have advised him to do. Everyone was staring at him. He looked down and wrote "Guilty," folded the paper, and handed it to the person to his left.

Mr. Cashwell gathered the slips and marked the piece of paper as he counted each one, finishing the last one with the exclamation, "Twelve guilty verdicts! That is indeed great news. Ladies and gentlemen, thank you. I will tell the bailiff we have reached a unanimous decision, and I am guessing that we will give our final verdict tomorrow morning. Now, and this is important, I don't want you thinking about this case, talking about this case, or watching TV or doing anything concerning this case that could affect your vote from where it is today."

Mr. Cashwell, looking at the sheet with twelve guilty marks, asked, "Let's see, what is today's date?"

Someone said "July 25th," which Mr. Cashwell wrote down.

Mr. Cashwell said, "Folks, technically, we aren't quite through. Everyone please plan on being here a little early tomorrow, maybe eight-thirty, so we can make sure we're all unanimous before going to report to the Court. There will be a little bit left for us to do in the sentencing phase, but we're almost wrapped up."

Paul packed up his few things and exited the room quickly, a couple of people patting him on the back as he walked out. He desperately wanted to get out of the room and felt much better as soon as the evening air hit him, though he wasn't sure if it was the fresh air or the Xanax kicking in. Either way, he was grateful for the relief. He felt little regret about leaving without speaking to Rebecca, still resentful about the exchange they'd had and the telling voicemail.

He tried calling Tom on the way home, but there was no answer, and he figured Tom must have headed home when he didn't hear from him. He drove home, arriving at about seven o'clock.

Daniel was watching television. "Hey, Son," Paul said as he walked in the door.

"Hey, Dad," Daniel said flatly.

"Something wrong?" Paul asked.

"Girl problems…Darla and I broke up."

"Sorry to hear that. Maybe things will get patched back up."

"Doubt it, but thanks. How is the trial going?"

"I think we're about done. I still can't talk about it but should be able to soon."

"I know you're looking forward to being done."

"I am."

Paul said, "Maybe you and I both need a change of scenery. Maybe we should plan a trip."

"Where to?"

"What would you think about a cruise? I had thought about one to Greece. Or maybe the Greek Isles."

"Awesome. I would do that."

"I'll let you look at the brochure I have upstairs when I go up."

Chapter 27

When Paul woke up at six o'clock the next morning, he sat in bed for a few minutes, thinking about the events that had transpired the day before. He was still troubled by the guilty verdict. *Could Maggie actually be right? Does how I vote really even matter?*

He rose from bed, walked downstairs, and ate a quick breakfast. At about six-thirty, he got in his car and drove to a shopping center not far from his house, parking in front of a twenty-four-hour grocery store that he knew had a floral section. At the refrigerated section of arrangements Paul reached in and pulled out a short vase that had an overflowing assortment of flowers and greenery.

Paul returned to his car, secured the arrangement in the bottom of his back seat, and pulled out of the shopping center. He drove about four miles to Richland Memorial Gardens, drove through the entrance, past a large section of holly trees and stopped. He picked up the flowers and walked to a large gravestone, which had an empty space beside it.

He looked down at it and read the name, Katherine Elizabeth

Nelms, Born May 2, 1968; Died August 15, 2018. He recalled the occasion when he and Katherine had bought the companion plots, and he now wondered if that space beside her would in fact be his final resting place. He noticed three fresh red roses lying beside her headstone. Daniel would not have left those, but he had an idea who had. He resisted the temptation to stomp on them or to fling them into the bushes, but instead simply lowered his vase beside them.

"Hello, Katherine," he said softly. "I've done a lot of thinking over the past few months, and I wanted to talk. Can you hear me? I've wondered that before, whether you can hear me, and I think you can. I hope so, anyway.

"I guess the first thing I want to say is that I forgive you. I know how easy it is to wander off course, to find yourself caught up in a mistake that grows, a deception that snowballs, even a relationship that may be a wrong one. And I think I understand the letter that you let me find. Honestly, I wish you had written one to me explaining everything, I really do. It would have been easier for me. I think I would have benefitted from reading that you still loved me…you did, didn't you? Or you do? I don't know exactly how to ask you that. Katherine, I guess what I'm saying is, I'm glad I married you. And I'm sorry for my own shortcomings. I probably failed to do some things I should have done."

He looked at the morning mist burning off the ground and added, "I seem to have gotten myself into a bit of a fix. I think it's all worked out now, but there are things about myself I've learned, and I'll need to live with that. I'm not as good a man as I thought I was. I realize that sounds prideful, to say I thought I was a good man, but I really did."

Paul closed his eyes and shivered at the early morning breeze. Then he heard, not in his ears but in his head, Katherine's voice:

Thank you, Paul. I was so sick. It wasn't anything that you did or didn't do. I was in so much pain. Hurt people hurt people, and you were one of those people I hurt. I am sorry. You were a wonderful husband, and I'm glad I married you as well. You are a good man, Paul. Don't doubt that. I have more perspective than you do now. Please believe me when I tell you that.

Then the voice was gone, and Paul wondered if the whole conversation had been in his imagination.

He stared at the flowers and felt the breeze pick up again, making some of the leaves in his arrangement vibrate.

"Katherine?" he said quietly. He walked to the headstone and touched it, tracing her first name with his finger.

It was peaceful and quiet, the only sound being a songbird in one of the holly tree branches above him. Paul picked up the arrangement to rotate it slightly, and as he did so, inhaled the faint scent of jasmine, reminding him of the time when Katherine told him she loved the smell. He sat the arrangement back down, and said, "Goodbye, Katherine."

A small butterfly, drawn by the colorful flowers and the fragrance of the jasmine, landed on the arrangement, opening and closing its wings several times before flitting off. He watched its random flying pattern as it investigated several sets of flowers and finally disappeared behind a row of bushes. For the first time in weeks, he felt at peace. He looked at his watch. It was almost eight o'clock, and he needed to get to the courthouse.

He pulled out his phone and dialed Rebecca. Several rings into it, she picked up, saying, "Oh, hi, Paul..." It was hard for him to read her mood.

"Hi, Rebecca."

"I'm glad you called; I'd been wanting to call you but wasn't sure if I should. I'm sorry for the way I spoke to you last night and was proud of you for changing your vote. I know how difficult it must have been."

"Listen, Rebecca," Paul said, "I'm sorry to do this this way, but I don't think things are going to work out."

"What do you mean?"

"Us. Not that there's really much of an 'us,' I guess, since we haven't even known each other all that long. But I am just starting to feel like maybe there isn't really a fit for us."

"Paul, is this about last night? Because please don't read that much into a few things I said. I'm sorry things escalated as they did."

"It's not just that. I just don't think I'm ready to be in another relationship yet. Or at least not one with you."

"Now you're just being mean."

"I'm sorry. I'm just being honest."

"Paul, I went out and bought everything over the past few days for our dinner, and here you are canceling at the last minute? I can't believe you're doing this." Her tone was a mixture of anger and hurt.

"Rebecca, you're a beautiful woman, and a man will be lucky to be with you one day. I just don't think it will be me."

"What am I supposed to do with all this mahi-mahi?" It was the same sarcastic tone he'd heard in the courtroom.

"Maybe you should eat it," Paul said. He hung up.

He regretted it momentarily, and yet, he knew that breaking things off was the right thing to do in the long run.

When he arrived at court about eight-twenty-five, he saw Rebecca drinking her cup of coffee in her usual spot at the table—her slightly puffy eyes avoiding contact with his. The other jurors made their way into the jury room and took a seat. Mr. Cashwell asked, "Ladies and gentlemen, has anyone changed their vote from last night?"

All eyes went to Paul, Maggie, and John.

Maggie and John said "No," and Paul shook his head no.

Mr. Cashwell said, "Paul, just confirming; you're still thinking a guilty verdict?"

"Correct, guilty," Paul responded.

"Terrific. Let's tell the judge we've made a decision."

Mr. Cashwell signed and dated the sheet to make it official and left to inform the bailiff. In a few minutes, the jury was led back into the courtroom where the judge conferred with the bailiff, Mr. Cashwell, and both attorneys at the bench. He then thanked the jury, concluded his private discussions, and looked at Mr. Cashwell, saying, "Has the jury arrived at a decision?"

Paul could feel his heart begin to pound. He reached for a Xanax but realized he had left them at home.

"We have, Your Honor."

Paul looked at Rebecca, Judge Mayer, and Levi, who was sitting stoically with neither relief nor anxiety in his face next to his attorney. His eyes shifted to the gallery and the little boy, thinking the little boy and he may have made eye contact, though it was difficult to tell. The little boy fidgeted, and the woman put her arm around him. Paul glanced at the other members of the jury.

"What say ye?" the judge asked.

Paul whispered, "I can't go through with this."

Jim, the juror sitting beside him, looked at him and whispered, "What???"

Paul stood. Judge Mayer stopped speaking and glanced at Mr. Cashwell, who looked at Paul and shrugged to the judge. Looking at Paul with mild irritation, Judge Mayer asked, "Yes?"

Paul swallowed. Why he chose to look at Rebecca at that moment, he would never know, but he did. The image of her face would become etched into his mind, and he could recall it years later with vivid detail: the curve of her lips, her eyes, like sea green pools of water that beckoned one's undivided gaze, her wavy hair that cascaded around her shoulders. She was so elegant, so beautiful, but so wrong for him at this point in his life. He looked back at the judge, whose expression signaled a growing consternation. The time had come.

"Your Honor," Paul said, "I need to address the Court."

He took a deep breath and began. "My wife Katherine was sexually assaulted in May of 2018…"

For the next several minutes, Paul spoke, beginning with Katherine's sexual assault by Marcus Roberts, then to the incident with the brick through the windshield and subsequent chase, Katherine's suicide, his sleepwalking experience involving him imagining a musket ball caught in his throat, his learning of the Marcus Roberts murder, his selection for jury duty and reluctance to exclude himself from jury service in that very case. He described his panic attack at having the sudden and shocking revelation that he may have been in the Marcus Roberts home that night. He mentioned Daniel's missing shotgun.

Paul said, "I don't remember pulling a trigger, I don't remember killing him, I don't remember anything about that night other than remembering that room." He looked at Levi, who was alternating between listening to Paul and whispering questions to Liam Olsen, his attorney. Paul even brought up Tom, and the fact that he could corroborate much of what had just been said.

Looks of incredulity were on the faces of the everyone in the courtroom, and at one point, Liam Olsen stood and interrupted Paul, saying "Your Honor, we move for a summary dismissal of all charges," but Judge Mayer waved him off and said, "Mr. Olsen, please sit down until the juror finishes; I'm the judge and *even I* am at a bit of a loss for how to proceed until I know more."

No one stirred during the 15 minutes that Paul recounted his story. Even the little boy, sensing something major was happening, was still. The stenographer quietly tapped away, audible gasps of disbelief occasionally coming from the jury and the gallery.

Paul finished recounting all that he could remember and looked at Levi, then to the judge, and said, "That's it. That's all I know. I think Levi Johnson is innocent." He looked from the judge to the little boy, who looked up at his mother as she put her hand to her mouth.

The judge, looking sternly at Paul, "Well, sir, I must say that you are in a passel of trouble. In addition to having a possible murder charge on your hands, you have obstructed justice, and while your actions this morning attempted to rectify that, you knowingly concealed many facts from this court. It's cost us a great deal of time and money, not to mention the emotional toll on the defendant and his family. Tell me your name?"

"Paul Nelms."

Paul looked at the other members of the jury and sensed outrage, and Mac mouthed several profane messages only Paul saw.

He looked back to Judge Mayer, who said, "Bailiff, would you please take Mr. Nelms into custody?"

At that moment, Liam Olsen stood and said, "Your Honor, the defense wishes to move for a summary dismissal of the case and that all charges in the matter of the State of Michigan vs. Levi Johnson, Case No. 08 CF 137 be dropped."

The judge responded, "I'm not going to rule on that just yet. We're going to take a thirty-minute recess. To the jury members, I'm not releasing you yet. Please report back to the jury room, and counselors, I want to see you in chambers." He slammed the gavel down with a loud *bang* and walked into his chambers.

Chapter 28

Friday, July 26, 2019

As the bailiff approached him, Paul looked over at Levi, standing and shaking his attorney's hand before waving to the woman and boy in the back of the courtroom. Rebecca gave Paul a cold stare and said nothing. He knew any chance of a reconciliation between them was over.

The bailiff ushered Paul to the fifth floor, where he was fingerprinted and told to wait in a small room. His wallet and phone were taken and stored for him, and he was led to an office where two detectives awaited him. They read him his Miranda rights, told him their conversation would be recorded, and began asking questions about his statement in court.

Paul said, "Before I speak, I'd like to have an attorney present."

"Up to you," one of the detectives said.

Paul said, "May I see my wallet? I have a card I need to get a number from."

The detective retrieved Paul's wallet and handed it to him. Paul found Mark Emerson's card, the attorney he had run into at the drug store. He returned the wallet to the detective, and the detective showed Paul into a room where he could make a call in private. Paul dialed Mark's number and to his surprise, Mark picked up.

"Paul, so good to hear from you," Mark said.

"Mark, I've got a problem. I've been arrested. I'm wondering if you can tell me who can help me with this."

Mark said, "Of course, Paul. I am so sorry to hear about this. Where are you?"

"At the courthouse. It literally just happened."

"What's the charge?"

"Suspicion of murder."

Mark was silent.

"Mark?" Paul asked.

Mark, recovering from his shock, said, "Paul, did you say *murder*?"

"Yes."

Mark said, "Okay, hang on a second," and in the background, Paul heard him yell to his assistant, "Marcy, can you call my eleven-thirty and reschedule?" After a pause, Mark came back on the line and said, "Paul, I can be down there in about twenty minutes."

Paul thanked him, hung up, and walked out into the hallway where the detective was waiting for him.

"My attorney should be here in about twenty minutes," Paul said.

"Okay, Mr. Nelms. You can wait in this room until he gets here."

Thirty minutes later, the detective walked into the room Paul was sitting in and said, "The cavalry just arrived. I'll show them in."

Paul just nodded.

The detective walked back out, and said, "Okay, you guys can come in."

Mark walked in, followed by none other than Tony Leone.

Paul stared at him.

Mark said, "Paul, I know you remember Tony. He's handled more capital crimes than just about anyone in the firm, so I thought I should bring him along."

"Hello, Paul," Tony said with a smile and outstretched hand.

Paul glared at him. Paul neither stood nor accepted his hand, but only nodded and said "Tony."

Tony's brow furrowed in a perplexed expression, and he slowly lowered his outstretched hand.

Paul turned to Mark. "Thanks so much for coming down."

The detective came back in and added an extra chair, saying, "I'll close the door. How long do you guys think you'll need?"

"Probably an hour. Thanks, Detective," said Tony.

The three sat down. Mark said, "Paul, what in the hell is all this about?"

Paul stared at Tony, the thoughts of his and Katherine's clandestine lives together preventing him from even hearing Mark's question.

"Paul?" Mark repeated.

"Yes?" Paul answered, his attention shifting to Mark.

"What is this about?" he repeated.

Paul looked at Tony again, then back to Mark and said, "Mark, I need to talk to Tony alone. Would you mind?"

Tony's trademark expression of confidence evaporated.

"Why sure, Paul," Mark said, standing up and looking at Tony. "Tony, I'll wait outside. Just come get me when you all are ready."

Tony swallowed, looked at Mark, and simply said, "Sure."

Mark walked out and shut the door.

Paul stared for a moment at Tony, who still had a slightly confused look on his face.

No one spoke for a moment, and then, partly to break the silence, Tony asked, "Paul, why did you want to speak to me alone?"

"I *know*, Tony," Paul said.

"Sorry?" Tony asked.

"I know. About you and Katherine."

Tony tried to convey an appearance of surprise, but a flash of alarm in his eyes betrayed it.

Paul went on, "I know about the affair. You know, I think that was what led her to kill herself."

"I have no idea what you're talking about."

"I know, Tony. You can drop the act. I have one of the letters you wrote her. The one where you offered to do something to Marcus Roberts if she wanted you to."

Tony looked as if he had been physically struck, and he sat back hard against his chair, processing the consequences of such a revelation. "Oh...my...." He chose his words carefully. "Paul, this could ruin me. I have a family; I have a career."

Paul sat resolute, not showing any change of expression.

Tony's countenance took on a look of desperation, "Look, Paul, what is it you want? Free representation here? You've got that. I'll help any way I can."

Paul said nothing, and simply stared at Tony with contempt and said, "I think she felt guilty about it. About the affair. I think that's why she committed suicide. She was learning to live with the trauma of the assault. She wasn't over it, but she was learning to live with it."

"Paul, I don't know what to say."

"Start by admitting it."

Tony looked down, as if contemplating what to say.

"You won't find the answer written on the table, Tony."

Tony looked up and said quietly, "What do you want me to say, Paul? That it happened? Yes, it happened. Do I regret it? Yes, I regret it."

"You visited her grave recently, didn't you? The roses were from you, weren't they?"

Tony nodded. "Paul, she was a wonderful woman, and I know this is painful..."

"Shut up. If you know what is good for you, stop the patronizing tone or I will jump across this table and break your neck. If you don't think I'm serious, try me. I really will."

"I'm sorry." Tony looked imploringly at Paul. "What do you want me to do at this point?"

Paul stared at Tony, who shifted uncomfortably in his chair.

Paul said, "Answer a question for me: did you kill Marcus Roberts…or have him killed?"

Tony looked shocked. Then he laughed. "Me? *Me* kill Marcus Roberts? Give me a break, that's the most laughable thing I've heard all week." The look on Tony's face shifted quickly from one of defense to one of offense. "Who are *you* to accuse *me* of something like that?"

"It's the same question a grand jury might ask you," Paul said, "All I know is that we both had a motive."

Tony looked at the door, and Paul wondered if Mark could hear any of the conversation.

Tony said, "Paul, look, let's figure out how to get you out of the situation you're in, then you and I can work out how I can try to make things right with you."

"I think I want Mark back in the room," Paul said.

"What, you are going to tell him?" Tony asked, his voice tinged with desperation.

Paul smiled. "I am, but it wouldn't matter if I didn't. A truth this large almost never stays concealed indefinitely."

Tony stammered, "I thought I was doing you a favor by coming down here. Mark comes in and tells me that you're in trouble, and I drop everything and come down to help, and this is the thanks I get?"

Paul smiled again. "Tony, I must say, I love watching you squirm like the worm that you are." Paul chuckled and Tony's face reddened as he slammed his hand on the table with a loud clap.

The detective opened the door and said, "Everything okay?"

Paul said, "Yes, everything's fine, and hey, would you send my other attorney back in?"

"Sure."

Mark walked back in, sat down and upon seeing Tony's face, so filled with consternation, quizzically looked over to Paul, and asked, "What's going on?"

Paul looked at Tony and asked, "You want to, or do you want me to?"

Tony took a deep breath and exhaled slowly. He shook his head, seemingly trying to figure out where to begin.

"Well?" Paul asked. "Want me to start?"

Tony looked at Paul, resignedly said "No," then shifted his gaze to Mark. "Katherine, Paul's wife, and I were having an affair."

Mark's jaw dropped. "What?" he asked incredulously.

"It's true," Tony said. "Paul knows about it, and I've as much as admitted to it."

"How...or why..." Mark began, trying to formulate a question.

Mark looked at Paul and said, "Does this somehow involve your arrest, Paul?"

Tony said "No" at the same time that Paul said, "I don't know."

Mark's gaze shifted from Paul to Tony and back again. He said, "Look, I am a little out of my league here. I'm usually doing commercial litigation work, but it sounds like we need some other folks involved. Tony, you are obviously conflicted here. Maybe the whole firm is."

"Mark, I do want you as a resource if that's possible," Paul said.

"Of course, Paul. You and Katherine were both good friends, and you still are a good friend. I will do whatever I can, within the limits of what I can do as part of the law firm, to help out."

"Mark, let me ask you this. How do I get out of here? I would like to go home."

"That I *do* know. We can work on posting bail immediately."

Tony added, "Yeah, we can get you out of here pretty quickly. It may be a few hours, but by the time you are wrapped up with the questioning that these guys want to do, you shouldn't actually have to go to jail."

Paul looked at Tony and said, "You preyed on her, you know. You took advantage of her. She was vulnerable."

"Paul, I didn't even initiate…"

"Stop. She may not have been thinking clearly but *you* should have been," Paul said, looking toward the door and adding, "I want you out."

Tony glared at Paul and left, slamming the door as he departed.

Mark said, "Paul, let me get Riley Boyce in here. He's a good criminal defense attorney, a younger guy but very capable. Hang on…" He dialed a number and said, "Katie, is Riley in? No? Well, tell him to get down to Room Six Twenty-Three at the courthouse if he can in the next hour, and to call me as soon as he gets free. Got it. Yes, that's right."

Mark hung up. "Okay, let's go over again how you got here. You may need to repeat this to Riley but give me an idea of what's going on."

For the next fifty minutes, Paul gave Mark the same account he'd given in the courtroom, adding details where Mark had inquiries. Mark nodded, taking copious notes on his legal pad.

After Paul finished bringing him up to date, Mark said, "I don't think they can make your charges stick, Paul. I mean…I don't know, but it sounds like a weak case if they don't have any stronger forensics or DNA linking you to the crime scene. To be honest, Tony may have a harder time not being implicated than you would."

Paul nodded. He looked at his watch. "Oh wow, I haven't even told Daniel yet."

Mark said, "Let me talk to the detective and see if we can arrange for you to call him," and he left the room. Five minutes later, he was back and said the detective had given the okay.

Mark handed Paul his cell phone and Paul dialed Daniel. "Daniel, hi, listen…" Paul began. "I'm downtown and have been arrested. I'm at the courthouse in Room Six Twenty-Three and I have an attorney with me, but I need for you to come down right away if you can."

"Oh my gosh. *Arrested?!* What for, Dad?"

Paul hid the dread in his voice, saying, "I'll explain when you get here, just come up to the sixth floor and ask to be taken to Room Six Twenty-Three."

"Be right there," Daniel said and hung up.

For the next twenty minutes, Mark asked Paul to go back over his story again, trying to fill in details that he could share with Riley and to better understand the situation. Riley walked in as they were wrapping up.

"Riley, I'm glad you got here," Mark said.

Mark introduced Paul and Riley, gave Riley a condensed version of Paul's account, and explained that they were waiting for Daniel to arrive, which should be any moment, and that Daniel could corroborate and possibly elaborate on the sleepwalking event.

"The detectives may want to talk to Daniel first," Riley said.

"True, good point," Mark said.

The detective opened the door and said, "Mr. Nelms, your son has arrived to see you. We thought we would ask him some questions if he doesn't object, and he said he wanted to ask you what he should do. Do you have any objection?"

Riley spoke up, "Detective, thanks, but I think we would want to have counsel present during the questioning, otherwise I think we'd advise him to plead the fifth."

"Got it," the detective said, starting to close the door, but before he closed it, Mark said, "Detective, I think we'll be posting bail so I'm guessing Mr. Nelms will be released within a couple of hours…Does that sound about right?"

"I think so, but we'll want to ask him some questions before he leaves. Just let me know when you guys are wrapped up. I'll go ahead and bring his son in."

The detective left the door ajar and a moment later showed Daniel into the room. Daniel walked up to his dad and hugged him, saying, "Dad, what's going on?"

Paul looked at his son, then to Mark and Riley. "Daniel, I am going to tell you some things I never wanted to tell you, some things about your mom you don't know, that you shouldn't have to know, but that you are going to have to know. They will come out one way or the other, and I'd rather you hear it from me." He waited for a moment, but Daniel said nothing. "Why don't you take a seat, Son," Paul suggested.

Daniel's face maintained a look of concern and confusion.

He tentatively said "Okay."

Paul began, "As you know, back in 2018, your mom was sexually assaulted…"

Paul went on to mention the times he had driven past Roberts' house thinking about harming him, about the chase, being selected to serve on the jury trying the case for Marcus Roberts' murder and his reluctance to recuse himself, then his recollection of details inside Marcus Roberts' home. Finally, he told him about discovering the letter. Daniel only said, "I can't believe this."

Paul responded, "I didn't know what to do, or what to even tell you." He hesitated, then added, "But anyway, when I realized your shotgun was missing, that sort of proved it in my mind. I don't know what I did with it. I did go out and get you a new one…the same kind."

Daniel said, "I'm confused. You picked my gun up from the shop?"

It was Paul's turn to be confused. "What do you mean?"

"Dad, it's been in the shop. The safety sticks. I took it in earlier this year to have it worked on. It's fixed; I just haven't picked it up."

Paul stared. "What?" he asked, incredulously. "Daniel, what are you saying?" He looked to Riley and then to Mark, then back to Daniel.

"Are you telling me that your gun hasn't been in our house for the past few months?"

"Yes, like I said, it's been in the shop."

Mark said, "Paul, you couldn't have killed him without a shotgun."

Paul sat back in the chair, a look of disbelief on his face, as he tried to process the implications of this new information.

Riley asked, "Daniel, how long ago did you take the gun in? Any idea about the date?"

Daniel responded, "Back in January. Like I said, I just haven't picked it up. Haven't had any hunting trips and just got lazy I guess." Turning to Paul, he said, "Dad, why didn't you just ask me where my gun was?"

"How could I? I thought I'd taken and used it…I couldn't…I would've had to tell you everything or else concocted some story about taking it out and losing it or something…I couldn't."

Riley asked, "Paul, if Daniel's shotgun was not accessible to you, would you still be of the opinion that you had something to do with the murder?"

"Riley, honestly, I don't see how I could have. I would have had to have access to a shotgun, and the only one I bought was the one I got *after* Marcus Roberts' murder. I have the receipt, and of course they have the records as well."

"What about this feeling you had that you were in the room? Do you think you were?" Riley asked.

Paul thought a moment. "I don't know why I had such a strong feeling of having been in that room. I had seen the photo of the room earlier in the testimony. Maybe I dreamed I was in it. I was having some hyper-realistic dreams…"

Paul looked back and forth at Riley and Mark. "What happens

if I now say I don't think I did it given this new information?"

"This is crazy," Mark said. "The judge is going to flip out. He might jail you for contempt of court anyway."

Riley said, "Well, they're definitely going to look into it. I mean…you've said earlier you think you might have murdered him. They probably will also look into Tony as a possible suspect. To tell you the truth, I don't think they're going to be able to pin this on anyone. There are so many reasonable doubts on this that I don't think any prosecutor is going to go back after this one. They might try to go back to Levi Johnson and try a lesser plea, but I seriously doubt it."

"Paul," Mark said. "Why were you so convinced you did it? I mean, to admit that you had done it when all you had was a recollection of being there, the missing shotgun and the musket ball comment?"

"I don't know…Maybe it was the power of suggestion." Paul thought a moment and added, "I think I tried to fit the truth into my own perception of reality; that's what we all do, isn't it? What's true to me is not necessarily what's true to you? And the more I repeated that possibility in my head, the more convinced I became."

"I'll tell you who I wouldn't want to be right now," Mark said.

"Who's that?" Paul said.

"Tony."

Paul shrugged and said, "I wouldn't want to be Tony *any* time."

Riley said, "Look, the first thing we need to do is to talk to the detectives and the courts and to try to straighten out this mess."

Paul looked at Daniel. "Daniel, I'm sorry I had to bring you in on all this."

Daniel had not said much, and he wiped his eyes, which were still damp from having heard Paul's emotional account. "No, Dad, I'm glad you told me" Daniel's voice began to crack with emotion as he added, "I'm sorry, Dad, that you've had to carry this by yourself all this time."

"It's okay, Son. I did talk to Tom Harris about it," Paul said, and then looking at Riley and Mark, said, "He's my therapist, who can corroborate a lot of this."

Mark and Riley wrote down Tom's name and number.

Daniel stood and walked toward the window, and said, "You think you know people. And sometimes you do." Paul heart sank, as this was precisely what he had feared would happen if he told Daniel about his mother's infidelity. Daniel continued, "But sometimes you don't, and when you find out you don't, it's good to know that sometimes you discover them to be even better people than you thought them to be."

He walked over to Paul, still seated, and leaned down and gave his father a hug.

Chapter 29

Daniel slid open the door to the lanai and walked out, a breeze greeting him as he rested his forearms on the railing. He surveyed the scene of Detroit, with Windsor, Ontario, in the background. The contrast between the two cities was striking, the former's much larger and imposing skyline dwarfing the latter's smaller, quainter appearance on the other side of the Detroit River. He glanced back at his father, who'd just gone inside to refresh a tumbler of lemonade he'd been sipping. Daniel looked over at the table where Paul's laptop computer and several legal pads were sitting. He glanced back inside and saw Paul disappear behind the bathroom door.

Daniel walked over to the table and began reading his father's scribbled notes. At the top of the page, Paul had written, "He wants this told in his own voice: i.e., needs to be in first person, starting with pre-gang." Below that were cryptic notes that were harder to decipher. He looked back to confirm that Paul was still in the bathroom, wondering if his dad would object to him looking at what he was working on.

The computer screen had gone to sleep, so he touched the

mouse pad to awaken the computer.

Clicking to the top of the screen, he began reading:

Part 1 – 2003 (From when he was 14) ...DON'T forget to confirm it was a 38 automatic.

We turn up the TV to drown out the sounds of rats scratching behind the walls. We used to try listening for their location and banging where the sound came from, but now it seems only to embolden them. At some point, though, we have to sleep, and that's when the whole pack comes out, and so we drift off counting rats when other kids are counting sheep. It isn't as bad as you think. Scratching, tumbling, fighting and jumping each has its unique sound, and sometimes I used to wonder if in that group of rats there was a young one that would be the equivalent of my age. By 1 AM or so they quiet down, and we all sleep, interrupted only by the occasional sounds of gunfire or a fight out in the alleyway.

One night Daddy got drunker than normal, pulled out one of his guns and started blasting the wall where those sounds were coming from. He had stolen a Smith and Wesson 38 Automatic(?) with a magazine that held 12 rounds, plus the one in the chamber. It was a nice gun. He emptied the magazine in that wall, plaster exploding all through the living room and leaving 13 massive holes. Momma came running and tried to settle him down, but she knew better than to press her luck when he kept firing. That was how the rats started getting into the house, through those holes. They chewed right through the cardboard Daddy taped up there the next night.

Daddy was a bad man sober, but a worse man drunk. He would sometimes hit us for standing in the wrong place, or saying something that crossed him, and so we all learned to stay out of his way, especially when he'd been drinking, which would come and go in spells. The drinking kept him from ever being able to hold down a steady job, not that he wanted a steady job to begin with. He called that "slow money." There are faster ways he would say, and for him, that was always true.

When he dealt in something illegal - drugs, or selling stuff he had stolen - he would take it upon himself to sample or try out whatever it was he was selling, like he had some sort of reputation to uphold. When he said it was good, he knew. He was dealing half the time, drunk half the time, but mean all the time. A woman told me once I was lucky to have a strong male figure in my life, but as I saw it, there was one thing worse than a young black male without a father figure in his life, and that was having a father figure like him in my life. He and Momma would get in big fights when he was sober, but she knew better than to mess with him when he had been drinking. She only had to make that mistake once, kind of like the time I threw a rock at a hornet's nest in the back yard.

He was drunk on the night I shot him. Momma had pressed her luck against her better judgment, mainly because she was protecting us. I've seen these nature programs on TV where a momma lion will fight to the death to protect her cubs. That's the way my Momma was. Daddy was on his knees straddling my older brother Tyrell, who was 17 at the time but a good bit smaller than Daddy, and punching him in the face. Tyrell's head snapped each time he got hit and I thought he was dead. Momma ran over and started hitting Daddy but he didn't even notice until she started clawing at his eyes. He screamed in rage and pain and then he threw her down. I was scared he would do the same to her that he'd done to Tyrell, who was moaning and bleeding and couldn't do anything. I ran and got Daddy's gun and by the time I got back in the room he was trying to choke her.

I shot him square in the back, and the force threw him right on top of her. For a minute I thought maybe the bullet had gone through him and into her, because when he landed on her, neither one of them moved. But then Momma pushed him off and rolled him over on his back. His right arm was twitching.

I was scared. Not from Daddy...I was pretty sure he was dead, but from the uncertainty of what I had just done. I wondered what would happen to me for shooting him. I was only 14, but I knew that kids my age could be sentenced. You make snap decisions like that in life, and in that blink of an eye, it sets off a string of events that you can't control.

Momma got up slowly and came to me and said, "Oh Levi." I started to cry. "Honey, it's OK, it's Ok. You had to do it. He was gonna kill me." Tyrell had blood all over his face, his right eye already swelling shut, and he walked over to Daddy and stopped a few feet away and leaned in to look at him, looking like he was scared Daddy would suddenly lurch up and grab him.

"Is he dead?" he asked.

I wasn't sure. "I don't know."

I walked over and kneeled beside my father, pointing the gun at his head with my finger still on the trigger. He wasn't breathing, and through his white t-shirt I could see a hole where the bullet exited his chest. It was pretty big...maybe the size of a half dollar, and I suddenly found myself thinking about those rats, and the holes in the plaster, and how the hole in his chest was about the same size. I got a little woozy and almost felt like I wasn't really in the room, like I was hovering above everybody. I stared at his face and sat down on the floor. If you only looked at his face, he actually looked peaceful, sort of like he did when he was passed out.

I realize what I am about to tell you will sound strange, but its true. Like I said, I was scared...but at the same time, with all that adrenaline surging through me...something made me also feel powerful. I felt like a protector, like I was maybe in control when I didn't think I ever could be. Like maybe there was something in me I had not seen before.

I even began to wonder what people would say about me when the news got out. And I started to think about gangs. There were several gangs in my neighborhood, and I figured this would attract some of their members' attention. Not that I necessarily wanted to get into one. I hadn't really thought about it all that much. But once I pulled that trigger, I pretty much gave up on staying on the "straight and narrow," a term Momma used to use. Killing my dad when he was attacking Momma would be something that would get me some instant respect. They would "get" that.

Most people don't understand gangs. For a young black male who isn't doing well in school, who has nobody tough to back him up, and who is under constant risk of being beat up if not shot, a gang offers an attractive alternative. Homies know you and all they expect in return is loyalty. Sure, they expect sacrifice, but what group worth anything doesn't? It's like our country's military. Both have soldiers who die fighting for a cause they believe in, for things and people they respect.

The protection was a big part of what appealed to me. Traditional law enforcement doesn't exist for people in my neighborhood. The police will show up, but nothing ever happens. And you don't want to report anything because you don't want to be recognized, period.

I had a neighbor who was an eyewitness to a shooting, and he had to testify in court. A year later, he was identified in a line-up of suspects for a robbery he didn't commit. I know because I know who did it. The eyewitness is doing time now for a crime he knew nothing about. Trust me, you want to stay off their grid, and never to have a cop's partner say he "recognizes you from somewhere." That's an automatic one-way ticket downtown.

I shot Daddy on a Saturday night. I spent a good bit of that night and early Sunday in the police station. I was fingerprinted and interrogated for hours, as were my mom and Tyrell. We were separated when they asked us questions, and I worried about some of our details not matching up, but they must have, because we were told we could leave by Sunday around lunchtime. Between Tyrell's swollen face and the marks on Momma's neck, there was enough evidence of self-defense that the district attorney ended up saying he wasn't going to press charges. It was one of the few times I have seen the system actually work for someone like me. But I know a lot of cops will now say, "I've seen him somewhere" if they see me on the street and suspect me of something.

We couldn't afford to bury him, or maybe it was Momma didn't want to bother. We weren't sure what to do, but we were told if no one claims a body, the state or sometimes the county cremates them. So we didn't claim the body, and we didn't have to pay anything. I guess they dumped the ashes out somewhere. In my mind, I picture those ashes just blowing whichever way the wind takes them, which is sort of how he lived his...

The writing stopped at that point. Daniel looked up as Paul was returning to the balcony. Daniel moved away from the laptop and picked up the catalog on cruises, sitting in one of the chairs. He asked, "So, remind me what day we leave?"

"November sixth, a Friday."

"You sure you don't want to take somebody else?" Daniel smiled. "A lady maybe?"

Paul laughed. "Like who?"

Daniel asked, "I don't know. Ever talk to Rebecca?"

"No. I don't think it was the right fit," Paul said. "But I'm glad she came into my life; I really am."

"How so?"

"I think she was the distraction I needed to jolt me out of the funk I was in." Paul looked off in the distance, thought a minute, and said, "It did occur to me to call Ginger Hammond. She's the art dealer who bought your mom's painting in the auction. I ran into her the other day, and when we were speaking, she referred to an ex-husband."

"Hmmm," was Daniel's only response. He looked at Paul's laptop and asked, "What are you writing?"

"A story about grief. Not exactly like the grief you and I have experienced, but the grief of a life that was not the one someone would have wished for, and the death of the dreams that this person had as a child. It's the first thing I've written in a long time that feels important, relevant. I'm helping this person give grief a voice. He said he didn't know how to do that himself, so I'm hoping it helps."

"It's Levi's story, isn't it?"

Paul nodded. "The idea came to me after all the charges for the Marcus Roberts murder were dismissed, both mine and his. I was able to get his address at SAIF."

"Wow. They let you communicate with him?"

"I had to get permission from the warden, but yes, once they knew the reason."

"Remind me what SAIF stands for?"

"Special Alternative Incarceration Facility. It's in Chelsea. I'm going to visit him next week for another interview. I am looking forward to it. I've always loved Chelsea anyway."

Paul resumed typing.

Daniel said, "You know, Dad, I think Mom would understand about everything coming out. You didn't have a choice."

"I had a choice. But I like to think I made the least bad decision given the circumstances. In the end, it brought us to where we are today. And for that, I'm grateful."

Daniel sat down in the chair next to his father, and he looked out over the skyline of Windsor, listening to the distant sounds of the city below.

"I'm grateful too, Dad. You know, I think sometimes you suffer, and one day, that passes. And when it does, what's left is a greater capacity for joy."

Paul looked at Daniel and smiled. "Maybe you ought to be the writer."

"I'm not sure I have a story to tell."

"Everyone has a story to tell."

Daniel shrugged.

"Do you think he did it?" Daniel asked.

"Who, Levi?"

"Yeah."

"I have a feeling he'll eventually tell me the truth," Paul answered. "It won't happen until he trusts me more than he does today, but one day, I think he'll tell me what happened."

Paul returned his attention to the laptop.

"Dad?"

Paul looked up.

"I'm proud of you."

Paul looked puzzled.

"As I think about all we've been through, all *you've* been through...losing your wife, the trial, everything...I mean, a lot of people wouldn't be able to sit here typing. You know, moving on with life."

Paul said nothing, but the corners of his mouth inched upwards almost imperceptibly. For a moment, he processed that thought before quickly returning his attention to his keyboard.

After several minutes, Daniel took a deep breath and listened to the calming sounds of his father's fingers as they returned to their rhythmic tapping, against a backdrop of "Moonlight Sonata," wafting outside—the player piano cycling through its repertoire of songs.

Daniel asked, "Should we get rid of that song?"

Paul stopped typing for a moment and listened, his eyes closed. He smiled softly and said, "No, I don't think so. I still find it…" He struggled for the right word, failing to complete the sentence.

He opened his eyes and stared at the skyline. "I love this place."

And the notes played on, blending with the sounds of overtime construction workers toiling on elevated platforms stories below, signaling the city's growth and recovery.

* * *

Several miles away, the woman and her son were just finishing dinner. "Finish those lima beans," she said, glancing over his plate.

"They taste mushy."

"They're good for you."

The television played on a counter in their small kitchen, the table where they were eating taking up much of the room.

The boy took one more bite of the beans, and she said, "You did pretty good, that's good enough." She took their plates and placed them in the sink to soak.

They walked into the living room, and she turned on the television for him, plugged in his PlayStation, and asked if he wanted to play Crash Bandicoot.

"Yes. Will it start where I left off?"

"I think so."

The game began, and he took the control from his mother. "Honey, I have to go outside for just a minute, okay? I'll be right back."

"Okay," he said, though he was focused on the game's opening scenes and the soundtrack from the game.

The mother went to a small closet and opened the door, reaching to the top shelf to retrieve a flashlight. As she opened the back door, she yelled, "Be right back!" and walked out into the backyard and went to an access door leading to a crawl space under the house.

She opened the door, shone the flashlight into the darkness and proceeded to crawl inside. There was barely enough height for her to avoid scraping her back as she crawled about twenty feet along the outside wall to a metal box secured by a combination lock. She held the flashlight in one hand and with her other, turned the dial to the right to 33, then left to 12 and then right to 30. The lock opened when she pulled down on it.

She opened the lid of the box and tilted the opening towards her, shining the flashlight into the top, which was filled with freezer bags. She pulled out one of the bags, unsealed it and placed her nose near its opening, a faint smile appearing as she slowly inhaled. *Money has a unique smell,* she thought to herself, *especially fresh bills.*

Pulling out one of the stacks of hundred-dollar bills, she laid the flashlight down, positioning it so that it provided enough light for her to watch as she placed her thumb against the edge of the stack and riffled it, producing a "fffttt" sound as her thumb slid over the edges.

After removing the wrapping that held the stack together, the woman took two of the bills and placed them beside the box. The remainder she reinserted into the freezer bag and returned the bag to the box and locked it.

The woman knew that Levi had said she needed to be careful

about that money, that this was the last hit he'd ever do for that lawyer, so it had to last. She stopped for a moment and listened to the sound effects of the game that her son was engaged in above her head. She heard him laugh.

She had no idea how long that money would last. But for at least the foreseeable future, she knew they would eat.

The End

Author's Note: The initial idea for this novel came to me in the late 1970s when I was a student at Wake Forest University. One evening (technically, early morning since it was after midnight), several of us walked into a nearby suite, which was in Taylor Dorm. We were standing around in the hallway, speaking quietly, when one of the residents (a friend) opened his door and silently walked past all of us and into the bathroom. He stood at the urinal and began making a hacking sound, like he was trying to clear his throat of some type of blockage. It was a bit alarming, as it sounded like he was choking, so we said, "Hey, are you OK?" He didn't look at us, but kept coughing, and said, "Yeah, I've got a musket ball stuck in my throat."

We looked at each other. "What?!" several of us exclaimed.

He answered, "I've got a musket ball caught in my throat, and I can't get it out," whereupon, he stopped hacking and walked back into his room and returned to bed.

His roommate started laughing. "He's sleepwalking again."

We were incredulous and peppered his roommate with questions. "How often does he do this?" (Not often, maybe once a quarter); "Does he remember anything the next day?" (No); "Have you ever tried to wake him up while he's sleepwalking?" (No).

The next morning, sure enough, my sleepwalking friend had no recollection of the previous night. It was one of the weirdest things I've ever seen, and I can still recall it vividly.

I'll never forget how "normal" he looked and sounded that night. It occurred to me: If he was imagining that he had a musket ball in his throat, and got out of bed to get rid of it, what else could he act on while sleepwalking?

Moreover, what if a sleepwalker committed a crime while sleepwalking? In an early version of this novel, I had Paul, the sleepwalker, commit the murder, but later decided to eliminate that version of the story on the advice of an agent I spoke to. In hindsight, I think it was good advice.

Yet it remains a provocative question: What happens if a sleepwalker commits a crime while sleepwalking? By the way, the cases Paul researches in the book concerning sleepwalking defenses are actual cases—a number of those defenses were successful, as mentioned.

Thanks for reading the book. I hope you enjoyed it.

Buddy Howard

Your opinion counts.
Please leave a review on the retailer's site where you purchased the book or any online platform where readers gather. Thank you for your support.

Discussion Questions

What was the significance of the opening section where Paul and Daniel are hiking on Grand Island? What do we learn about Paul, his state of mind and the challenges in his life?

When Katherine comes in after the assault, how did you feel about the steps Paul took to learn the attacker's identity? Should he have simply honored Katherine's wishes to forget the attack and move on with life?

What is Daniel's significance to the story? Did you ever consider him a suspect? Why or why not?

Toward the end of the book (before the final scene under the woman's house), who did you think killed Marcus Roberts?

What purpose was served by Rebecca in the story? What were her motivations? Did you not really trust her early on?

Why were the art auction and Ginger Hammond in the story?

Paul initially is leaning toward a not guilty verdict. What causes him to change to a guilty verdict? And then what makes him return to a not guilty verdict?

What of significance occurs at the gravesite?

What two or three words would you use to describe each of the following: Paul, Katherine, Daniel, Tom, Rebecca, Tony and Levi?

Did your view of Katherine change at all after the scene at the graveyard?

During the trial, Levi looks over at Paul and Paul thinks there could have been a hint of recognition in Levi's gaze. How could there have been any recognition?

Were any of the jurors memorable and why? Did any of their arguments resonate with you?

Why was Detroit, MI chosen as the setting for the book?

What is the significance of Paul writing Levi's story at the end of the novel, both in terms of what it meant for Levi but also Paul? How does this relate to the beginning of the book?

What are some of the themes that emerge from this story…about truth? …about deception? …about grief?

Did you like Paul? Why or why not?

If you had to project a sequel, what would the story line be? What would happen?

To find the more information about the book or to read the author's response to common book club questions (see follow, please visit www.birchandquill.com or www.burdenofevidence.com.

www.ingramcontent.com/pod-product-compliance
Lightning Source LLC
Chambersburg PA
CBHW020123120726
47903CB00007B/2070